BITTER INHERITANCE

Facing eviction from her Yorkshire farm after the death of her parents, red-haired Sally Mason refuses to accept that a woman is not capable of independence. In doing so she must fight her formidable aunt, and worse still her grim landlord, Oliver Radford, who maintains a bitter feud with the Mason family over a murder committed fifty years before. Sally finds an ally in her new friend Marcus, but when she discovers he is Oliver's son, the barriers between them seem insurmountable. Can they solve the murder mystery and lay the feud to rest?

BITTER INHERITANCE

BITTER INHERITANCE

by

Ann Cliff

Magna Large Print Books
Long Preston, North Yorkshire,
BD23 4ND, England.

British Library Cataloguing in Publication Data.

Cliff, Ann
    Bitter inheritance.

    A catalogue record of this book is
    available from the British Library

    ISBN   978-0-7505-2817-7

First published in Great Britain in 2007 by Robert Hale Ltd.

Copyright © Ann Cliff 2007

Cover illustration © Len Thurston by arrangement with
P.W.A. International Ltd.

The right of Ann Cliff to be identified as the author of this work
has been asserted by her in accordance with the Copyright,
Designs and Patents Act, 1988

Published in Large Print 2008 by arrangement with
Robert Hale Ltd.

Magna Large Print is an imprint of Library Magna Books Ltd.

Printed and bound in Great Britain by
T.J. (International) Ltd., Cornwall, PL28 8RW

ONE

'A woman can't farm on her own. You must get out, sooner the better. Farm's run down bad enough as it is.' The gravelly voice grated on the ear and Sally moved away a little. 'I can't say I'm that sorry. You Masons have never done me a good turn. Sell up and clear out!' The heavy jowls shook as the man turned away.

'Oh, no!' Sally felt her heart sink, a physical pain in her chest. This was her home; the little grey stone village of Thorpe was the only place she knew.

'It's our farm – *my* farm, now that Father's gone. I love it. And it's not run down, Mr Bartram, you can't say that. We've looked after the land for two hundred years!' There were few families who could go back that far. Even in their part of Yorkshire, overlooking the Vale of York, people had moved about over the years. But the Masons had stayed in one place since 1694 – exactly two hundred years, in fact.

They were standing outside the house because she wouldn't invite the man inside. Sally was aware of the lovely sweep of the land, rising with fields and patches of

7

woodland to the skyline and then dropping down to the river Ure over the back of the ridge. It was a beautiful place, a farm to be proud of.

'Don't be daft, lass.' Sol Bartram shook his heavy head. 'A woman can't run a farm, least of all a young woman. It's not natural. Yer not strong enough. And what would a woman know about such things? Specially a Mason! Yer mother were a teacher – that's no help!'

Yes, Mother was a teacher. Pity yours didn't teach you better grammar, Sol Bartram, Sally thought furiously, her anger rising from her toes to the tips of her red hair. No one should speak like that of her dead mother.

'What's wrong with Masons? This was our farm. We owned it and you know we did. Until the Radfords bought it when Father lost his money, and had to sell.'

Sally had been fifteen at the time. She remembered with awful clarity how they had held on with very little to eat and the poorhouse looming. And then a buyer was found and they had money for food again. Her father leased the farm back from the buyer; all they had left were the livestock and some farm implements.

Sol jeered. 'Masons! Think they're better than other folks with their books and big words – and yer Uncle Samuel, he's a stuck-up parson. Yer dad always had his head in a book and it's not practical. You can't farm with book learning ... look at them thistles in that hedge! Radfords don't like weeds.' He pointed with his stick to the other side of the road.

'That's not our land, Mr Bartram.' If it wasn't so tragic it would be funny, but Sally didn't feel like laughing.

Sol turned to go. 'Any road,' and his tone was final, 'Radfords won't let you rent the farm so that's the end of it.'

'Why not?'

'Yer've got no lease, see. Better sell up, get Watson's auctioneers to sell yer cows and sheep. I'd do it now while stock's fat, well before winter. It'll need to be before Lady Day, if I was you. But it's nowt to do with me.'

Lady Day! That must be the deadline, the day in April when traditionally farms changed hands. They could have said Michaelmas, which was September ... now it was only June. She had ten months to fight the Radfords. Sally took a deep breath and mentally tensed herself for the fight.

'I'm glad you noticed the stock's fat, Mr Bartram. They are in good shape and the land is, too. I'll thank you not to go round telling folks that we've run Badger's Gill down. And you needn't bother telling them I'm leaving, either. Not just yet!' Sally

9

turned on her heel and marched away up the pasture, red head held high.

'Get yerself married – you need a husband to keep you quiet!' His coarse voice followed her up the hill.

The air felt fresher when Sol had shuffled off back to the Crown Inn, where he sat behind the bar like a big spider manipulating the business deals of Thorpe as he ran the village inn. Sally knew he was a dealer in livestock and dead stock and acted as agent for several landowners, including the Radfords. It had been Sally's job to go to the Crown with the rent every quarter day, begrudging every penny paid out to stay on the farm that had been theirs, and hating any contact with greasy Sol Bartram, who looked at her with little piggy eyes in a way that made her blush.

With Sol as their agent, the Radfords were invisible. Nobody ever saw them in Thorpe and Sally had never met them, although she'd imagined them to be like Sol: fat and greedy and completely heartless.

Sally Mason looked around slowly and felt the tension drain away. Dewdrops hung like jewels on the cobwebs in the hedge, glinting in the morning sun. There was the quiet sound of cows munching happily on their fresh patch of grass. The bees were in the clover ... she'd been enjoying the summer day until Sol came along to sully it. If only

Father hadn't died so young. But Sally had always tried to keep to the bright side of life, to count her blessings. She wasn't going to sit down and weep. Her mother had sometimes told her that she tended to ignore the sad side too much and only wanted to hear happy stories. Sally had always felt that if you concentrate on what is good and happy, life will be brighter. She'd never needed this philosophy so much as she did now.

It was seven years since her father had reluctantly decided to sell the farm after a run of losses. Nobody had mentioned that the Radfords would ever want vacant possession of the property; they had plenty of land themselves. What had changed to make them decide to turn her out?

'No, Mr Landlord. I may be only twenty-two, but I'm not leaving. I will ask for the tenancy of Badger's Gill to be passed to me, and I'll show everybody that a woman can run a farm and succeed. Starting from now!' Her voice rang out over the pasture.

The cows looked up in mild surprise, not used to raised voices. Sally laughed. 'Sorry, girls, but that feels better.' She picked up a bucket as she went through the gate.

The sheep were waiting to be moved, having eaten off the orchard grass. Lavinia looked up and bleated softly and Mary moved in a purposeful way to Sally's side. Soon the others followed, drawn by the promise of food. 'And I'm not selling you lot, wicked though you may be!' The sheep looked quite unconcerned about their fate, jostling each other to get to the bucket. She often talked to the animals, especially now that she lived alone.

Sally's flock was a motley collection of different breeds of sheep. Some had black faces and legs, some had horns, some had long wool. It was time they were clipped, she thought as she looked them over. The wool wouldn't fetch much, but it would be a little bit of income. These were special sheep because each one had been hand reared, on cow's milk from a bottle. They'd all been orphan lambs, given to the girl by shepherds who had too many lambs to care for. These sheep thought that Sally was their leader. They had grown up to be a tame flock, wayward and mischievous but easy for her to handle. They escaped when they could, being sheep, just for a change of scene and diet but never because they were hungry. Sally's animals were always well fed. The sheep had been trained to eat a little grain from a bucket. One rattle of that bucket and Lavinia, Mary, Prudence and the rest – they all had stately names – collected their lambs and followed Sally.

She took them down the lane and into the gill. Badger's Gill, after which the farm was named, was a small hidden valley with a stream in the bottom called the Thorpe Beck. Sally counted the sheep out of habit, knowing it was unlikely that one of them would stray. When they escaped they always went in a group, all twenty ewes, eighteen of them with lambs. All of them in top condition. She smoothed back her unruly curls and sighed. 'If I sheared, say, three of you every day... I could get through you all in a week! We'd better start today.'

The sheep shearing was slow, but it went well. In the old days, shearing day had been fun; several shearers would come to help her father to deal with the much bigger flock they'd had then. Sally and her mother would produce a good dinner and the men would tease the little girl and tell jokes and stories. By contrast, today there was only Sally, shearing by herself because it had to be done.

The day was warm and the ewes sat quietly as the wool rolled from their backs while Sally made smooth movements with the sharp pointed shears that her father had taught her to handle. Her main concern was that the sheep were not cut. Sally loved the smell of clean wool and her hands felt soft from the lanolin within. The only problem was her aching back. She was thankful that she wasn't a professional shearer, travelling round the farms all summer doing the same back-breaking job.

'There, Mary, you'll be cooler with that wool off your back!' But Mary was more concerned with getting back to her lamb, which had been wailing for twenty minutes.

Three ewes shorn, seventeen to go. But that was enough for one day and it would soon be milking time. Once more Sally realized as she wiped her hot face, how hard it was going to be without her father. During the month since his death she'd been occupied with getting through one day at a time. But now, she looked down the years and thought of all the work that the three of them had shared: Sally and her mother making cheese and butter, baking and washing. Sally and her father had done some of the farm work between them. In the good times they'd employed a couple of workers and hired a labourer for hay-making. There was a great deal of work at Badger's Gill for one pair of hands. But she would have to get through it if she wanted to keep the farm. And maybe, if she were successful, she might be able to pay a labourer to do the heavier jobs ... in time.

Sally was rolling the fleeces into bundles in the barn when she heard a raucous shout. There in the cobbled yard was Sol Bartram again, this time leaning from his trap. He was wearing a collar and tie and looked important. The old farm dog, Moll, was growling in her kennel. Moll was too old now to round up the sheep, but she'd appointed herself as Sally's guardian. And she made it obvious that she didn't like the visitor.

Most folks would have jumped down from their trap to talk to her, but Sol seemed to like the superior feeling of looking down at her from a height. Or perhaps, Sally thought with distaste, he was too fat and breathless to exert himself. He beckoned Sally over and she went unwillingly. What now?

'I'm off down to Ripon. Got a meeting, a dinner to go to. Do you want me to call at the auctioneers and ask them to put on a farm sale, right away? You'll need to sell the cows and sheep and yer've got an old hoss and a plough....' He sounded as though he'd already calculated what she was worth.

'No, thank you. I am not selling anything.' Sally's mouth set in a straight line.

Sol went on, oblivious, not listening. 'I forgot to mention – rent's overdue. Mr Radford'll only give you a fortnight to pay, or never mind Lady Day, you'll be out now!'

In the stress of her father's death Sally had forgotten about the rent. But it was not overdue; the quarter was up at the end of June – in a couple of weeks. Another thing to deal with, on top of this morning's news. Sally stood up as straight as possible and stared at the man. 'I know the date very well, Mr Bartram. The rent is not overdue – it's to be paid at the end of the month! Surely the Radfords wouldn't throw me out into the street?'

'Wouldn't rely on it.' Sol laughed harshly. 'They're hard men, business men. They drive a hard bargain. And then there's the bad blood between ye. Radfords and Masons have been fell out a long time. They'll not likely help a Mason.'

The man was trying to bully her, making things even worse. There was not a scrap of good feeling in Sol Bartram. Sally kept up an unwavering stare with her blue eyes. 'I have to milk the cows, Mr Bartram. Good day.'

Sol shook the reins and the pony moved off. 'Aye. Well, think on. You're a hard piece yourself. Bad as yer grandfather most likely! Most women would be bawling their heads off.' Passing through the gate, he turned and said, 'Fetch rent by end of month.'

The grey stone village of Thorpe was calm and quiet, bathed in afternoon sun as Sally crossed the green to collect her cows for milking, trying to calm her jangling nerves. Two interviews with that man in one day was too much for her peace of mind.

The cows were standing in the village pond for their afternoon drink and it was a slow job to persuade them to walk over the road and into the milking shed. Cows shouldn't be hurried, they seemed to say as

16

they sauntered along, udders swinging. Ducks ran flapping out of their way, just as they always did. It was the same scene that Sally had known every day of her life. Thorpe was her world, in rain and shine, in snow and hail. A peaceful way of life, now threatened. She was trying to be brave, but she might have to sell up. It would all be over. It was unbearable that the cattle might have to go to a farm where they'd be treated like – like animals! In spite of her anxiety Sally laughed at the thought, but it was true that the Mason livestock were treated almost like people. They had always been handled with respect for their dignity and thought for their comfort. 'They are our workmates, Sally,' her father had said once.

Most of the cows had been born on the farm and Sally's father had been proud of his home-bred herd. Sally knew each cow by name and they knew her. In the past, they had won prizes at shows, but there was no time now for frivolous outings like that.

Selling them would be very hard, she thought to herself every time she remembered Sol and his threats. Let's hope it doesn't come to that. Keep busy, Sally. But when Bluebell the lead cow nuzzled her gently as she was milked, Sally buried her face in the soft flank and wept. She cried for her father, who had battled so long with failing lungs. She cried for her pretty mother who had died two years before of a septic throat. And she felt quite alone and overwhelmed by the heavy responsibility of the farm.

By the time milking was over, Sally was calm again. She carried the milk into the dairy and set about the evening chores as she'd always done. Increasingly, Sally had done more of the work as her father's illness had progressed. She knew all the routines and had more experience of the farm work than most women. But she only had female strength. And she had all the house and dairy work to do as well.

To pay the rent, Sally would have to dip into the family savings. Thursday evening was the time for the Penny Bank to open in Thorpe. Hastily washing her face and putting on a clean dress, Sally flew up the street to the Reading Room where the banking session was held.

The bank was opened each week by John Pickering, a serious, kindly man who was the unofficial village leader. Villagers could organize their savings without needing to go to Ripon and they knew their money was safe. The Yorkshire Penny Bank had imposing buildings in the big towns and John Pickering was himself rather monumental, thought Sally, just as a banker should be.

'Mr Pickering, I don't know where Father's bank book is. But could you – could you let me have some money out of the account to pay the rent? I do know it's a joint account, him and me.' Sally pushed back a stray red curl.

'Surely your father told you all about the financial affairs of the farm? And where the records are kept?' Mr Pickering sounded alarmed. Concerned grey eyes looked into hers.

'Well, no. We never talked much about money. I think he didn't want me to worry.' A tear splashed onto Sally's hands. 'The only thing I know is that he'd put everything in both our names when I turned twenty-one.'

There was a pause and the banker looked out of the window. Then he sighed and opened a ledger. He ruffled through the pages. 'I hate to have to tell you this, my dear, but there's no money left in your account – just a few pence, to keep it open.' He looked up.

Sally sat absolutely still with shock.

'But surely this won't be the only money in the family. I know Robert talked about saving up to buy back the farm one day.' Mr Pickering spoke deliberately, slowly, perhaps giving her time to recover.

The girl fought the rising panic. No money! 'And where do you think it might be? Another bank, perhaps? Father used to bank in town as well.'

'He never told me. I think you'd better go home and look through all your father's papers and you might find out. You see, Sally, the Penny Bank account was only used for saving up spare money from selling eggs or cheese. It couldn't have been his main account. Your solicitor will probably know something about it. Have you no money in the house?' Most farmers kept a 'bob or two' under the mattress for emergencies. Sally knew all about that and she also knew where it had gone.

'I used it all to pay for the funeral. And the headstone.' ROBERT MASON, 1841-1894, OF BADGER'S GILL, AND HIS BELOVED WIFE, LOUISA, 1845-1892. A simple headstone was all she'd been able to afford. Another tear rolled down her cheek. It was all too raw, too savage for the girl, thinking of the earth over their grave. This time there was no bright side to look upon.

John Pickering's sympathy showed in his face as he closed the ledger. 'You could ask your Uncle Samuel – he could know something about your father's affairs. I think he'd be a good person to advise you.'

Sally realized that she didn't want anybody to know about the embarrassing shortage of money. But she should visit Uncle Samuel and Aunt Bertha. Her uncle would be grieving for his brother and would surely be sympathetic.

'Thank you, Mr Pickering, I'll see Uncle Samuel. Don't worry about me, the farm is going well. Soon be selling the lambs. Goodnight.'

Sally went slowly back down the village street, much more slowly than she'd gone up it earlier. Badger's Gill was the last house on the Ripon road, facing the village with its prim front windows but open to the rolling countryside at the back. Sniffing the scent of roses from the village gardens, Sally tried to put the thought of the rent out of her mind. Masons were not very good with money; they were not very interested in it. But unfortunately she would now need to take a keen interest in it ... how did one do it? She thought about the lamb crop. They could be sold before the end of the year, but not yet.

'Hello, Sally, are you going to pass by without a word? Come in and have a bite of supper with us!' came a strong, cheerful voice, from a village garden.

Sally looked up. 'Sorry, Martha, I didn't see you.' She crossed the dusty village road. Martha, plump and comfortable in a white apron, opened the little gate into her garden, which was crowded with summer flowers.

'Come on in, now. George has just lit the lamp. George, here's Sally, you were just wondering how she was getting on.'

Soon the three of them were sitting round

the table, with ham, cheese and pickles and hot, strong cups of tea. Sally began to feel hungry and remembered that she hadn't eaten since midday. The lamp cast a warm circle of light round them and as she looked at the kind faces, her feeling of loneliness receded.

George and Martha Dawson were of her parents' generation and she'd known them all her life. Sally's father had often called George 'medieval' because of his old-fashioned ways. He was tall and rangy, but beginning to bend a little with age and from lifting heavy weights. Sally had always liked his kind eyes, hidden under his pulled-down cap. George's farm was a few scattered fields on the outskirts of the village, where he kept sheep, and grew a few carrots or cabbages to sell.

As she ate Sally could feel the couple's concern for her, but they asked no questions. Martha smiled when she heard of the sheep shearing. 'George would have done it for you, love!'

'Aye, lass. I'll shear the rest for you next week.' However much she protested, Sally had to give in. 'That's what neighbours are for,' he said quietly, lighting his pipe.

These kind people would want to lend her money if they knew she had none. It was most important that they shouldn't know. They described themselves as comfortable, but they would have little to spare. The winters were long at Thorpe, with little chance for selling produce, and anything they could save in summer would be needed for the dark months when the wind whipped in from the North Sea and nothing grew in the fields until spring.

Looking up from her plate Sally saw that Martha was watching her closely over her glasses in a motherly sort of way. 'Not much money coming in lately, I expect,' the older woman now ventured almost diffidently. She smoothed the white apron. 'But I was thinking you'll have some milk to spare, very soon. Those calves'll be big enough to live on grass any day now.'

Sally blushed at the forbidden mention of money, but then she smiled. 'That's a good thought, Martha. I've been so busy, I didn't think of weaning the calves. But if they're not to feed I can go back to making butter, maybe.'

'You've kept up the cheese-making, haven't you?'

'Yes, there's been enough milk to make cheese twice a week.' Sally thought proudly of the Wensleydale cheeses in her little store-room, quietly maturing, all laced into their calico covers and waiting for the factor to call in the autumn to buy them. But until then they would not earn any money. 'I might make a bit of butter and take it to Ripon market next week.' How many pounds of butter would pay the rent?

Martha beamed. 'You used to make grand butter, lass, I'm sure folks will fall over themselves to buy it. Now, if you're taking the pony and trap down next Thursday, can I have a ride with you? I could help you with the baskets maybe.'

Sally's heart lightened a little as she thought of selling butter. High Side butter from the villages on the moorland side of Ripon was thought to be far better than that produced by the fat cattle of the valley. 'We'll be a couple of real High-Siders, striding through town with our big baskets! Are you sure you want to be seen with me?' Sally's laugh was almost cheerful, and it made George smile.

'There's worse things than being a High-Sider! Nowt to be ashamed of. But you'll nearly have forgotten, it's a long while since butter was made at Badger's Gill.' George shook his silver head.

It was true. Sally couldn't remember the last time she'd made butter, but it would have been before her father had such difficulty in breathing that he'd had to leave most of the farm work to his daughter. After that there had been no time for making butter. Maybe that was why there was no money in the bank.

'I'll need to set the cream to rise, I'd better be off,' said Sally once supper was over, feeling tired after the ups and downs of the day.

'Don't forget the butter stamp. Your Ma had a good one for the tops of the bricks. A badger, it was, for Badger's Gill... Your father carved it for her when they were first married.'

Sally promised she would find the stamp and all her bricks would carry the badger trademark. It was a small link with her parents and a nice idea.

'And when they taste how good it is they'll come back for more. The badger will remind them who you are,' said Martha, evidently afraid that the Masons were not quite business-minded enough, but Sally was quite grateful for the advice. She had a week to skim off the cream, let it mature and make it into butter, before the market next Thursday.

TWO

You have to eat to live, my girl. How about that? Walking home through the long June twilight, Sally realized that there would be no money to buy food for herself, for quite a while. Maybe Martha had already thought of that, and this was why she'd invited her to a meal and watched her eat. Like the other farmers, the Masons had usually bought their groceries on market day, using the money they earned from eggs, butter and other produce of the farm. Rabbits, too, if they could snare them. Ripon folk liked a fresh rabbit. But there had been no visits to the market for some time, either to earn money or to spend it.

After the funeral there had been little food left in the house. The whole village had been there and most of them had come to the tea afterwards. Robert Mason had been well-liked and everybody, while lamenting his passing, had enjoyed his funeral – a real community event.

Sally thought about her stores. The hams, cured last autumn, had been baked and eaten. The flour bin was nearly empty, but there could be some oats in the granary, she thought. The garden vegetables were coming along nicely but only the gooseberries were ready. That left milk and eggs; the cheese should really be kept for sale. Since the funeral there had been so little time that Sally hadn't worried about proper meals, or buying in more food. Not until now. Although she could clearly remember the time before the farm was sold, when there was little to eat in the house, Sally had never needed to think about where the next penny was coming from. Her father had handled the money in both their names. 'R. and S. Mason, Badger's Gill' was a respected family concern with good credit anywhere in Ripon. But that was when they were selling plenty of cheese and butter. Tonight she'd discovered that their savings had gone, or had been stored elsewhere. Well, she'd better make some more! It was summer, the cows were milking well, so there was a bright side if you looked for it ... hard.

Turning in at the gate, Sally decided to take a last look at the sheep before going to bed. It was almost dark enough to visit the badgers, so first she went down into the bottom of the gill. The Masons had always been interested in the badgers and her father had loved to watch the young cubs playing at this time of the year. In a way, Sally thought, the Masons guarded the badgers, checking on them from time to time. They'd been there before the Masons came, maybe for thousands of years, but they were at risk from cruel men. Although the sport of badger baiting had been illegal for almost half a century, there were still sessions held in secret at country inns, and so badgers were in demand. Dogs were set on them and bets were laid as to how many dogs would be killed before the badger died. It was barbaric, but it still went on. The Masons had seldom mentioned the animals to anyone else, wanting to keep their home a secret, but the farm name, Badger's Gill, gave them away.

Their habits varied, probably as a protective device. Badgers were unpredictable creatures and tonight, no young cubs were about, the place was eerily quiet. In the silence Sally stood quite still. She could hear the distant hoot of an owl and a dog barking. Her old dog, Moll, up in the farmyard. Something was wrong ... and then she heard a creak. It was the creak of a swinging gate and Sally knew what it meant. She ran to the top of the bank and saw the gate swinging open into the green lane. The sheep had gone! With a sinking heart, Sally wondered what kind of trouble the flock was in this time. A few months ago they'd found a hole in the hedge, scrambled through and gone off to eat in the village gardens. Sally had needed to apologize to a few irate gardeners and give them plants from her own garden. She blushed to think of it.

Where were the sheep this time? The worst thing of all was the open gate. It had been deliberately opened by a human – no sheep, however determined, could open that gate.

Mist crept up from the river as dawn broke, curling through the oak trees in Hack Fall, moving up Badger's Gill and touching Sally with its cold fingers as she strode down the bank. After a nearly sleepless night worrying about the sheep – and the unknown enemy – Sally was rounding up the cows for milking. You had to trust people in the country. You had to believe that they wouldn't steal stock or let them out. Most folks would put animals back in their field if they saw them on the road. But whatever else happened, even if the sky fell down, the cows had to be milked every morning and every night. It was an imperative that shaped the day, that had always called farmers from village events, and it came before and after a day's holiday or even a funeral.

The missing sheep were weighing on Sally's mind and she rushed through the milking as fast as she could. But peering out of the cowshed door she could see that the mist was thickening into a fog. It was hard to find sheep in a fog; they merged into the background too easily.

With the milking over, the girl munched a piece of bread and cheese – no time to make a cup of tea – and threw on an old shawl. Catching sight of herself in the mirror she grinned at the image of the slight figure swathed in grey, with the red hair hidden. Suitably anonymous, although everybody in Thorpe knew the sheep only too well.

Where had those wicked sheep gone? Sally didn't blame Mary and Lavinia so much as the person who let them out, and she shivered when she thought of the ill-will behind the action. What had she done to earn such treatment?

A quick survey of the gardens on Thorpe's main street revealed nothing; not a petal out of place, thank goodness. Prudence had a fondness for roses and if she got the chance she led the flock straight to Mrs Bentley's garden at the vicarage.

Sally remembered how last year the sheep had adventured along the green lane. Gertrude had led that day and they'd gone carefully round the backs of the houses, crossed the road to Masham and ended up on Nutwith Common. The Motley Flock, as her father had called them, liked variety in their lives.

With some tempting grain in her bucket Sally set off at a trot, slowing down to a more ladylike walk when she saw anyone coming. There were few folks about in the foggy morning but she heard the rumble of a cart halfway along the street.

'Robin, the sheep are out again!' Sally's cheeks were just a little pink and she was breathing a little faster. 'You haven't seen them, have you?' She felt conscious of the old shawl and her farm boots and the dowdy impression she gave. It would have been better to appear cool and collected. She would like to impress Robin Scott.

Robin laughed and shook his curly brown head. 'Not again! How clever of them. No, I haven't seen them, unfortunately. Wish I could help you, lass, but I've got an urgent job to do this morning. Tell you what, though, I'll keep an eye out. I'll let you know if I spot them.'

'Thanks.' Sally couldn't keep the dejection out of her voice and Robin must have noticed it. It would have been good to have Robin's help.

'I nearly forgot, Ma says you should come to supper on Sunday. It'll be lonely for you at Badger's Gill all on your own. I'll tell her you'll be there, then!' He shook the reins and the carthorse lumbered off.

Sally watched him disappear into the fog and sighed. She should have got over Robin by now. They'd played together when they were small and Sally had hoped they could be more than friends. Gradually her feelings for him had deepened as she grew up, but Robin, jolly light-hearted lad that he was, had never even hinted at romance. And after years of waiting Sally had slowly realized that he probably never would. To him, she was like a sister. Robin's mother was aware of the whole situation and Sally thought she must sympathize a little. She often invited Sally to join them and Robin was still good company, still her friend, but somehow detached.

As she plodded up the road Sally saw Robin's image in front of her, the flash of a smile in a thin brown face, the dancing light in his eyes behind his glasses. Robin Scott was one of those who were born lucky, apart from poor eyesight. The Scotts owned three or four farms and Robin's enthusiasm had led them into modern farming methods. They ran the farms as a business and the Masons had sometimes envied their success. Robin was just a year older than Sally and she wondered sometimes whether he would ever fall in love. It was almost time for him to get married and take over one of the family farms, but he never talked of the future.

There was something on the road. Sally reluctantly jerked her thoughts away from Robin, back to the task in hand. There was the imprint of a cloven hoof in the soft earth at the side of the road and here were some more. Sheep had passed this way recently. It would be very hard to find the sheep on the common in fog, but better for them to be there than nibbling away at gardens or farm crops.

Halfway up the hill there was a farm gate and the sheep had milled around there for a while and then gone in. Sally followed their tracks all the way up to Camp Hill Farm, shivering at the thought of what she would find. There was a new tenant at this farm, an unknown quantity. Collecting a bunch of strays would be the worst possible way to meet a new neighbour. Sally imagined the scene. 'Good morning, Mr Farmer, how nice to meet you, I've just come to pick up my sheep. So sorry they've trampled your young corn, I hope it will grow again soon.' She would avoid the farmer if at all possible.

Skirting the farmhouse and buildings warily, Sally made her way up the hill and memories flooded her mind, so that for a while she forgot about her troubles. Up here on a clear day you could see across a wide sweep of farmland, over to the east from the ridge of the High Side. But at present she could see nothing but the rectangular shape of the Roman camp, looming at the top of the hill. Sally had loved to come up here with her mother and hear about how the Roman soldiers built a small fort so that they could watch out on all sides. Only the stones of the outer walls now marked the place, but inside the walls was a sheltered hollow where the grass was green. The Romans out of the history books had actually been here and Sally had tried to imagine their lives at Thorpe, far from their homes in the sunny south.

Camp Hill was a nice little place for tired sheep to rest up and Sally had a feeling she would find them there. She peered down into the hollow. Of course, there were Prudence, Lavinia and the rest, all sitting comfortably chewing the cud with innocent faces, their lambs at their sides. They looked up at her with composure. At the far side of the bank that had once been the wall of the camp, a tall figure stood watching over them. The figure came and went through the mist like a dream. Head up, shoulders back, with short hair and a stern profile. For a fleeting moment, Sally imagined a Roman soldier stood there, unreal, a phantom from long ago. Just as she'd always imagined one to be.

Tired and hungry as she was, Sally laughed at herself for the thought. 'You don't believe in ghosts – don't be daft!' She drew the shawl closer round her, shivering in the cold air.

The Roman turned his head and saw Sally through the fog. The figure changed instantly into a real young man, and an irate one. 'GET THOSE SHEEP OFF THIS LAND!'

Well, that's a farmer! A ghost wouldn't yell like that, what a relief, Sally thought as she braced herself to deal with this new problem. What if she denied all knowledge of the flock? A slight breeze shook the leaves of an overhanging oak tree and suddenly the fog began to roll away. A misty sun shone through and as Sally stood and trembled, the grand vista appeared at her feet, over to the Vale of Mowbray and beyond. It was a miraculous moment.

In the morning light Sally stood, exposed in her old shawl – a slim young woman. The man's jaw dropped. 'Sorry, miss! I couldn't see in the fog.' But the dark face still looked stern. 'Where's the shepherd?'

'What shepherd?' Sally tried to look vacant, as if she didn't know what he was talking about.

The man pointed to the Motley Flock. 'These sheep are strays and I assume you know something about them. What about it, Bo-Peep?' His voice held an ironic tone.

It was time to create a diversion and the mist had parted just in time to enlarge their world. 'What a beautiful morning!' Sally said as she turned her face to the east, to the sunshine and the view of the valley. 'I used to come up here when I was a child ... and, do you know, for a moment I thought you were a Roman soldier!'

It worked. The man laughed, jumped down lightly from the bank and came to stand beside her. 'Marcus, at your service. Ninth Legion! No doubt you're Bo-Peep from the nursery rhyme?'

He was an attractive man when he stopped scowling. And he seemed to know about the Romans. Well, at least he'd forgotten the bad temper; Sally hated to be shouted at. She smiled vaguely. No good admitting she was a Bo-Peep.

'That's what the fog does for you! I thought

you were a shepherd at first. And I'd like to find the owner of these strays. It's not good enough, letting them wander like this.'

Sally kept quiet and looked attentive. Don't mention sheep, don't look at them... She was willing the man to go away.

The Roman relaxed a little. 'I've wondered myself about what went on up here, two thousand years ago. It was probably a summer camp – too cold up here in the winter, I should have thought.'

'That's what we've always thought. But there was a big Roman town over there, of course.' Sally pointed to the valley in the direction of Boroughbridge. 'My mother said this was probably a lookout for them.'

'You're very well informed, Bo-Peep!' The tone was still slightly ironic, but the man gave her a friendly look.

They looked together over the summer landscape, at the varied patchwork of fields and woods, rising in the blue distance to the Cleveland Hills. Near at hand the last shreds of mist were dissolving in the sun. Sally stole a look at him. The man spoke well, although he was dressed in plain riding clothes and boots. He looked to be in his late twenties; tough, but there was a hint of humour in the firm mouth. What would he think of a dowdy little female that couldn't control her sheep?

Marcus looked down at Sally and she felt

very conscious of the shawl, now dripping with moisture from the fog. Why did she always have to feel so inelegant? Because she was a farmer, she supposed.

'I am just looking over the farm for the new tenant,' he explained. 'He's not living here as yet. I must warn him about leaving gates open. Sheep are obviously a problem here.' He gave her a sideways glance and Sally nodded her head vigorously.

'Oh yes, they are! I'm just passing by, taking a short cut over the hill; there are footpaths here as I suppose you know. That one,' and she pointed to a narrow path leading to a stile, 'leads over Nutwith Common, it's the quickest way to Masham from Thorpe.' This bit of the story was true, at least.

'I like to ride these cross-country tracks. I'm a historian, only an amateur of course, but I try to read the landscape for clues. Now do you think those footpaths are medieval, or are they even older? Prehistoric, perhaps?' He looked at her, considering.

Sally laughed. 'My mother and father used to wonder that too. They read a lot of history, you see, and tried to make it alive – my mother was a teacher; she often brought the children from Thorpe school up here in summer to show them the fort, before she died.' Tears came into her eyes and she blinked them away.

Marcus turned away tactfully. 'So the place

has a lot of memories for you. I feel the same way about Lofthouse, over in Nidderdale. The Nidd was a magic river, when I was a child!'

They looked at each other and Sally felt an attraction of a new kind, as if she wanted to know more about the mysterious 'Marcus'. Not many local farmers were interested in history. He must own the farm. Her father would have known who owned the land here, but Sally couldn't remember. 'It's your land, I suppose? You actually own a Roman fort?'

'My family does. We have a few farms scattered over the High Side. Sometimes I think we should sell them all, the sheep runs, and buy some good land down yonder.' He pointed to the valley of the River Ure. 'Folks down there are already thinking about the hay harvest while we've only just started shearing. It's more civilized, down on the river flats. But then, you don't get views like this one. Are you interested in farming?' The question was so sudden that Sally jumped.

Meeting his thoughtful dark eyes with her own blue ones, Sally said, 'I've lived on a farm all my life. It's hard work but I'd hate to live in a town, even a small one like Ripon.'

Marcus smiled and Sally felt more at ease. He looked quite human when he smiled. 'But Ripon is an ancient city, plenty of history there. It might be easier than following footpaths in the fog. For a young lady, that is.'

It would be hard now to admit she was the owner of the sheep. If only she'd not been dressed so shabbily! But she would probably never see him again, so it didn't matter.

'It was good to meet you, Miss Bo-Peep. I'll collect my horse and be off. Just tell the shepherd to get the sheep off, will you?' Marcus raised a hand in salute and dropped down the bank to where a tall chestnut, horse was tied to a tree. Sally hadn't noticed the horse before; it was very well bred.

Sally decided to walk away from her delinquent flock and try to retrieve them later in the afternoon, when Marcus was out of sight.

They seemed happy enough in their hollow. But the flock had other ideas. There was a sharp clink of the bucket as Sally turned away and that was their signal. They jumped to their feet and assembled in a fairly orderly bunch round her, like children ready for a treat. The Motley Flock had had their fun and they wanted to go home. Sally ignored them and swung down the path, walking as fast as she could, but Mary and Lavinia followed, with the rest tagging on behind. The game was over, it was time to go. They bleated happily at Sally as they trotted along, peering up at her through their woolly fringes.

'You horrible sheep!' Sally was exasperated. But she was also proud of her flock at the same time.

Marcus came up on his horse and to her surprise he was laughing, bending over his saddle and trying to catch his breath. 'Caught you out! You can't deny ownership now, Bo-Peep!'

Blushing furiously, Sally went off down the farm track, the sheep behind her, following closely with their eyes on the bucket. The lambs galloped to keep up. Marcus let her go ahead but then caught up as she came to the road. 'Would you like some help to get them home, Bo-Peep?'

'No, thank you. I'm sorry I wasn't entirely truthful... I was so ashamed.' Sally's face was hot and when she raised it to look at him, she saw the ironic glint in his eyes again. 'I don't usually set out to deceive, but do you know, someone deliberately opened the gate and let the sheep escape!'

The horseman shook his head. 'A despicable trick. Report him when you find out who it was. And put a padlock on the gate. We can't have this happening again!' He swung the horse to face her. 'Perhaps I should follow behind to make sure they don't stray?'

To make sure they were well clear of the farm more likely, Sally thought. 'They follow me very well, thank you. I apologize for them and I'm grateful for your – tolerance. I'm sorry that they strayed on to your land.' It sounded strained, a formal little speech, but Sally felt she had to say something. He'd been quite kind. The sheep stood still, waiting for Sally to make a move. Mary, as usual, was standing very close, hoping that the girl would stroke her woolly head. How embarrassing!

'I've never seen such a well-behaved flock, I must say. Most impressive!' His voice softened a little. 'You must be a good shepherdess, Bo-Peep.'

'Thank you. I reared them all myself and now I'm ashamed of them!' Sally saw the funny side of the situation and in spite of herself, laughter bubbled up. Her shawl fell back and stray curls came tumbling round her face. 'Oh Marcus, I am so sorry!'

'Don't let it happen again, miss.'

Reluctantly Sally turned to go back down the hill to Thorpe. She wanted to get home as soon as possible, away from this dreadful situation. But at the same time she had a strange feeling that she wanted to stay on the damp hilltop, talking to this interesting man. Who was he? Marcus, too seemed slow to leave. He was busily adjusting his girth, fiddling with the stirrups and then leading his horse out on to the track. Perhaps he was keeping an eye on her. Did he suspect that she'd take the sheep back up the hill, as soon as he'd gone?

'I hope that we may meet again in better circumstances! And more comfortable surroundings, too.'

'Could hardly be worse,' Sally muttered as, with a wave, the man turned his horse and cantered off.

The Motley Flock was severely reprimanded by its owner later in the day, not for the first time. The sheep stood in a circle, back home safely in the paddock, and gazed up at her, as Sally told them what she thought of them. 'And made me look so stupid in front of – in front of a stranger!' She blushed again at the thought. There was an old padlock in the barn and Sally locked up the gate with a big chain that night. She'd have to remember where she put the key. Marcus would be pleased that she'd taken his advice.

She couldn't find out who he was because Camp Farm had changed hands in the last month or so and nobody seemed to know who'd bought it. 'Some big farmer from Ripon way,' said Robin laconically. She would probably never see him again.

THREE

'I am sorry to have to say this to the mistress of a respectable household.' The doctor looked over the top of his glasses and the respectable Mrs Bellamy looked sternly back. She sat upright in rustling black, thin and elegant, waiting for the verdict.

'This young woman is almost certainly pregnant. Either that or she has a large tumour. Pregnancy, taking into account all the symptoms, is the more likely.'

Mrs Bellamy's icy calm was broken. Her hand flew to her mouth and her voice was high. 'Surely not! The child is only sixteen and young for her age! She goes nowhere alone! We are her guardians! How can she be ... have you told her?'

'Not yet. I thought it best to speak to you first.' The doctor looked out of the window, wondering how soon he could make his escape. On a fine June day such as this he would rather be out of town than in grimy Sheffield, even in the upper-class suburbs. The sun filtered weakly through the smoky haze of industry. You never saw real sunshine in Sheffield.

Emma stood up nervously as the doctor

and Mrs Bellamy came back in. Her hands twisted together and she looked at the floor as her guardian spoke in a stern, quiet voice. 'Emma Jane! Is there anything you are hiding from us?'

'N-no, Mrs Bellamy.' What could she mean?

'Dr Murray says that you may – you may be with child!' It was a terrible whisper. 'How can this be?'

Emma flushed crimson as the light dawned. She should have realized that it could happen. That young Mr Steele, a business acquaintance of Bellamy's, had stayed in the house on his way to London. Had stayed a few weeks in the end, as they had made some business arrangements. She had hated Mr Steele.

'I will leave you now, Mrs Bellamy.' The doctor packed up his bag. 'It seems that the young person has something to tell you. I will examine her again in a few weeks. Good day.'

When the doctor had gone Mrs Bellamy turned on Emma in a fury. 'Is this how you repay our kindness: taking you in as an orphan after your parents died? Making you a member of a respectable family in Sheffield, a leading family of cutlers with a reputation to uphold? I never thought, never ever thought that you would bring us to this disgrace!' She paused. 'You will be whipped, 'of course.'

Emma looked at the carpet and tried to concentrate on its pattern. There was nothing she could say.

'Who is the man? He shall be made to marry you! Tell me this instant, Emma Jane! With whom have you besmirched our name?'

She could still smell the drink on his breath, hear his excited giggle as he climbed into bed beside her. They'd given Mr Steele a room next to Emma and she had no lock on her door. She'd tried to wedge it with a chair after the first night, but he'd still managed to get in. Emma had cried, but he had threatened her. 'I'll kill you if you tell anybody at all. Remember that.' Strong hands had closed round her throat. Small and pale, Emma had never expected to be in danger from a man. She hadn't thought very much about where babies came from, but had a hazy memory of what had happened last year when a maid got into trouble and had to be married off quickly.

'I can't say.' Hot tears forced themselves out from under Emma's closed eyelids. Her head ached. How she wished she could feel well again.

Her guardian shook her arm roughly. 'I demand that you tell me. Where have you been? Did you sneak off somewhere while Mr Bellamy and I were away in April? That must be it! I don't know what Mr Bellamy will say when he hears this, but you are in deep trouble, you stupid girl! Brazen hussy, for all your meekness. You must have provoked some poor man, led him on ... you slut!'

Emma remembered those awful nights, the dread that he would come again: he usually did. She remembered the pain and the shame of it and the way he'd laughed when he left her shuddering. He was on the way to business deals abroad, thank goodness. She would never see him again so long as they didn't find out who did it. That much Emma held on to, as she looked at the carpet. She didn't want them to pursue Mr Steele. It was possible they'd make him marry her and she would have that dreadful nightly ordeal for the rest of her life! Anything was better than that.

'To think that after we gave you a home and a family, you should behave like this.' Mrs Bellamy went on and on, but eventually she ran out of breath and Emma was left alone in the morning-room.

It was true the Bellamys had taken her in after her parents died. But they had also taken over the business interests and money built up by her father, a property owner, who had been a distant relative. Emma was given a small room and allowed to eat at the Bellamy's dining-table. But she was not encouraged to join in the conversation. There was a maid for the rough work and a cook, but Emma did much of the housework and all the sewing for the household.

Emma was often severely disciplined 'for her own good', which meant that she was whipped. Mr Bellamy took a small horsewhip to her of the kind used by jockeys, for the slightest reason. If Emma dropped a plate, she was whipped. Mr Bellamy seemed to enjoy it, although he said it was his unpleasant duty. She was a drudge and she knew it. Her parents' money had disappeared and the only escape Emma could think of was to try to find a post as a governess. But she looked so young and small, it would be hard to find work. The whipping took away her confidence. And since those nights of torment she'd felt even less confident about asking anyone for a job. She felt guilty somehow, and very frightened of men.

The next few days were a nightmare for Emma. Why had she not realized what was happening to her body? Why did nobody explain these things to young people? Mr Bellamy was appalled, of course. He wanted to get rid of Emma as soon as possible, and told her so.

Gradually through the gloom, a faint hope glimmered. They talked of sending her to the country. Somewhere remote so that her disgrace would not affect their respectable standing. In Sheffield they were pillars of the church, known for their gifts to charity. 'We try to set a standard for the workers to follow,' Mr Bellamy said smugly at board meetings.

Emma had been to the Dales for holidays in the days when she had loving parents and a happy life. 'The country' always had a sort of golden glow for her. If she could get away from the Bellamys even for a few months, perhaps her head wouldn't ache so much.

'It will be a just punishment for you.' Mrs Bellamy obviously hated the country. 'You will have to put up with horrid smells and uncouth people. There will be no polite society and no drains. And in any case your condition will be obvious. You will be in disgrace and ostracized by all decent people. It serves you right.'

'Yes, Mrs Bellamy,' Emma whispered. She would try to pack a few books in her luggage. She had not yet begun to think about the baby; such thoughts were pushed away.

For the next few days Sally had no time at all to think of Roman soldiers. The old farmhouse dairy echoed with the swish, thump of the butter churn as she made batch after batch of butter. It took her most of a morning: skimming the cream off the top of the milk, churning in the big barrel churn, washing and pressing the granules together and finally – the best part – shaping each lump of butter into a perfect, rectangular brick with the badger pattern on the top.

The weather continued to be fine and while Sally made butter, George finished shearing the Motley Flock, with dear Martha helping to wrap the fleeces. Afterwards they sat in Sally's kitchen, eating thick slices of Martha's fresh crusty loaf with some of Sally's plum jam. It was the first bread Sally had eaten for a week and she was ravenous. Oatcakes made with stale corn were now her main diet, but they were not the same as bread.

However, they wouldn't eat the butter. 'Nay, you'll need to sell it all!' Martha had inspected the butter and approved of it. 'It should sell well, you've done a good job. Your mother always said you were a good little dairy worker!'

George grinned across the table, satisfied with his day's work. 'Now Martha lass, where's that gooseberry pie you promised?'

'Here it is. Well, those sheep'll be glad to get their wool off. Weather's warming up. I just hope we don't get a storm.'

After milking that night Sally went down the gill to see her beloved sheep, unfamiliar now without their wool, although quite plump and well fed. They gathered round the bucket as usual and she noticed that the lambs were learning the same behaviour.

About half the lambs were females. 'And I think I'll keep you girls, if you behave yourselves!' Sally told them. 'We'll have a bigger Motley Flock next year and more lambs.' She sighed, remembering that all the lambs should really be sold to help to pay the rent.

Thursday dawned without the dreaded storm, cool and cloudy. Summers on the High Side were generally cool, with a slight breeze off the moor on even the hottest day. Thorpe was on a windy ridge with valleys at either side, but in the west there was a long line of moorland on the horizon, turning purple with heather in the late summer and white with snow in the winter. Sally knew that they were farming on the edge: any higher up the hill and the soils were too poor for a dairy. Ripon was a different climate, soft and sheltered in the Ure valley, the huge old trees indicating the depth of soil. But the High Side farmers had to compete down in Ripon with those who had life easier.

As Sally drove the trap carefully down the Ripon road the sun came out and she could feel the heat increasing, the warmer air coming to meet them as they went downhill. With her unruly red hair tied back with a ribbon and a clean cotton dress of light blue, Sally felt like a different person from the girl in the grey shawl. True, she'd lost weight and the frock was a little too big for her, but it was quite pretty and more feminine than any of her farm clothes. Perhaps she should stop worrying just for today and enjoy the change of scene. But that was impossible at the moment. There was too much at stake.

Martha sat beside Sally, glancing from time to time at the butter baskets. They were covered with cool cabbage leaves, which was all they could do to protect them. The butter was firm and chilled, kept on marble slabs in the dairy to cool it down as much as possible. Slowly, Jed the pony picked his way down the hill near Sutton.

'It's a long time since I stood in the market to sell,' Sally admitted to Martha. 'The eggs are easy, Thorpe folks come to the door for them and I have regular orders in the village. It's the same with milk, if there's any to spare. The cheese is collected – so there's only butter to sell in Ripon.'

'Well, there'll be lambs to go to market in a few months and maybe some of the calves. George will help you find a buyer and he says prices are quite good this year.' Martha sounded reassuring but once again, Sally felt the weight of the farm on her shoulders. There was a lot to think about.

A pheasant crossed the road and the young pony shied slightly. 'Hey, Jed! Steady!' Martha grasped the sides of the trap firmly, but said nothing.

'He tries hard, this horse, but he has a lot to learn,' explained Sally, as Martha re-adjusted her bonnet and smoothed her grey dress. 'Father used to manage him better than I can.'

'How do you know when a horse is try-ing?' Martha enquired, but Sally couldn't explain herself. She just knew sometimes what animals were thinking.

In spite of her worries Sally felt a lightening of the heart when they reached Ripon and unyoked in Wells' Garth, as her father had always done on market day. Farmers could leave their traps in the Garth and their horses in the nearby stables. A narrow 'ginnel' led straight out to the large market square, dominated by the imposing Town Hall. You couldn't see the square itself for the mass of stalls, people and produce. In the very middle was a tall obelisk with a horn on the top, the badge of Ripon. That was where butter was sold; other towns had their butter cross, but Ripon had the Wakeman's Horn.

The women had to push their way through the crowd to reach the stone butter benches. It was good to be back for a while in the bustle of the town, a quiet cathedral city for the most part, but a place that came alive every Thursday when the market was held. 'I sometimes think that folks come here more for the gossip than anything!' Martha was watching two women avidly listening to a third.

Sally was not in a hurry, just for once. People bought their butter later, after the other groceries, to sit on top of the basket as they went home. The morning was very warm. When they reached the square Sally took off her jacket and draped it over the baskets. She was sorry that the shady side was already taken. The baskets were heavy and Martha was obviously pleased to put hers down. Sally was used to heavy weights but even so, she stretched with relief as they looked around.

Martha offered to stay with the baskets while Sally walked through the market place. She had no money to spend, but it was good to see the amazing variety and to know that you could buy almost anything on Ripon market. Martha went off next, taking her string bag. The day grew warmer and the High Side farmers were mopping their faces with big handkerchiefs. 'Hottest day for years!' one neighbour said to her, with a kindly smile. Too hot for the butter, maybe. Sally lifted the cabbage leaves and saw that the bricks were very soft, almost slumping. Oh somebody, please buy my butter soon!

Robin's mother came by and stopped for a chat, a cheerful woman with a lot to be cheerful about. She had three wonderful sons, a doting husband and plenty of help in the house. She probably didn't know what it was to be really tired, Sally thought enviously.

'Dear me, Sally, it's a bad day to sell butter!' Mrs Scott could see the problem at once. 'But never mind, next week will probably be quite cold. We hope to see you on Sunday after Evensong – Robin asked you?' The Scotts, unlike the Masons, often had time to go to church.

'Thank you, it's kind of you.'

If only a cool breeze would come in from the North Sea ... but the air was still and the heat increased as the day wore on. It was obvious, Sally thought after an hour or so of crowds sweeping by ignoring her, that nobody wanted to buy butter on a very hot day. The townsfolk could easily get some at the grocer's any day of the week. High Side butter was superior, they all agreed, but not if it was too soft. It might spoil the other groceries in their basket; best leave it for today. She had no regular customers who might be loyal to Sally Mason through good weather and bad. When Badger's Gill butter was on sale regularly – her mother had tried to sell every fortnight – there were Ripon folk who looked out for her and always bought from her. But that was in the past and those customers had gone.

Half an hour later Sally saw a thin trickle coming from one of the baskets. The butter was melting into oil, running through the wickerwork as a liquid. Even if she could catch it, once butterfat melted it was worthless. Her butter could never be sold now. Soon both baskets were empty.

When Martha came back Sally was weeping. There was a pool of oil round her feet, the ruin of her hopes. All that work, starting with milking the cows, had been for nothing. And there was still no money to pay the rent. They would go home no better off. If only they'd put the butter in a pail of cold water! But the morning had been cool when they left Thorpe. Sally felt hopeless. She was not meant to struggle on at the farm. She should give up now and walk away from a task that needed a strong man, and a man with a good wife at that. It was all too much.

'Don't cry, Sally love!' Martha put an arm round her shoulders. 'It's bad luck, I know, but we'll think of something else. I rarely saw butter do this before! But I heard of it, from my granny. It used to happen often in the old days.'

Prompted by Martha, Sally dried her eyes and ate a piece of bread and cheese, but it was stale, dried out by the heat of the day. All around them stallholders were trying to escape the sun, rigging up shade where they could. Food was obviously growing stale quickly; a woman on a cake stall sold off everything at half price to get rid of it. Martha bought some gingerbread. She couldn't make it for that price.

'There's no profit today,' the cake woman sighed. 'And those poor lasses with the butter, I feel right sorry for them. We must live on our losses.'

Several other women were trying to sell butter at Ripon that day and even though they were in the shade, their butter melted too. They shrugged and smiled at Sally with fellow feeling even though they were competitors.

'I've lost the butter, but thank the Lord I've sold some eggs and a few herbs,' a woman from Kirkby said to Sally. 'And you've come all the way from Thorpe for nowt. Life's hard, at times... You'll be Robert Mason's daughter, that right? You look just like your ma.'

Sol Bartram walked past, his piggy eyes darting everywhere. He looked past Sally at the crowded market place, smiling craftily. 'Hear yer sheep were out on the road again. You should mend the fences! And feed 'em better. They must be starving!'

With red-rimmed eyes, Sally looked straight at him. 'And did *you* open the gate for the sheep, Mr Bartram? Somebody did!' Until this moment Sally hadn't thought of Sol. But he was the only enemy she had, after all. Who else would wish her ill? And why was he so against her?

The little eyes jerked back to Sally's face. 'That's slander, you can get yerself arrested for accusing folks of things like that.' He looked towards the road on the outside of the square and pointed to a smart trap, driven by a well dressed man with grey hair. 'Know who that is?'

Sally was not very interested. 'Well, who is it?' The face was thin, ascetic, rather grim.

'That's yer landlord. That's Mr Oliver Radford, that is. I was talking to him only yesterday. He was saying how pleased he was that you're going, how he hates Masons, always has, and is looking forward to getting a proper tenant in Badger's Gill. Masons did Radfords some dirty tricks, years ago. He's a hard man is Mr Radford and he won't worry if you're thrown on to the street. I should make other arrangements, if I was you.'

Sally could believe Sol when she saw the face of Oliver Radford. That stern, handsome face belonged to a man who was ruthless, set on getting his own way, she could tell. There was no mercy in it. Not for the first time she wondered what had happened to set the two families against each other. It seemed ridiculous to be enemies without even knowing the whole story. And it was hard to believe that her family did 'dirty tricks'. The Masons had their faults, but they were not vindictive or dishonest. Sally's father had spoken rarely of the Radfords, and then always with a gentle regret as though the feud was inevitable, but not his fault. Her mother maintained a steady silence on that topic. They had both been shocked to find that the Radfords had bought Badger's Gill. That was deception if you like, thought Sally. A bad harvest and then the cattle plague had forced him to sell, and the auctioneers had found him a 'secret buyer', someone who would lease back the farm to the Masons. Only when the sale was completed did the Masons find out that the Radfords were their landlords. After two hundred years of independent small farming the Masons had gone down in the world. They were farm tenants, dependent on the landlord's whim – a landlord who was hostile to them. It was a bitter pill to swallow and Robert Mason's health had begun to decline from then.

Watching the retreating, tweed-clad back of Mr Radford as he moved slowly through the crowded street, Sally realized that in fact he'd been quite reasonable until now. The Masons had paid the rent to Sol at the Crown and the Radfords had left them alone. If only that could continue! But of course, her father was gone, and a female tenant was unusual, unconventional. Her main problem was being a woman. The Radfords must have known of her father's illness; they'd probably been waiting to grab the farm back when he died.

Sol looked down and saw the oily pools round the baskets. 'Lost yer butter, have you? Typical Mason, selling butter on a hot day!' He laughed and Sally could have hit him.

'The rent will be paid on time.' Sally's mouth set in a determined line and she spoke through clenched teeth. 'What's a bit of butter, anyway? There'll be more next week.' She tried to sound braver than she felt.

Martha came back from the cake stall, and Sol Bartram shuffled away. Martha was furious, having heard the last remark. 'I know what it is! He wants the farm for himself.' Martha laughed the real High Side laugh – mirthless, ironic. 'That's what he's up to. I can see it now.'

I must be very innocent, Sally thought. Martha's right. Sol Bartram is putting up as many hurdles as he can to get me out of the farm. He must have a reason for it and knowing Sol, it will be something to benefit himself. They might as well have gone home, having nothing to sell. But Sally's brain was beginning to work again and she realized that with the little time in hand she could visit her uncle, the Reverend Samuel Mason, at the vicarage. He might know something about her father's financial affairs.

With her hair hanging limply now and her dress likewise, Sally had lost the confidence of the morning. It took a lot of determination to drive up through the laurels to the vicarage. Martha looked after the horse and the girl knocked on the door. It opened sharply and a maid of about fourteen peered out. 'Vicar's out, miss!'

'I'm his niece ... Sally Mason. Perhaps Mrs Mason is at home?'

The vicar's lady was probably at home, but she might not be 'At Home' – willing, that is, to receive callers. Aunt Bertha was a large lady who liked a little nap in the afternoons.

'I'll just go and see.' And the maid vanished.

Sally stood on the step, running her fingers through her hair and tugging at her dress. Pity Uncle Samuel wasn't there, he was always quite sympathetic. It took about ten minutes for the maid to come back and let Sally in. As usual she was enveloped in Aunt Bertha's bosom which smelled strongly of camphor.

'My poor dear girl! We have been so worried for you! Come and have a cup of tea,' she gushed, leading the way into the drawing-room.

'No thank you, Aunt, I have a friend waiting outside with the pony.'

Bertha snorted and threw her head back. 'Not a man friend, I hope? It will not do, you know, to go running about the countryside with a man!'

Tired as she was, Sally smiled. 'No, it's my friend Martha from Thorpe. I drive the trap myself, you know. We've been – been selling butter at the market.' It's nearly the twentieth century, Aunt, she thought to herself. Women can drive themselves without waiting for a man. Especially when there is no man in the family, any more. Drooping with weariness, the girl looked round the room, which was heavily draped with expensive curtains and full of big heavy furniture. Every surface was crammed with china ornaments, crystal and silver. The effect was oppressive, especially in the heat.

'Well, I hope all that nonsense will stop very soon! How soon can you leave the farm?' Bertha fanned herself and sank on to the sofa.

'I'm not leaving, Aunt, I intend to keep going. But I would like to see Uncle Samuel, to ask about Father's finances.'

'NOT LEAVING?' Bertha's voice was shrill. 'My dear child, you have no choice! We have planned it all for you. You will sell all the stock and implements and Samuel will invest the money for you. And you will come to live here with us.'

It was an appalling thought. Live at the vicarage?

'But I must earn my living, Aunt. Farming is my way of life, you see.'

Aunt Bertha was all sweet ruthlessness. She got her own way in life by drowning everything in syrup, Sally thought.

'You must realize Sally dear, that women are not formed for this kind of thing. Exercise is most unhealthy for women, you know!'

Her aunt looked in need of exercise herself, Sally thought, and felt ashamed. Aunt Bertha was only trying to be kind, but she couldn't know the wonderful feeling of being able to run up the field, to move and lift and swing. Activity, she felt instinctively, must be good for everyone.

'And as for business, for dealing and that kind of thing, you know, women have absolutely no aptitude. Especially in farming, which can be quite crude, haggling over prices at markets. You should not have to worry your little head about anything except running a household. That is quite trying enough. No doubt we'll find a husband for you one day, my dear. But meanwhile...' the syrupy voice took on a slightly harder note, 'you will remember, dear Sally, that we have an older maid as well as young Jenny who let you in. Sarah is ready to retire and you will take her place. So you see, you will be able to earn your keep and Sarah can go to live with her sister. It is all arranged. Your uncle thought it a splendid idea.'

'But–' Sally spluttered.

'You can have the attic bedroom all to yourself, and half a day off every week. Church three times on Sunday of course, this is the vicarage after all. And you can help with visiting the sick. Dear Sally, you will be so much better off here than struggling on that poverty-stricken farm! Can you cook?'

Sally was saved from replying by her uncle, who now appeared. 'Young Sally! It's good to see you.' This hug at least was a little bit of real affection.

'I have told Sally of our plans,' Bertha announced grandly. 'And I suppose she will be able to give up the farm at the end of September – that's quarter day, is it not? And then we can hire the carrier to bring down anything that we want to keep from the farm. Samuel, I think you always liked the old oak desk ... and the dining-table, of course. And anything else that you want from the old home. The rest can be sold.'

FOUR

The old trout's planning to take our furniture already! They'll take over the lot! I'll lose everything, all my own possessions. Sally felt herself staring into a black pit of

63

despair. It was bad enough to contemplate losing the farm, but to be condemned to live with her dear relations was just too horrible to think of. Uncle Samuel was dear to her. Aunt Bertha – well, she meant well, no doubt. But Sally didn't want to live with them. Surely she had come of age, she couldn't be made to live with her uncle and aunt against her will? It was the convention, of course; Sally knew that. Young, un-married females were expected to live with relatives and to make themselves useful until such time as they could get themselves married. But the Mason family, apart from Uncle Samuel of course, had never been very conventional and Sally had never tried to get herself married.

This was not the time to argue; Sally would have to go home to milk the cows very soon. She must concentrate on her pre-sent mission. Surprised at her own coolness, she took a deep breath. 'Uncle, I wonder whether you know anything about father's – er – money arrangements? Where he did his banking, that sort of thing? I really need to find out as soon as I can.'

Samuel's mild face showed alarm and a cold feeling crept over Sally. What if nobody knew? She might never be able to find out.

'Dear me, child, did he not tell you about it? I understood that he had made you a partner in the business ... even though you are a woman!' Uncle Samuel smiled slightly, taking the sting from the words. Bertha shook her head disapprovingly.

'Well yes, he told me that and he talked about saving up – to buy back the farm one day. He always did the banking, that sort of thing – but then he went so suddenly, there was no time to...' The hot tears were beginning to flow again. Really, thought Sally, I am having a very weepy day and tears will get me nowhere.

'And you've looked in the desk?' Samuel was obviously concerned for her. 'Robert kept everything in the desk, I believe.'

Sally's shoulders drooped. 'There's nothing about bank accounts in the desk.' She had relied on Uncle Samuel to know something about her father's affairs.

Aunt Bertha bustled out of the room to order tea for her husband, and Sally looked at her uncle. 'Aunt Bertha can't believe it, but I want to stay at Badger's Gill. I am a farmer, you see. That's why the money is important, for the business. To pay the rent first of all.'

The Reverend Samuel Mason stroked his chin thoughtfully. 'I know how you feel, in a way. It was a wrench at first for me to leave the farm. Robert would have worked in partnership with me, but I was always set on the Church, you know. I was lucky that the family was able to pay for my education, in fact I feel slightly guilty that it depleted the farm resources. That's why I feel responsible for you, Sally. And I must admit that it's been a much easier life here in Ripon. Better social standing, all that kind of thing. Bertha would have hated to be a farmer's wife!'

They both smiled at the thought. Sally remembered that her grandfather had sold off some land to pay for Samuel to go through theological college. That was why he wanted to help her now. If only he could see that she didn't want their help if it meant giving up the farm.

'Well, Uncle, I must ask you to explain to Aunt Bertha how I feel. I'm going to try to keep the farm on. If I can sort out the finances.' Sally shut her mouth tight, not wanting to say any more about money.

When Aunt Bertha came back Sally excused herself and Uncle Samuel came with her to the door. His brow was furrowed and she noticed for the first time that he was more stooped and his hair was turning grey. 'I'm trying to remember whether Robert said anything about money. We Masons are not good at that sort of thing, as I suppose you know. Bertha looks after all ours, of course!'

Looks after the money very well, in spite of being a woman, with no aptitude. She stifled the thought. 'Of course.' Sally beamed at her uncle. 'Do your best to remember, and please come to see me when you can spare the time.'

Samuel Mason looked at his niece sadly. 'I am sorry, Sally. But I believe you have no choice. Your future is here in the vicarage with us. You will get used to it, and used to Bertha in time. I did.'

Plodding home from Ripon with empty baskets and an empty purse, Sally was almost inclined to believe her uncle. What hope had she for the future? At that moment the outlook was bleak. With no money and no help on the farm she wouldn't last very long, however passionately she wanted to keep going. Determination was not enough. But how did determined people succeed? Martha could think of nothing to say and so it was a silent journey, the seven long miles back to Thorpe. It was not until they came to the Kirkby Lane end that the older woman stirred in her seat.

'You won't like this, Sally. But I think you'll have to consider giving in.'

'No!' Sally knew what she had to do to find the rent. 'I'll have to sell the sheep.' The Motley Flock would have to go. The creatures she had reared from birth, and planned to keep into their old age, represented vital money. Sally's vivid imagination saw the pens at the market: a nice shepherd might buy them, or a big, fat butcher might make them into mutton pies. Sally turned to

Martha. 'As soon as I can.'

'It will be sad to see the last Mason leave the village. Your family has been here for a very long time, my dear.' The vicar took her hand gently, as if it were made of porcelain.

Sally was startled. They were all trying to talk her into leaving. Convention seemed to hang heavily over Thorpe, especially on Sundays. It was going to be hard to convince her friends and neighbours and even herself at times that she could survive at Badger's Gill. But surely determination was worth something? It might help her to find a way. She tried to smile at the vicar in a confident, successful way.

The vicar had been in Thorpe a very long time himself, but not so long as the Masons. Sally could not remember a time when Dr Bentley had not preached the Sunday sermons; he had married her parents and christened Sally herself. He always stood in the porch after the service and made polite conversation with his flock.

'What makes you think that I am leaving, Vicar?' It seemed the safest thing to say, while Sally pushed the stray curls under her Sunday hat and tried to control herself. The old boy was jumping to conclusions, but she must respect his age and position and not be too impatient.

The vicar looked round at the departing

faithful and sighed. 'Mr Bartram told me, and I must say that I was quite relieved. I have been most concerned about you since your dear father passed away.' His faded blue eyes looked concerned, Sally could see that. 'No doubt you needed time to adjust to – the situation, but change comes to us all, of course. It is often for the best. One or two people thought that you were intending to try to farm by yourself. Now that would be unwise, my dear. Most unwise.'

Trust Sol Bartram to run to the vicar with his story and to get God's representative in Thorpe to take his side against Sally. This was convention working against her again. Was it so sinful to be rather unconventional?

Sally had rushed through the milking in order to get to church in time for evensong; she hadn't stopped rushing all day. It was the proper thing to do and kept up a show of normality. But she was tired and distraught, although the ancient ritual of the service had calmed her down a little. The last thing she wanted was to take advice from the vicar, unless he agreed with her. She didn't want opposition. 'But I remember you taught us that we should … accept the station in life to which it has pleased God to call us. That's what I want to do!'

The vicar beamed. 'Precisely, my dear girl. Precisely my point. A young woman is called to the domestic life, to be a helper, a comfort. Not to compete with men in a man's world!' He shook his silvery head. 'Farming, my dear, will always be a man's world. But, as I said, we will be sorry to see you go.'

Sally inclined her head and moved on and the vicar shook the hand of the next villager. It was no use arguing.

'Come on, Sal, supper's waiting!' Robin came up and slipped his arm into hers just as usual. 'Evening, Vicar!' And he walked Sally down the churchyard path past the graves of Masons long gone. What would they think of her? Sally wondered: Joshua, Benjamin and Samuel Mason ... not to mention their wives.

'You're looking a bit thin, my lass. Ma's supper is just what you need.' Robin looked very handsome in his Sunday suit, freshly shaved, grinning down at her. 'Fancy the vicar telling you to settle down to the domestic life. Not likely!' His fresh young laugh rang out. 'Doesn't sound like Sally Mason!'

That hurt, much more than the vicar's conventional comments. Oh dear, Sally thought, I don't like either of their views of me ... what's wrong with me?

It was only a few yards down the street to the Scotts' farmhouse. As they turned into the drive Sally said quietly, 'You don't think I'm ladylike enough, perhaps?' That was the other side of the coin; if she succeeded as a farmer, folks would think she was unwomanly. In fact she would need a certain toughness, not just physical strength but the ability to bargain with men on their own terms, buying and selling. Robin seemed to think that she wasn't cut out for 'the domestic life' and Robin's opinion was important to Sally. Maybe she should take shorter steps when she walked and try to be more graceful in her movements. It was so hard to remember, busy as she was. She picked up her skirt daintily as she walked down the path.

The young man paused at the farmhouse door with his hand on the knob. 'Lord, Sally, don't be so serious! That's your big problem, you know. You take everything far too seriously.' He laughed again.

Sally wished that Robin were a bit more serious, but she wasn't going to tell him so. Life at Badger's Gill had been all too solemn recently. Without realizing it she'd become more serious and thoughtful, as she became more responsible.

Supper at the Scotts' was a cheerful affair. Mrs Scott welcomed Sally with a smile and drew out a chair for her at the big dining table. Robin's father handed Sally a plate of thinly sliced cold beef and gave her a kindly look. She took both gratefully; she hadn't had meat for a long time. The diet at Badger's Gill was not quite adequate, come to think of it. These days she thought about food as little as possible. Sitting at the noisy family dining-table, Sally was unobtrusive. Robin's twin brothers were conducting an argument about fishing and it was easy to keep quiet for a while. Still thinking about being feminine, Sally looked down at her black Sunday dress and sighed. It needed some lace at the cuffs and neck to make it less severe. She hadn't thought about clothes, or how she looked, for months. That was a mistake, it seemed. There was an old lady in Thorpe: gaunt, work-worn with patient, suffering eyes. She wore black dresses like the one Sally wore. In a few years, she'd look just like Mrs Peterson. She'd have the same huge, long-fingered hands and joints swollen with rheumatism from milking. Already her face in the mirror was gaunt, with prominent cheekbones, Sally had noticed. People would soon know that she was poor.

Deep down, Sally Mason wanted to get married and to have babies. She supposed that every woman had the same dreams. But apart from Robin, she had never got to know a man who appealed to her and it didn't seem at all likely that he would ever see her as a potential wife. Possibly, no one would ever fall in love with a determined woman who lived on her own and milked cows for a living, unless it was a young man without land who wanted a farm. A few young men on the High Side had 'married farms', sometimes taking plain wives as the price of advancement, but Sally was only a tenant and therefore not a good catch. If she owned the land she might find herself surrounded by suitors. But Sally wanted to marry for love, not convenience. Did she love Robin? She rather thought so.

It wouldn't do to think of such things, Sally decided. Women who got married and were happy, women like Mrs Scott across the table, were incredibly lucky. Meeting the right person was such a gamble; some people never did. And she herself had quite enough to worry about without including the distant future.

Mr Scott beamed down the table at Sally. 'Things going well for you, lass?' He didn't wait for an answer. 'I've been wondering whether you know how to keep accounts?'

Looking down at her plate, Sally said awkwardly, 'I don't think Father kept accounts. We just knew roughly how much profit we made...' she tailed off.

'Not many farmers write things down!' Mr Scott shook his head reprovingly. Sally thought how much this man knew; he had worked as a legal clerk in his youth and still earned some money from writing legal documents. Part of the Scotts' success, she guessed, must come from keeping records. She knew that Robin was in charge of pedigree records for their cattle.

'There isn't much time for records, I'm afraid.'

'I suppose not. Will you take another helping of beef?' Mr Scott waved the carving knife above the meat. She shook her head and he laid down the knife and leaned over the table. 'I can give you a ledger, Sally, to start you off. One page for expenses and one for income. Then you will know what pays and what doesn't. Whether you should keep more cows, or more sheep for example.'

'Thank you, Mr Scott.' It sounded complicated; how did you separate the sheep costs from the cow costs? Sally sighed. She didn't have time for keeping accounts.

After the pie and cream the men of the family disappeared and Sally was left with Mrs Scott, sitting comfortably by a small summer fire. The older woman looked at Sally keenly. 'Sally, you're getting quite thin, you know. Can't you hire a labourer for the heavy work? Joe Marsh is looking for work and he's a good cowman. If you're determined to stay, that is. It's going to be tough. I think you need some sort of help.'

Sally looked down at her hands, roughened with farm work and red with scrubbing to get clean for church and Mrs Scott looked at them too. 'My dear, let me give you some elderflower cream for those hands.' She bustled out and Sally relaxed a little, pleased to be sitting down. She tired more easily these days. Was it the poor diet, she wondered.

When Mrs Scott came back the stream of good advice was resumed. 'I really think that something should be done. Shall I speak to Joe for you?'

'I know you're trying to help me, Mrs Scott, and I'm grateful. But I can't afford to employ anyone. At least not at the moment.'

Susan Scott looked guilty, as though she hadn't thought about money. There was a short silence and then she smiled. 'Of course, that will be a problem. I wonder what you could do.' She looked into the fire, thinking. 'The only women I know who make a success of any kind of business – well, they do the planning, the managing. They have people to do the heavy work. I believe that's the only way for you, Sally. You'll have to think like a manager!'

Sally smiled at the thought of Aunt Bertha. 'My aunt says that women's brains are not capable.'

'What nonsense! Many a man relies on his wife to do the thinking. Who d'you think runs the Crown? Sol, or Mrs Bartram? Women are practical as a rule, if they've been brought up like you have. And they can think of more than one thing at a time. Men can't do that!' They both laughed.

Sally could see the sense of this approach. It would mean that she could be a farmer and still be reasonably feminine. It was impossible to carry on as she was for very much longer. If only she could find some money! She decided to be honest with Mrs Scott. 'I – I'm going to sell the sheep,' she said firmly, trying to make it sound like a business decision. She looked round. 'Should we be talking like this on a Sunday? And I am quite sure that I want to keep the farm. What I need is some way of earning money to pay Joe or someone like him.' Sally pushed her shoulders back and sat up very straight. 'But I can't think of how to get started.'

A maid came in to clear the dishes and Susan Scott suggested a walk round the garden, which Sally always envied because it was so well-kept. They went out into the fragrant evening. It seemed after a few minutes that Mrs Scott had been struck with an idea. She stood in the middle of the shrubbery walk and laughed. 'That's it! Now, Sally, this is what you must do.' They sat on a garden seat together in the soft evening light. 'There are a few women in your sort of position – widows mostly, of course. Not many young girls lose both parents so early in life; you've been unfortunate. But the point is, some of these women take paying guests. It's not so hard as farm work, although it can be hard enough. But it can pay quite well. Think about it.' Mrs

Scott sat back, pleased with her idea.

'Paying guests! You mean ... lodgers? Keep a boarding house?' Sally was horrified. It sounded so much like drudgery. And anyway, who would want to board at Thorpe? It was too far from the town for travelling salesmen or any kind of travellers. That much was certain. 'They might be drunks, or ... dangerous people! How could you know?'

'Not at all! Paying guests are genteel. They are often wealthy city people who come to the country for their health, or on a walking tour, or, sometimes a family needs to have someone cared for. You remember Mrs Thackeray on the moor? She looked after a blind man for years, gave him a good home. His family paid her very well for it.'

'Well ... it would depend on whether they could look after themselves, I suppose. I've too much to do as it is!' Sally frowned. 'I could spring clean the rooms and offer very plain food. It would all depend on whether the person, or people, would like to live in the country, on a farm. Some folks wouldn't care for it, at all.' She thought of Aunt Bertha.

Susan Scott jumped up. 'I will try to find someone for you, Sally. It could enable you to pay a farm worker, to make life easier. A discreet advertisement in the *Yorkshire Post* is the thing! I will take care of all that.'

The delicate scent of elderflowers hung in

the air and Mrs Scott described how she made the cream, changing the subject tactfully to give the girl time to get used to the new idea. 'I'll make you some more while the flowers are out. I prefer the berries for wine making ... elderflower wine smells so odd.'

'Thank you, Mrs Scott.'

Perhaps she sounded ungrateful, but Sally could not find very much enthusiasm for Mrs Scott's idea about the paying guests. Had Robin's mother ever managed with no indoor servants at all? Probably not. A stranger living in her house would be a burden, a great deal of sheer drudgery. Sally thought of carrying endless buckets of coal upstairs for a bedroom fire, endless jugs of hot water for the washstand. There would be extra washing and ironing. And she'd have to think up and then cook different meals every day, to be served on crisp white tablecloths ... it was months since the silver cutlery had been taken out and cleaned.

On the way home, Sally decided it was too late to call on Martha and George. But tomorrow she would have to ask George to sell the sheep for her as quickly as possible. The rent must be paid on time no matter what else happened. Long shadows fell across the grass as Sally went down the gill to say goodnight to the sheep. The flock clustered round as usual, nibbling at the bucket and there were tears in Sally's eyes as she looked at them. The sun went down but the girl lingered, unwilling to go inside to the dark, empty house.

I'll ask if they can be kept together, she said to herself. And go to a good home ... and maybe, later in the year... no, it was no good. She would never be able to get the sheep back again.

The evening sky was a clear green, merging gradually through blue into the pink of the sunset. The air was calm and from the hedge the scent of the elder bush reminded her of Mrs Scott and her kindness. The Scotts had been good to Sally since her father died. From Badger's Wood an owl called and there was a movement in the grass. Suddenly, there they were, a young family of badgers, tumbling and fighting in a little hollow. Sally held her breath and watched them and the flock watched with her, curious, but quite used to these quarrelsome neighbours. The badgers played for some minutes and then the parent called and they set off in a line, presumably to learn hunting. Sally watched them go with a smile. She did not want to leave this place, ever. And if she had to sell the sheep to pay the rent, that was the price. She stroked Lavinia's furry ears and walked slowly back to the house.

What if Mrs Scott were right, and a paying

guest could solve the farm's cash crisis? Sally lit a lamp and wandered round the familiar rooms, seeing them in a new way, as a visitor might. The house was old, with low-beamed ceilings and panelling on the walls. Would city folks find it attractive? Or just shabby and old-fashioned? The parlour was a pleasant retreat, lined with book-shelves and with a large stone fireplace. Roses peeped in through the open window. Sally had spent little time in the parlour since her father died.

There was an old-fashioned, panelled dining-room with the dining-table that Aunt Bertha coveted. Her father's oak desk took up much of one wall. The kitchen was large, with a big cooking range, a separate pantry and dairy and a row of geraniums on the broad stone windowsill. A paying guest could eat in the dining-room. In fact, it could also be used as a guest's sitting-room. And upstairs the big main bedroom stood empty. She would need to clear the wardrobe of her father's things, give them to the church bazaar, perhaps. The curtains could be washed and the carpet needed attention. The sheets should smell of lavender and tomorrow, Sally decided, she would gather lavender flowers for the linen press and pick some roses for the vases.

Sally had lived in this old house all her life and never really looked at it objectively before. She had the feeling that women like Aunt Bertha might turn up their noses at her home. But some people might like the peace and simple comfort of Badger's Gill. If Mrs Scott had her way, Sally was about to find out.

FIVE

George Dawson considered himself a hardened old farmer, but there was a tear in his eye as he watched a sad little procession cross the green on Thursday morning. Under a grey and cloudy sky, Sally was leading her little flock to be loaded into the cart to go to market.

The horse was standing ready yoked and there was no time to lose. Sally sprinkled a little grain from the bucket and the Motley Flock ran easily up the ramp and into the cart. George threw a net over them and tied it down, hardly daring to look at Sally. She gave a last pat to the curly heads and turned away. 'Try to find out who buys them, George–' Sally choked, and stopped.

'Good young ewes with lambs at foot, should fetch a good price today,' the farmer said gruffly, pretending that this was a normal market day.

Martha came out, wiping her hands on her apron and put a hand on Sally's shoulder. 'Let's go and turn out yon parlour of yours. I've not much to do today, myself.'

The Motley Flock, quite composed, peered out of the cart. George moved off down the road and they looked surprised that Sally was not going with them. As he clopped down to Ripon, George rehearsed his list of things to do. Top of the list was a pig. They really needed a pig to eat scraps and unsaleable vegetables. A little sow would be ideal.

The stock market was full today, George found, and he had to queue to unload the sheep into a pen. Several auctioneers were moving round the pens and he soon realized that the pigs were nearly all sold. Hurrying over to the pig lines, he spotted a likely sow, ready to have a litter soon. He waited for the pen to be sold and managed to buy it for a good price. Then he saw a couple of neighbours and stopped for a chat. He arranged to sell a load of turnips and some carrots, to be delivered next week. All this took some time and the sale was nearly over. To his dismay, when George got back to the sheep lines, Sally's flock was gone. 'Who bought 'em?' He clutched at the auctioneer's sleeve. Sally wanted to know where they went!

'Dunno. Don sold them, not me. Went to a chap from the High Side. Don't worry, your cash is safe in the office.'

The money was important of course and George collected it immediately. But he regretted not watching the sale. He'd have to keep asking every week at the market, until he could find out where they'd gone.

The Roman soldier was in Ripon that day and had taken a stroll through the sheep pens. He spotted the Motley Flock immediately, even though they had now lost their fleeces. He reached over and tickled the friendly inquisitive one under the chin, just to make sure. The whole group moved towards him. Normal sheep didn't behave like that.

Marcus had not been able to forget the girl on Camp Hill. He remembered her shawl blowing in the wind, her expressive blue eyes and her slim figure. Don't be too romantic, he told himself, just because you liked poetry at school! You didn't often meet anyone like Bo-Peep. She spoke politely even though she looked like a homeless waif. And he liked the way she'd handled her predicament, caught with strays on private land and standing up to him. Lonely himself, Marcus thought he'd recognized a certain loneliness in the girl.

The auctioneer came over. 'Buying today, sir? That lot's a bit small for the likes of you!'

Why had she sold the sheep? Perhaps they'd escaped once too often. But he might be able to find out more about the girl. Pride had prevented him from asking anyone local who she might be. But then he remembered the way she'd spoken to them, rubbed their heads ... that girl loved her sheep. If she had to sell, that must mean she was in trouble. Marcus looked at the sheep thoughtfully. There were rather too many for what he had in mind, but they'd be better left together, in their group. A butcher hovered, appraising the flock. Marcus could see that he was weighing them mentally; the ewes were fat, but the lambs were too small. Marcus raised a finger, caught the seller's eye and the sheep were his.

Just then Marcus spotted a livestock carrier in the crowd. 'Here Tom, take these up to Mrs Jameson's, at Dallagill, will you? Tell her they're mine – she'll understand. They can go in the orchard for today.'

'Aye, that I will. If I can get going right now there'll be time for another load afore night. Give us a hand, boss.' The sheep were decanted, slightly puzzled but not at all dismayed, into Tom's cart and whisked off down the road.

The day before Marcus had called on Mrs Jameson and found her in a right pickle, as she told him. 'Grass is growing and nowt to eat it. And I'm too lame to go and buy some stock and too old to chase round 'em, in any case. But I don't want to give up, not yet!' Dan Jameson had been their best stockman and his wife had worked in their house when Marcus was a boy. They'd always lived in this cottage, with a few fields at the back, next to the chapel. Marcus was fond of them and had tried to look after Mrs Jameson since her husband had died.

'I'll put a few sheep on, they might be company for you,' Marcus had promised before he left. He sometimes wished he didn't have the gift of letting people get under his skin. It was downright uncomfortable at times. The flock would eat the grass for the widow, provided they didn't escape. He would tell her to get a bucket of grain; that seemed to be the secret.

When he did call to see her, Mrs Jameson was indignant. 'This lot's been hand reared! They're somebody's pets! I'll bet they've all got names! Who did you steal 'em off, you wicked boy?' She patted Lavinia lovingly. The flock had made itself at home from the start and settled down to eat the widow's grass as a serious business. They looked as though butter wouldn't melt in their mouths.

'I don't know, Mrs J. But I'd rather like to find out.'

Sally mourned the loss of her sheep, but she was too busy to sit down and cry. She trotted up to the Crown with the rent on the due day and Sol seemed rather disappointed.

'Oh, so you found it in the end.' He didn't offer any more threats and Sally only waited for the receipt before leaving as quickly as she could.

Mrs Scott called in to say that the advertisement for a paying guest had been placed. 'But don't hold your breath, it's only a small one. It may take a while to find the right person.'

Rather too soon for Sally, a woman drove up in a trap the week after the advert went in and asked to see 'the rooms'. She pulled up with a flourish and threw the reins imperiously to Sally, evidently thinking she was a servant.

'What rooms? Oh, you mean the guest rooms.' Sally stammered a little and blushed. She was on her way to see Martha, but she turned back and opened the front door, which creaked a little. They didn't use front doors very often at Thorpe.

Sally herself thought that the old house looked pleasant if a little faded, smelling mainly of the flowers she'd picked that morning. It was always better in summer, after the traces of winter damp had gone. This was certainly the best time of year to start the new business. But she felt nervous under this woman's hard stare. 'We're not ready for visitors yet, of course. In a few weeks, perhaps...'

The woman's stony face soured a little more. 'Obviously not!' she sniffed. She drew a white-gloved finger across the dressing table and examined it critically. 'Dust! Not very professional, are you?' Her purple bosom swelled.

Sally stood straighter. 'As I said, we're not yet prepared,' she said quietly.

The woman sniffed again. 'I am looking for a temporary home for a relation of mine. She is perfectly respectable of course, just a little – strange. Especially at the time of the full moon.' She watched Sally's face for a reaction.

Not over my dead body, Sally was thinking. It's not your relation that worries me, it's you, madam. Smoothing down her curls, Sally said blandly, 'Surely the – lady will need professional care?'

'Not in the country, she won't. It can hardly matter how anyone behaves out here! With only the villagers and the farm animals. A few screams will no doubt go unnoticed up here!' She looked around at the uncouth farmyard.

'I hardly think you understand country life, madam, if that is what you believe. People here are a community and take a great interest in each other's affairs. Strange behaviour would probably be much more noticeable here than it would in a town.'

And I hope that puts you right off me and the farm, Sally added silently.

The long purple dress trailed from room to room, following Sally, critical at every step. But at the end Mrs Smythe decided that Badger's Gill would do. 'The doctor told me that country air and fresh food might improve her a little. I will bring my relation here next week, for six weeks in the first instance.'

Sally's eyes widened when the rate of pay was mentioned. A few shillings a week would help, but it was not much after the cost of food was deducted. And when Sally heard that Mrs Smythe lived in Ripon and would inspect the house every week, she made up her mind. 'I am afraid it will not be possible.' And that was that.

'Of course you did the right thing. You can get much more money than that!' Mrs Scott advised Sally later in the day.

With a melancholy whistle the train chugged into a gloomy tunnel and Emma felt it was somehow symbolic of the way her life was going. The girl leaned her aching head on the back of the seat. Sheffield was behind her and the future ahead was dark. She was determined about one thing: they would not make her cry. Years of living in the Bellamy household had made her quiet and withdrawn. She had learned not to cry, ever, even when she was whipped. The whippings had started when she first went to live with the Bellamys at the age of twelve. It had been hard not to cry, then.

There was nothing that strangers could do to affect her; Emma felt frozen, incapable of emotion. That was the best way to be.

'We're going under the Pennines!' The gentleman in a waistcoat beamed. 'A wonderful achievement, this tunnel.'

'Yes, it is.' Emma was polite, but nothing more. She went back to wondering what her new life was going to be like, and in particular about Miss Mason. Mrs Bellamy had harped on the subject of Miss Mason all the time that Emma's trunk was being packed. This formidable lady lived far off in the Dales and she was prepared to take Emma as a paying guest. From the Bellamys' point of view, the older and grimmer Miss Mason was, the better. Certainly, as Mrs Bellamy pointed out to her husband, S. Mason (Miss) wrote a good hand and must have had some education. Several letters had been exchanged before the transaction was complete. Miss Mason had assured them that there was no man in the house; they pictured her as old, soured by living alone, prim and proper and most critical of fallen women. Just the thing to put the girl in her place and to remind her of her folly, every day.

'You will mind your manners and only speak when you are spoken to. Miss Mason will not wish for idle conversation!'

What is she, a nun? Emma wondered. But a silent old lady would be a distinct improvement on her present company. Emma had tried, but it was hard to love her guardians. She realized that from their point of view she was a great disappointment and a burden to them. They told her so, very often. Would Miss Mason be told to whip her? It might be in the Rules.

The Bellamys had stopped her from packing anything valuable, 'in case it is stolen'. With regret, Emma had left behind her mother's jewellery box and her father's gold watch. How dangerous were these wild villagers going to be? She had little to remind her of her parents and of those far-off days when she had a family and they were happy together. Emma knew that she was being sent to Thorpe to get her out of the way, so that no breath of scandal would touch her respectable relations. She would have the baby at this place called Badger's Gill, among strangers and with no one to support her. Obviously, it was also meant to be a form of punishment and a time for repentance. 'The child will be sent for adoption immediately,' her aunt had said with distaste. 'And in due course I suppose you will have to resume your duties in this house, with a solemn undertaking that this will never happen again.'

The baby was still unreal to Emma, a horrible accident, the result of torture. Sometimes she was tempted to tell them the truth. It was so unfair to be branded a slut. But there was a strong possibility that they wouldn't believe her. Or if they did, they might make her marry that monster. Silence was the best course and Emma stuck to it.

It looked as though rain was about to come in from the west and the clouds were so low on the Pennines that you could almost touch them. Industrial Yorkshire was not very picturesque, Emma decided as the train went north, first to Leeds, and then she changed for a train to Harrogate. She was glad that her trunk had been sent on ahead and she had only a light bag to carry. At Harrogate she had a drink of water and found the train to Ripon.

The mill chimneys had disappeared and the dark brooding hills were left behind. Here the countryside was much more attractive, with a patchwork of fields and woods, little red-roofed villages and even, here and there, a ray of sunshine. There were people and horses working in the fields.

All too soon they steamed into Ripon station. This was the tricky part of the journey. The Thorpe carrier had been told to look out for her, but would he find her? Emma stood forlornly outside the station, feeling very alone. The Bellamys had at least been familiar, but here she was among strangers.

'Miss Wakefield? Let me take your bag! We leave for Thorpe in ten minutes.' A burly man in a bowler hat and side whiskers beamed at her and led her round the corner to where a wagonette with two horses stood by the side of the road.

Emma climbed up into the vehicle and sat down gingerly. Two women broke off their conversation and looked round at her. 'Looks like rain, doesn't it? Hope we don't get wet! Are you going to Thorpe with us?'

Emma said she was and turned away to look at the street.

'Travelled far, have you, dear?' The woman with baskets looked hard at Emma.

'From Sheffield.'

'Ooh, that's a long way! Never been there myself. You'll be staying a while at Thorpe, maybe? Who're you staying with, then?' They looked Emma up and down and she shrank in her seat. The baby was showing, but she'd made herself some loose dresses and was wearing a concealing long coat.

'I'm not quite sure,' Emma stammered. She wasn't going to tell them everything, although they'd be bound to find out before long. The women rolled their eyes at each other, but they left her alone.

Rain still threatened but they got to

Thorpe before it arrived, jogging through some pretty countryside, climbing all the time out of the plain, heading towards the purple line of moors.

Thorpe, when eventually reached, was built of stone: the houses, the walls and the barns were all stone, some a sunny yellowish colour and others dark grey and rather forbidding. Houses and cottages were grouped round a village green, which had a rather large pond. Fields rose steeply at the backs of the houses beyond the green at one side and the street wound uphill and narrowed, presumably to more houses and perhaps a church.

'Put me down on the green, please,' Emma asked firmly. And when the horses jogged off, she felt another wave of loneliness. There was no one about, nothing on the street except some ducks heading for the pond. Badger's Gill was supposed to be near the pond, so Emma followed the ducks.

The house was easy to find, standing foursquare to the street with a tiny metal badger on the garden gate. Emma went up the path slowly and forced herself to knock on the big front door. Nothing happened. The loud knock sounded hollow, as though the place was empty. She timidly pushed open the door and saw her trunk standing in the hall. This was the right place, then. Where was Miss Mason? There was a clatter of hooves and the creak of a cart, somewhere out of sight. Emma went round the house and saw a procession coming into the farmyard: country people doing farm work. 'It's going to rain, we did well to get the last load!' An older woman smiled at a young red-headed girl, who was riding on top of a load of hay. A girl on a load of hay!

'Just time to stack it in the barn before milking time.' The two men with them agreed and the horse was led into the stone barn. Emma could hear jokes and laughter as the workers unloaded the hay. Why were they so cheerful? Especially when the drizzle started. Why would they be pleased to see rain?

After a few minutes, Emma thought she should go to ask for Miss Mason. Peeping round the barn door she was immediately spotted by the young woman, who came towards her with a wide smile. 'Emma Jane Wakefield? So you've got here at last. Was it a good journey? If you can wait a few minutes, I'll make you a cup of tea.'

Emma decided to wait until later to ask about Miss Mason.

'Martha, pull the fire together there's a dear, and put the kettle on!' The red-haired girl led the horse out of the barn and unyoked.

A peasant, she must be, thought Emma.

'Come with me, my dear!' Martha sounded kind as she steered Emma towards the kitchen.

Feeling small and pale beside this vigorous woman, Emma drew back. 'I'm not supposed to go in the kitchen. I might get in the way. Mrs Bellamy said I was to stay in the dining-room.'

Martha raised her eyebrows. 'Well, suit yourself, lass. You'll be ready for a cup of tea, any road.'

Laughter and conversation continued in the kitchen. The rain beat on the windows and Emma sat on a dining-chair with her back straight, until the girl brought her a cup of tea and a big scone. 'I'm sorry you didn't get much of a welcome, but we're just finishing the hay – and we've beaten the rain! That's important on a farm. We need rain for the pastures now, you see. So we're happy.'

'Yes.' Emma took a sip of tea. She did not see.

'Now Emma Jane, don't be shy. You've had a difficult time, I'm sure,' the pleasant voice went on. 'But we want you to enjoy your time here.'

'I'm not here to enjoy anything.' It seemed safest to stick to her instructions; no good being friendly with this girl, it could get her into trouble with Miss Mason.

The redhead laughed and called into the kitchen. 'George, Robin, will you come and carry this trunk upstairs, please? Emma Jane will feel better when she's settled in.'

The trunk was wafted upstairs immediately. The young man called Robin gave Emma a friendly smile as he passed her, but she looked at him stonily. It could get her into trouble if she smiled at anyone.

The tea was hot and refreshing and the scone was very rich, with plenty of currants. It was smothered with deep yellow butter and Emma, who had not eaten since leaving Sheffield, found to her surprise that she could eat it all.

'I'm Sally,' the redhead explained, 'and Martha and George have helped me with the hay ... and Robin came to cart it in for me. Now, Emma Jane ... do you have a shorter form of your name?'

'I'm usually Miss Wakefield.' It was one of the Rules that her Christian name should not be used.

This Sally looked so healthy! Her blue eyes shone and her face was browner than was fashionable, but most attractive. Emma was conscious of her own pasty complexion and dull, lank brown hair.

'You poor lass, to come such a long way on your own! But never fear, we'll look after you. We can help each other, you know.' The blue eyes looked at her with compassion.

Emma turned away, the tears welling up, tears she'd sworn not to shed. People couldn't hurt her by unkindness, but sympathy was making her cry! She must keep her distance. 'I don't think so.' Emma kept her voice cold and hard. 'And now if you please, I am to report to Miss Mason. Where is she?'

Sally's laugh rang out. 'I'm so sorry! I'm Sally Mason, there isn't another Miss Mason! You'll have to put up with me!'

'You! Miss Mason?' Emma was shocked. True, the girl spoke reasonably well, but she looked like a farm woman. Not like the head of a household. 'There must be some mistake!'

'No, your people arranged it all with me. You're to stay here until ... for a few months. Now, there were pages of Rules with a capital R, instructions on how you should be treated, but I don't intend to bother with them. We can please ourselves here in Thorpe. Make our own rules!'

The blue eyes were pleading. Why should this girl want to be friends? Emma stood up. 'I feel it will be better to stick to the rules, Miss Mason. Please show me to my room. I wish to unpack my things.'

In the trunk, Emma found a package addressed to Miss Mason. When she'd finished putting her clothes away, she took it downstairs. She'd better hand it over at once, in case she was accused of stealing. That was the way she had come to think. It was also time to explain what the Rules were, in case Miss Mason had not read them properly. Emma was quite clear about them; she was to stay out of the kitchen, indoors in the dining-room, and do sewing for Miss Mason, who would make sure she had plenty of work. She was to clean her bedroom and the dining-room. She was to speak to nobody outside the household. And that was all, except for church on Sunday. There was nothing in the Rules about punishment. She was hoping not to be whipped or beaten, but she couldn't count on it.

Martha heard Emma reciting the Rules, as Sally opened the package. They were standing in the hall. 'That's daft, you look as if a bit of fresh air would do you good. And some company, if I'm any judge! You don't want to shut yourself away.'

Emma looked at her critically. What did this old woman have to do with it?

Sally looked up from untying the many knots and seals on the package. 'I had hoped we would be company for each other,' she said softly. She seemed genuinely disappointed.

This was strange. Why would anybody want Emma Wakefield for a companion? 'I'm afraid that won't be possible.' Emma turned on her heel and marched upstairs, before they saw the hot tears on her face.

SIX

'Well!' Sally sat down suddenly at the kitchen table. 'Another cup of tea, please!' She was looking at the package. 'They've sent me the whole amount – all the money for four months' board, all at once!'

This was going to solve a lot of problems. They could buy some sheep in the autumn sales, for a start. Hopes of finding the Motley Flock and buying them back had faded, but the farm needed sheep, as part of the rotation of grazing. And maybe she could hire some help.

Martha beamed. 'And so they should! It's not going to be easy, my girl.'

Sally shrugged. 'She'll come round, I'm sure. She's got problems, though. Must have been treated very badly...'

'Downtrodden, if you ask me.' Robin spoke unexpectedly. 'If you want my scientific diagnosis, only if you want it, mind, she's been kept down so long that it'll take her a long time to get back to normal. Another cup for me too, please!'

'She's only sixteen and she looks younger, although she speaks like some old bird of forty.'

'And she flinches when I look at her. Poor lass!' Robin held out his cup.

'Just think, Sally,' Martha was beaming, 'if the money is there you can go and get help–'

'Old Joe Marsh, just as Ma suggested!' Robin chipped in.

'That's fine. But how should I deal with – Miss Wakefield?' Sally felt inadequate, faced with this – child, she seemed – who was so much more complicated than her beloved cows and sheep.

Robin stood up. 'I'd better be off, but I know what my Ma would say. It's a commercial arrangement, Sally. You don't have to take this person into your life. Let her stay in the dining-room and get on with your own affairs.'

When he had gone, Sally looked across the table at Martha. 'But that poor girl! She'll surely need some help, before we're through.'

Martha sighed. 'Don't worry about that just now. I think I agree with Robin. My cousin in Ripon, now, she takes in lodgers in a respectable sort of way. She has a gentleman in the front room, you see. Takes his meals there, has a bed there. Goes out to work every day and sings in the church choir on Sundays, at your Uncle Samuel's church, Sally. But Mr White never comes into her part of the house. They live separate lives. And it's the best way to be.'

Sally was still worried. 'It's different for a man, perhaps. But what about a young lass, about to have a baby and all on her own? She hasn't got a life of her own. And she doesn't look at all a bad sort of girl, to me. Just very young, somehow.'

Martha agreed. 'I was surprised to see how young and pale she looks. Most lasses in trouble as I've known them have been bold and bonny, maybe matured early. They've fallen for a handsome face and had a fling, then paid for it later. That lass has never had a fling. You can tell by looking at her. That's another type, entirely.'

They looked at each other and George went out. 'Got to feed the stock,' he muttered. 'Had enough of women's talk!' But he winked at Sally as he went through the door.

'If she hasn't had a fling,' Sally spoke slowly, 'that means...'

'That she was forced.' Martha's mouth set in a straight line. 'If you ask me, that little lass has been taken advantage of. But the woman allus takes the blame.'

Before she went home, Martha washed the tea things; Sally had already gone to milk the cows. Looking into the cowshed on her way out, the older woman suggested that Sally should call in a doctor.

To her surprise, Miss Wakefield agreed to see a doctor the next morning. It was one of the Rules. 'Mrs Bellamy said that I should see your doctor. For him to take responsibility for my health.' She sounded to Sally like a little parrot. She sat upright at the big dining-table, staring straight ahead, her swollen little body looking sadly amiss.

'Well, I think we should all be responsible for our own health.' Sally decided that she too could be dogmatic.

Luckily, Dr Bishop was a modern thinker and agreed with Sally. He summoned her into the dining-room after his examination of Miss Wakefield. He looked concerned, Sally thought, under the bracing manner. 'Pregnancy is not an illness,' the doctor began briskly. 'In my opinion, this young lady needs fresh air and exercise.'

Miss Wakefield looked even paler if anything. 'But I can't go outside. I never do, you see.'

'Well, it's time you did!' Dr Bishop was just a little impatient.

'I am frightened of animals!' The brown eyes looked genuinely scared.

Sally felt about to fizz, but she controlled herself. 'Emma Jane – Miss Wakefield – I can show you where to walk without meeting the cows. If you don't care to go down the village street, there's a green lane by the side of this house that leads you through the back of the farm, you can go right down to the river. You can pick flowers and listen to the birds!'

For a moment, Sally thought she saw a flicker of feeling in the girl's face. 'Just as I did when Mama took me to Ilkley, a long time ago.'

The doctor pronounced Miss Wakefield healthy enough, although rather under-developed for childbirth. And she appeared to be a little anaemic. 'She should eat liver and black pudding,' he said with a smile.

Sally was surprised at the efficient way her lodger set about sewing. All the household mending, long neglected, was soon being attended to and the standard was high, better than Sally could achieve. When a week had gone by Sally decided to tempt the guest out of doors. It was a fine day and Miss Wakefield donned a large bonnet and gloves, at which Sally repressed a smile. She agreed to borrow some boots, in case her shoes got muddy. But the green lane was enclosed, safe and full of summer flowers. The next day Miss Wakefield agreed to go by herself.

The walks and fresh air had a noticeable effect, at the end of her first month at Badger's Gill, Emma Wakefield was a different person. Her hair was fair and shining, her skin was clear and she seemed to be sleeping at night. But she still kept Sally at arm's length and Martha said it was a good thing.

'Why should you suffer, lass?' Martha was protective of Sally, not wanting her to be too much involved with the guest's sad story.

Casually, Sally left a few books in the dining-room for Emma to look at, some of them were books about birds and flowers and she was heartened to find that the girl took to them eagerly. The summer was fading into autumn, a pleasant time of year on the High Side. Above the village, the moors were purple with heather. It was hard to imagine life in a town, but Sally realized that this girl would not recognize the most common birds or wild flowers. Studying them might be good for her, to take her mind off her troubles.

The cows were in their slow progress to the milking shed one afternoon when Sally saw Sol Bartram waiting in the lane like a fat spider. Miss Wakefield was due to return from her walk and she came up to Sol just as the cows reached the shed. Sally pretended to go back for another cow and went by the hedge. She heard Sol clearly taunting the poor girl, who was walking slowly now, dragged down by the weight of her pregnancy.

'Come to live in Thorpe with yer immoral ways, have you? We've no time here for the likes of you! And any road there won't be a bed for you soon. Masons are out of the farm and onto the street, come quarter day!'

Miss Wakefield, head high, ignored him. She stalked past him and into the house.

'How dare you speak to my guest like that!' Sally was so angry that she forgot the power that Sol wielded.

The agent laughed. 'You're no better, encouraging fallen women! I'm going to tell Mr Radford about this, bringing his farm into disgrace. So much for the Mason family quality.' He spat the words at her over the hedge.

'What I do is no business of yours, Mr Bartram. Please go away.' The cows were waiting outside the shed, long faces turned to her in slight annoyance. Their routine was being interrupted and they did not approve.

'Oh yes, it is!' The agent's voice rose to a shout. 'I can tell yer landlord how bad weeds are at Badger's Gill and what with neglected walls and fences – have you seen that wall down bottom slope? Mr Radford's got to hear about this!'

The wall, inspected later, had indeed fallen down and there were huge gaps in the boundary. Fortunately there were no animals in the field. Sally knew the damage was recent and suspected Sol himself of inflicting it. So now she had walling to do as well as all the other jobs. Drystone walling was an ancient art that Sally would have loved to master, but the big boulders were too heavy for her to lift. She'd have to find another way.

'That's it. I'll have to find Joe Marsh!' Sally told the cows next morning as she milked.

Joe lived with his wife in a little cottage in a hollow on the Masham road, but he wasn't at home. Walking back past the church Sally heard the sound of mowing and there was Joe, cutting the churchyard grass. He was a small man with the huge hands of a worker, batlike ears and a shy smile. Sally knew him by sight, but he'd never worked at the farm before. How would it go? The girl was nervous as she opened the churchyard gate.

'Aye. I can come tomorrow, if you want.' Joe was brief and to the point. 'Pay me same as Scotts do, that'll be right enough. How many days did you, say?' He lifted the old cap and scratched his head.

They agreed that Joe should work at Badger's Gill for a week to start with and attend to all the jobs that Sally couldn't manage. And Miss Wakefield's money would pay his wages, for the moment at least. As she was leaving, Joe gave Sally a wry smile. 'Well, miss, we'll have to frame ourselves, that's for sure. Sol Bartram is after your place and I've heard he means to get it.'

Sol was evidently as good as his word. Several days later, Sally received a letter in thick intimidating spiky writing on good quality paper. She could hardly believe her eyes.

Dear Madam,
I write to inform you that your tenancy of Badger's Gill shall be terminated on 6 April 1896. You are probably not aware that under the Real Property Act of 1845, a lease is void unless made by deed. You have no lease, and I do not propose to grant you one. I have taken the decision in view of the adverse reports I have received.

The charge of immorality I shall leave to a higher authority than my own. I suggest that you consult the Church for guidance as to your future conduct. Your management of my property is my business however, and evidently it leaves much to be desired. Walls are fallen down, hedges overgrown and weeds proliferate. There has been no crop rotation.

I have some sympathy with your position, and had been considering allowing you to retain the tenancy so long as the farm was properly managed and the rent paid. But my agent informs me that you are not capable of maintaining a farm, and this bears out my own opinion about the suitability of females in such a role.

Yours faithfully,
Oliver Radford

Sally let out a howl of rage, then looked at the dining-room door. No doubt Miss Wakefield wouldn't approve of such unlady-like noises. 'Just look at this! The villain! I can't believe it!' She choked back a sob. Sally felt crushed, as though someone had dealt her a physical blow. She leaned over the kitchen table speechlessly and passed the letter to Martha, who sat opposite. It was mid morning and they were drinking tea in the kitchen with autumn sun stream-ing through the window. Martha had called in on her way to deliver some vegetables. Joe Marsh sat beside her, quietly enjoying a brief respite from cleaning out the stables. Martha read the letter aloud, deliberately. There was a silence while they digested this new blow.

'Poor lass! You've enough worry, without this!' Martha was looking over her glasses with concern. 'Is it – final, do you think?' She looked at Joe.

'Nay, never say die! If the old bugger knew the truth, sorry miss, he'd be only too pleased to let you stay! There's nowt wrong with farm, nowt at all! The real villain is not Radford – it's Sol Bartram.'

Sally was so angry she couldn't keep still, couldn't think straight. 'Suitability of females! What a horrible man! No wonder the Masons quarrelled with such a family.

But I'm going to fight him.' The only problem was that she had no idea how to make such a man change his mind.

Joe stood up and pulled his cap down low. 'Well, miss, I'd best get on. I reckon we've got a tidy farm here, there's a good argument for staying.' He hesitated a moment. 'To tell the truth I'd like to help you, miss.' Joe went to the door and seemed to struggle with emotion. He looked back at Sally. 'It happened to me, back in '63. Turned off of a farm, we were. Never got back. I'd like to see you stay at Badger's Gill.'

Swallowing, Sally tried to smile at her helper. 'Thank you, Joe. I appreciate it. It wasn't Radford that turned you off, was it?'

Joe shook his head. 'Nay, it were his Lordship. Him as lives up in London and only comes down for grouse shooting. But ... it's an old story.' He sighed and stumped out.

By the time that Joe had been at Badger's Gill for two months, all was neat and tidy. The stone boundary walls stood firm and the hedges had been trimmed. One field had been ploughed for spring corn. He was a slow, steady worker, economical in his movements, with long experience of farming. Joe never hurried, but he got through a great deal of work in a day. And best of all, he was another pair of hands. Sally now realized that she could not have carried on much longer without help.

The old farm worker had a shrewd turn of mind and he'd talked quietly about what might be done every time they stopped for a break. He was always respectful and insisted on calling Sally 'miss', but he let his opinion be known about how the farm should be run.

Sally had decided to be honest with Joe and tell him how matters stood. She explained about the paying guest. 'So I've got this money for now, but when it's gone I might not be able to pay you any more.'

Joe had scratched his head and looked at the ceiling and coughed politely. 'Well, miss, why don't we buy a few more cows with some of the money, and mebbe some more poultry? We could rear a few geese for Christmas. Farm could do with more production, if you know what I mean.'

'But there'd be more work and less money to pay your wages. But ... I suppose with more production, we might earn more money.' Sally frowned. It was sensible enough to spend the money on expanding the 'business' as Mrs Scott had called it. But what if things went wrong? She still shuddered when she thought about the melting butter at Ripon market. 'Farming's a gamble, you know.'

Joe ignored her last remark. 'Aye. It's not

just for me, mind you, but if I was to work for you full-time and milk cows and all, you could make more butter and cheese. There'd be more money for you and for my wages on a regular basis.'

Robin, when consulted, agreed that Sally should buy more cows, as long as she was sure that Joe would continue to work for her. 'It's a form of investment,' he said in his 'business' voice and then laughed. 'But yes, all farming is a gamble, I agree!'

There happened to be a farm sale soon after this and Sally took George with her to look at the milking cows. The owner was retiring to Ripon and George said this was the best place to buy farm stock, when you knew there was a good reason for the sale.

The cows sold cheaply that day and Sally bought four, which increased her herd, and also the work. But Joe was now the milker, night and morning except for Sunday, his day off. The cows had accepted the change of milker placidly, just turning round to stare at Joe for the first few days.

Things had started to go right for a change and Sally could hardly believe her luck. Robin gave her a book on scientific dairy production, all about bacteria. It merely justified the things she'd been taught by her mother about scalding the pails with boiling water, but it was good to know that she was being scientific. The new cows milked well, her butter was in demand, they sold more eggs than ever and the young farmer was able to put some money in the Penny Bank, to save up for next rent day.

The autumn air was bracing and Sally felt happier than she had for many months. With Joe to take care of the heavy work, she felt able to cope. Mrs Scott had been right; Sally realized she'd have to be a manager. The next task was to buy some geese and perhaps a pig or two.

And then the blow fell; Mr Radford's letter arrived to remind Sally of the problem of tenancy. The night after the letter came, Sally could not sleep. And awake in the middle of the night, she heard the sound of quiet sobbing from Miss Wakefield's room. If only the girl would relent a little! The baby was due quite soon, but nothing had changed in the way that Emma Wakefield lived apart. To relieve her feelings, Sally decided to write back to Mr Radford. Eyes blazing, she sat down with pen and paper in her bedroom, quite impervious to the cold.

Sir,

I received your letter with disgust. I am thankful our families were never friends and that we have always regarded you with a hearty dislike. I was prepared to accept you as a landlord, but this letter bears out my estimation of your unsuitability for such a role. I think you are extremely misguided and ill-informed, because you rely on the word of a man like Sol Bartram.

You are careless of what you call your property, that you never once visited Thorpe. This farm is mine and I intend to stay here, no matter what you do. I consider that you are a brutal, heartless old scoundrel and I will tell everybody so!

Yours faithfully,
S. Mason (Miss)

Sally threw down her pen with relief. Her mother would have been proud of this eloquence! She'd been taught how to write all manner of letters by Mama at the kitchen table. On the other hand, she had also been taught never to be rude, no matter what the provocation. But Mama hadn't been dealing with horrible old Oliver Radford! Worn out, Sally blew out the candle, climbed into the big feather bed and fell sound asleep.

The letter was posted. Nothing happened. But after about a week Sally saw things rather differently. The way to achieve her aim was perhaps not to tell him the truth about himself, but to persuade him that she was a good tenant. The only glimmer of hope in the letter was that he'd been considering her as a tenant until Sol told him how bad she was. But then, there was also the problem of the family feud. It was going to be a hard battle and she needed to write another letter.

Sally went downstairs in the dark one morning to light the fires, shivering in the chilly air. Mornings were darker now and it was hard to get out of a warm bed. She prepared the paying guest's breakfast and when she took it to the dining-room, Sally was struck with pity for poor Emma Jane. The pregnancy was surely nearly over; behind the swollen belly the girl looked young and frightened.

For the first time, Miss Wakefield spoke about her condition. She turned a pale face to Sally, a face that had probably been pretty before this ordeal. 'It won't be long now?' It was a question.

'Not long. We'll get the doctor when you need him – and I'll be there too, if you want me.'

'Yes, please.' It was a whisper, but Sally heard it and was thankful that her guest was trying to be a little more human.

'Try to eat a little more. You need to keep your strength up!' Back in the kitchen, Sally made her own toast on the fire and boiled an egg, thinking all the time about Oliver Radford. The best approach was probably a polite letter, explaining the true situation. Why not ask him to visit Badger's Gill? Then they could talk to each other without

Sol interfering. They could show him round the farm; Joe would be an asset, his ideas were always sound. And if Mr Radford saw that she had a good worker, a man who'd been a farmer himself, that might make a difference.

After work that night, Sally sat by the paraffin lamp at the kitchen table and wrote her second letter. Polite, respectful, but firm: asking the enemy to come and see for himself how the farm was run.

Dear Sir,
This is to request you to reconsider your decision with regard to the tenancy of Badger's Gill. The farm is in good heart, the buildings are maintained and the rent is paid on time. Your information to the contrary is not accurate and should be ignored.

We believe that your requirements for a tenant are being met. The gender of the tenant, I respectfully suggest, should make no difference to the situation.

We would be pleased to show you round the farm, so that you can see for yourself that it is being managed properly. Please visit, at your convenience.

Yours faithfully,
S. Mason (Miss)

That might be more effective.

The cattle would soon be housed at night, now that the weather was cold. There was a stack of good hay in the barn and plenty of turnips for winter feed. The farm buildings were clean and tidy and all was as it should be. Well, not quite all. Sally was still hankering after some sheep. It was hard to keep back the tears when she thought of her Motley Flock, which had never been seen since the day they were sold in Ripon. The lambs would have been sold off by now and whoever bought them might have sent the ewes off too, to make mutton pies. Sally was sure she'd never see them again. You have to move on, her mother always said. So Sally had already decided to rear some more lambs in spring, but spring seemed a long way off. There was a gap in the farm that could only be filled by a few sheep.

Pulling on her old shawl, Sally skipped across the green to tell Martha and George what she'd done about the dreadful letter. Martha was relieved to see that Sally had recovered her spirits. The couple both agreed that it was a good idea to ask Mr Radford to see for himself. Meanwhile, said George, the sheep sales are on. 'Will you take a gamble, lass, and buy a few ewes?'

Sally smiled at him. 'I'm going to farm as though I will live for ever, as Papa used to say! And at Badger's Gill, too! Yes, I'd like to come to the next sale with you.'

It was agreed that they would all go to Masham sheep fair the next week and take George's cart. It was a great social occasion for the whole area. The High-Siders came down from the moors above the town with their little Swaledales, mingling with the lowland farmers from the valley of the Ure. There was even a cross-bred sheep called the Masham becoming popular, but Sally thought it might be too expensive.

It was cold and breezy as they clopped over the common in George's cart and down into the little town by the river. Everyone was heading for the market square, where temporary pens had been set up with hurdles and hundreds of sheep were bleating. Sally wore a warm winter dress, ladylike boots and a fairly new warm coat. She felt quite equal to competing in the sheep auction. She hadn't heard from the landlord, but once the letter to him was posted she'd felt quite optimistic. And since Joe had been working with her, she was much less tired and was getting back some of her former brightness.

The sheep fair was a holiday, an outing, a little bit of excitement in a hard-working life. Sally walked round the fair with her friends for a while and then Martha went off to visit a relative and George did some trading in turnips. When they had gone, she wandered by herself, quite happy, sniffing the smell of sheep. She bought some toffee at a stall to give to George and Martha. Robin was there with his brothers, friendly and detached as ever. Suddenly, Sally stopped dead by a pen of ewes. They were a mixed group, some big and some small, some with curly coats and one or two with horns ... the Motley Flock, large as life! Composed as usual, watching the passing crowd.

SEVEN

'Mary, Lavinia, Prudence, Gertrude!' Sally called softly and the ewes rushed to the side of the pen. She leaned over and stroked them, laughing and crying at the same time. 'I'll buy you, I promise I will!'

Gertrude the Wensleydale looked up through her fringe of crinkly wool as though she understood Sally's excitement. Mary's black face was inscrutable. But whatever their recent experiences, they'd all been well fed and were in fine condition.

'Well, I never!' Martha was overjoyed, and amazed.

George said, 'You'll know just which sheep you want to buy now, lass.'

The unknown buyer from Ripon had evidently now decided to sell. What luck, that now she had some money, she should find them again! After that Sally could hardly contain her impatience until the sale began and the pens were slowly sold off, one by one. Prices that day were not too high, she noted with relief. She would probably get them back for the same price.

Martha and George had gone off to take an old lady home when the crucial time came and the auctioneer started on the line of pens that ended with the Motley Flock: Lot 210. Eagerly Sally took up her position by the pen. He father had taught her how to bid at sales. She looked round quickly; not many people interested in Lot 210, except perhaps the tall man beside her. Head up, shoulders back... 'It's the Roman soldier!' It was months ago, back in early summer that they'd met, but Sally had not forgotten.

Marcus turned to look down at her. 'Bo-Peep! I was hoping to see you here today. And you look quite different, you know, from the girl on Camp Hill.'

It was spoken quietly, but the words sent a thrill through Sally. Robin, bless him, had never spoken to her with that tone in his voice, ever. It sounded as though he'd been looking for her. 'I'm here to buy back my sheep ... they were sold, you see. And I've missed them, naughty though they are. Do you like sheep, Marcus?'

The tall man's grave face lightened. 'I've

always lived with sheep, we're a sheep farming family. And I was working with them from the start, except for when they sent me away to school.'

The auctioneer was creeping nearer. Sally looked over at the progress of the sale and when she looked back, Marcus' eyes were on her. She felt suddenly nervous. Her mother had wanted to send her away to school, but they couldn't afford it. 'We've always had a few sheep, to graze after the cattle. It hasn't been the same without them.'

Marcus laughed. 'I know the feeling. Yes, we've been improving our flocks, the breeding side is most interesting. But look, here he comes to sell your sheep. You'd better get ready to bid for them if you want them back.' Sally was grateful that he didn't offer to bid for her, as most men would have done.

There were few bidders and soon the auctioneer raised his hammer. Sally's was the last bid. He looked across at Marcus before the hammer came down and the tall man nodded. 'Good enough.'

The hammer fell and Sally turned to Marcus, her cheeks burning. 'You bid against me! How could you? You bought them!' She felt betrayed. He was teasing her, snatching them from her with a last minute bid and he was laughing.

Marcus took her right hand. 'You shake hands for luck, you know. You are the buyer and I'm the seller. I wasn't bidding against you, Bo-Peep, just confirming that I'd take your price.' The crowd had drifted to the next pen and his quiet, deep voice was heard by nobody else.

Marcus was the owner. The Motley Flock had been with him all this time. No wonder he was amused! Sally looked up and saw that his laughter was genuine, not mocking. The quiet voice was almost apologetic. 'I'm so pleased you were here. I didn't know how to contact you. But of course, I didn't know, either, that you would want them back. Although I did suspect it, since they were so tame.'

'You bought them!' Sally was still trying to get used to the idea.

'Yes, I bought your sheep at Ripon and they've been up at Dallagill, keeping an old lady company and living well. She needed some sheep to eat the grass, yours were just right. But they finished the grass, so they had to go. They're in lamb again for next spring. We used a good tup, you'll get some fine lambs.'

'I suppose you didn't know that they were my sheep, the ones that strayed. You wouldn't want that type of nuisance!' Sally was still struggling with shock. It was embarrassing, just as when they met before. But she didn't feel quite so bedraggled this time and her hair was tied back neatly, thank goodness.

'Yes, I knew them all right. There's no mistaking that mixed bunch!' Marcus looked over them indulgently and they looked back, quite happy as usual. Standing in a pen for hours at a sale did not upset them, as it did some sheep. The Motley Flock was used to people and they watched the sale with interest. 'I thought of keeping them until I found you, but time and the grass ran out. We didn't want them to go hungry this winter.'

Marcus had been looking for her. The attraction she'd felt could be mutual. How embarrassing had the sheep been? She began timidly: 'Did they stray when you had them? Were you all over the countryside looking for them? I know how bad they can be!'

Marcus looked down at her. 'Don't worry, they behaved well, Mrs J has good strong hedges and walls round the field.' He hesitated, as though not sure what to say next. 'But – I've been wondering about you. Why would you sell your little flock, Bo-Peep, when you were so fond of them? There must have been some trouble.'

Sally, embarrassed, stroked Lavinia's head. 'You've certainly looked after them, they're in top condition. I am so glad to see them again! They're only sheep, but they seem like friends, when you–' How could she tell him of her poverty and loneliness? That living alone, she'd got used to talking to sheep?

As the girl hesitated, another man came up to Marcus urgently. 'You're wanted, lad. Meeting in the King's Head, remember? They're waiting for you.'

'Very good, Martin.' Marcus turned to Sally with a shake of the head. 'I'm afraid it's unavoidable, I have a Show Society meeting, which is a pity, now that I've found you again. I hope to see you in about half an hour, and we could perhaps talk over a cup of tea? Even though we haven't been introduced!' With a quick smile, he was gone.

Sally was left with a warm glow. Marcus spoke of finding her again, he wanted to come back to talk to her. It seemed that he, too had remembered their meeting at Camp Hill. In a daze she walked round the fair again and saw some Thorpe people who wanted a chat. She saw her mother's old friend, Mrs Russell, who lived at the far side of the square. 'Yes, I'm still at Badger's Gill, Mrs Russell. I hope to stay there, if I can.'

For some reason Mrs Russell approved of Sally. 'Well done, my dear. Not many young women would be able to do it. My own Maggie never dreamed of taking over when her father died. And neither did I have the courage, to be honest. So we sold up and came to live in Masham. It was the easiest thing to do, of course. But I still miss the farm.' And as they parted, the older woman gave Sally a warm smile. 'The best of luck to you, Sally.'

This meeting put some heart into Sally. Another woman approved of her and it was encouraging to think that not all respectable, middle-aged ladies were like Aunt Bertha.

The shadows lengthened across the square. Carts were coming to collect the sheep. The afternoon was passing, but Marcus did not come out of the meeting. George and Martha came back, worried that they'd missed the sale. 'We'd better make tracks for home. I'll fetch the cart and load up these girls ... my, they look right well!'

Sally would have liked to see Marcus again. They still didn't know each other's names or whereabouts, which was silly, but everything had happened so quickly! They might never happen to meet again. But George and Martha were keen to get home before dark and she didn't like to hold them up. So they went back with the flock, who seemed quite happy with the arrangements, netted up in the cart, jogging through the twilight to their home at Badger's Gill.

Marcus went home thoughtfully after a long, slow meeting. He was president of the local show society and was keen on making the event a way of improving the local livestock, by rewarding the best breeders of sheep or cattle with cups and rosettes. But there was still much to be done to persuade the average farmer to breed for improvement. The young man sighed rather wearily as he left the little town behind and headed for the moor. Marcus was in no particular hurry; there was no one waiting for him to come home. Things would have been different had Elizabeth lived. His life had seemed set on a successful course, but just before he was to be married to the attractive young woman he loved, she died of pneumonia. That was three years ago; Marcus still felt lonely at times, but Elizabeth's memory was fading. Life had to go on.

The big horse knew it was going home and quickened its pace. Colsterdale was home: a big sheep farm belonging to his family, who lived at Pateley. The little dale was not far from Masham but it was separate, a different world. Marcus and the farm workers saw few outsiders in the dale and he was used to his own company. Of course, he reminded himself, he was lucky to have the Browns to look after him, husband and wife who had a cottage on the farm. Jesse Brown was a very good shepherd and his wife Jeanie cleaned the house and cooked for the boss, not without a certain amount of grumbling about his untidy ways.

No doubt it was time he thought again of marrying, but after Elizabeth's vivacity, other lasses seemed insipid. Until, that is, he'd met the girl at Camp Hill. Miss Mason of Badger's Gill. He knew who she was, now.

As the meeting ended, Martin, the man who'd come to call him, had teased Marcus about the motley pen of sheep he'd sold. Not quite the family standard, Marcus had agreed. 'D'you know who bought them?' he'd enquired casually.

The other man had laughed. 'There you were, shaking hands and you hadn't been introduced! That's Robert Mason's daughter. Farmed Badger's Gill. He died early this year ... a bonny lass, too. Now, can you tell me where to buy a good tup? We had no luck at the sale today.'

It was strange, thought Marcus as he turned in at the familiar farm gate, that he couldn't forget Miss Mason. Today she'd seemed beautiful, her heart-shaped face framed with chestnut curls. He shook himself. Must be spending too much time on his own.

There was something about the Masons that he had almost forgotten. An old quarrel, and they'd never mixed with the family. He must ask his father about it. Shut away in Colsterdale he was not up to date with what the old boy was doing, but he knew that

Radford Estates had owned that farm, Badger's Gill, for a few years. Presumably Miss Mason's father was the tenant. Had been... Martin had said he'd died. Perhaps he should read the death notices in the paper more often and take more notice of what was happening outside his own boundaries ... surely the poor little lass wasn't farming on her own?

Ripon Cathedral clock was booming the stately hour of one o'clock as a party set out from Trinity Vicarage on a solemn mission. In the outside driving seat of the old-fashioned barouche was the corpulent Jeremiah Jones, the vicar's gardener and handyman, who had been at the vicarage for twenty years and who sang with Welsh fervour in church on Sundays.

Under the vehicle's hood, the vicar tucked up his wife in her many rugs and settled back to watch the familiar autumn landscape slide past. They had waited for a fine day to make the trip to Thorpe. Jeremiah drove very slowly, as Mrs Mason preferred, and her husband noticed that they were outpaced by an energetic walker. 'Do not hurry, Jeremiah!' Bertha reminded him again as they passed the city boundary and came into open country, as though the man would make a sudden dash. 'You know how it affects my poor nerves!'

Samuel commented on the scenery and talked about the plans for a Christmas concert: anything, to keep his wife off the topic of Sally. They were going to visit Sally at Bertha's insistence and he hoped that at this pace, they'd manage to get back to Ripon before dark.

It was good to visit his niece, Samuel agreed, but he did not like the agenda; he hated disagreements of any kind and they were certainly heading for one today. Bertha thoroughly disapproved of Sally's farming ambitions and was still determined that the young woman should be brought back to Ripon, for her own good. She would also make a useful addition to their household. Sally would have to be brought to heel, and quickly, she told her husband in the sweet voice that so misled some people.

Samuel worried about Sally, but he had no idea of how to help her. The absence of bank books was odd; where could Robert have kept his records? Did he have any money left? Bertha was probably right: there was no future for Sally at the farm.

Samuel settled down in his seat with a sigh, glad that he didn't have to argue with Bertha, which made his head ache. He hoped Sally would come quietly. The old horse plodded on, making heavy work of the hills. It was dark and claustrophobic under the trees at Thieves' Gill and Samuel was glad when they reached the top of the bank and could see the line of moors against the sky. It seemed a long way to Thorpe.

Sally had no idea of the doom that was slowly drawing nearer to her, jogging up to Thorpe on the Ripon road, because nobody had told her it was coming. She knew at the back of her mind that the business was not settled and that Aunt Bertha had her sights set on Sally and her furniture. But it was easy enough to ignore for the present, in favour of more urgent problems.

The young farmer was busy making blackberry jam, stirring a large cauldron over the kitchen stove. The scent of blackberries hung in the air, a fragrant, warm, purple aroma. The last of the autumn sunshine was being bottled up for winter use. Jam and scones were useful for a paying guest. Sally's hands were purple from handling the fruit and eating some of it, and her face was flushed. Stray red curls escaped from under her white cap. She was perfectly happy, secure in the moment, knowing that out in the cold afternoon Joe was getting through the necessary farm work. And best of all, the rent had been paid.

A few apples were needed to bring out the flavour of the blackberries. Sally went to the pantry, where her apples were laid out in rows on the shelves. She stretched up to take one and heard a knock on the door.

Uncle Samuel's booming parson's voice left Sally in no doubt as to what would happen next. Aunt Bertha swept into the kitchen, trailing rugs and threw her arms round Sally, recoiling as she realized that blackberry juice would stain her coat. Sally's uncle followed, calling a greeting and Jones took the trap into the farmyard, where he managed to terrify the geese. The old dog barked and the peace of the afternoon was gone. But that was only the beginning.

Hurriedly taking off her apron and washing her sticky hands, Sally led the visitors into the parlour where she had a small fire, mainly to keep the books from getting damp. She was glad that the furniture was dusted and the room was tidy. The visit already had the feeling of an inspection.

'You know why we are here, of course?' Bertha's eyes were darting round the room, lingering on the piano, which was a good one and positively feasting on the little corner cabinet in which Sally's mother had kept her china.

'But Aunt, I've already said that I want to stay here.'

'You can't afford to stay here, my sweet! You have very little income.' The voice, powerful and sugary at the same time, echoed round the room and down the hall.

Sally couldn't get a word in, as her aunt took the floor and told her how her future was going to be. 'You will come to live with us as soon as it can be arranged, my dear girl, for your own good, as we agreed when you visited us in summer. Your room is ready. We are waiting to welcome you with open arms!' There was a dramatic pause and a reply seemed to be expected, but Sally was speechless. How dare she! They had agreed on nothing!

Bertha whipped out a tape measure from her bag and measured the cabinet. 'This will go nicely in my drawing-room.' She smiled and turned back to the matter in hand. 'Now, Sally, you must defer to our experience, you know. There is danger here. Your reputation could be compromised, my dear, by living alone, young as you are. What if some young man quite innocently called at the farm? There would be gossip about you immediately and as a clergyman, your uncle cannot allow that sort of thing to happen. Sally, my dear, we think only of you!' Bertha paused for breath, bosom heaving. 'Just look at you, like a scullery maid in a dirty apron, you poor child! This is not the life for you. You need to be living more as a young lady should. At the vicarage, we have a maid for such rough work as this!' Her aunt waved a hand through the door at the jam, which was in danger of boiling over.

Thankful for a diversion, Sally dashed back into the kitchen to attend to the jam, her face crimson with suppressed rage. Was it the red hair that made her feel such emotion? Sally had often wondered what she would have been like with dark hair and a calm disposition. She pulled the jam off the stove and went back dutifully to her guests.

'I realize that the animals will have to be sold and the landlord informed that you are leaving. But I have arranged for a carrier to call next week, to remove such items of furniture as we will require at the vicarage. Please don't look so alarmed, dear Sally. This is all for your own good, no thought for us at all.'

'But I'm not...' wailed Sally.

Bertha rolled on, inexorably: 'Of course, we will leave dear Robert's furniture to you, in our wills, so you will eventually inherit. Watson the auctioneer can sell the rest, when the farm animals are sold. I have already been to see him about it. He will deduct his costs from the proceeds of the sale and give the remainder to your uncle, to invest for you.'

'He what?' Anyone would think she was simple, unable to look after her own affairs. Sally turned to Uncle Samuel, who had the grace to look uncomfortable.

'And now, I need to measure the dining-table,' Bertha announced majestically, drawing the tape measure from her bag once more. She made for the dining-room door.

Sally flew across the hall. 'No! Don't go in there, it's private!'

Ignoring Sally, Bertha swept into the dining-room and the first thing she saw was the fire, blazing merrily. 'What extravagance! Surely, my sweet, you don't need a fire...' her voice died away as she saw Miss Wakefield, sitting with a straight back at the table, primly sewing.

'Who may this young person be?' Bertha demanded. Samuel shrank back in the doorway as his wife surveyed the young person from head to foot, taking in the obvious pregnancy – and the ringless left hand. 'What is the meaning of this?' For once the sugary tones were forgotten and Bertha's voice was hard.

Sally stood in front of Emma as if to protect her from Aunt Bertha. 'Miss Wakefield is staying with me, for the present. So you see, Aunt, I'm not alone in the house.'

Bertha sat down suddenly on a dining-chair, as if overwhelmed. 'Miss! Miss! A fallen woman! You have taken into your house a fallen woman! We will never live this down – never! You have disgraced us all. Sally Mason, you are not fit to organize your own affairs, this is proof of your folly! Get rid of this female immediately and come to Ripon with us tonight!' She fanned herself with a handkerchief.

Sally was nearly fainting from a combination of rage and horror. She felt the blood drain from her face as she opened her mouth to defend her guest.

Miss Wakefield stood up, quite composed. Her young face was also hard as she looked at Bertha. 'Please do not speak to Miss Mason like that, whoever you are. She has been most kind to me, have you not, Miss Mason?'

This was so unlike Miss Wakefield that Sally paused.

'But obviously you are with child – Miss Wakefield. Putting yourself forward in the presence of decent folk! Who are you to talk to me, girl?' Bertha quivered with indignation.

'What do you know, that you accuse us so unjustly? My name is Emma Wakefield and I am not immoral. I was a victim. I was raped. Forced against my will, and got with child.' Emma spoke simply, staring at Bertha. 'I cannot allow you to blame Miss Mason, or me, for anything. I am staying here quietly until my time is over, and I will thank you to go away and leave us alone. I am not going to be a victim any more.' She went quietly to stand by Sally. 'I couldn't help overhearing some of what you said. The financial arrangements between us are private, but I can tell you that Miss Mason can afford to stay here. And obviously, she should be allowed to make up her own mind.' Emma walked out and they heard her going upstairs in the horrified silence that followed.

'Well, Sally, perhaps we should leave you in peace. You seem to have solved at least some of your problems!' Her uncle looked over his glasses at his niece, obviously glad that the crisis was over.

Sally managed to find her voice. 'Thank you, Uncle Samuel. I'm grateful for your concern for me, but I can manage and I want to stay here.'

Her uncle looked relieved, but Bertha was not. 'I am most upset that our offer of a roof over your head has been rejected. And I am very concerned that you are not living the life of a lady. And now, we shall have to find another maid. It is all very vexing.' She sobbed a little.

Uncle Samuel tried to calm his wife down and Sally went into the kitchen to make them a pot of tea. Aunt Bertha admired the old china cups, but sadly, as though beaten. Sally thought she would find it hard to give up the dining-table, even if she could live without her niece. Slowly, the atmosphere returned to near normal and soon the visitors decided that it was getting late and they ought to go home. While Jeremiah Jones was bringing round the horse, Sally cornered her uncle in the hall. 'Please will you tell the carrier not to come and cancel the auctioneer? I hope you won't be offended, Uncle, but I'm staying at Thorpe.'

Uncle Samuel gave her a brief hug. 'I know. How like your mother you are, Sally.'

The ordeal was over and Sally had won – with the help of her little friend. Emma's change of character was amazing. Sally was left feeling limp by the visit, but she felt a deep gladness that her paying guest had shown a human, caring side.

EIGHT

Emma Wakefield sat on her bed weeping tears of relief. After all this time, feeling was coming back to her. The person she used to be was returning as if from a long journey. Feeling meant pain, but it was better than the terrible ice. To speak out, after months, years of silence, had lifted a weight from her, had somehow freed her from the worst of the memory of what had happened. The admission that she'd been raped and was innocent had been instinctive, to help Sally. Emma had listened with horror to Bertha's booming voice telling Sally what she must do and it reminded her of her own experience at the Bellamys' house.

Emma had been too young to defy her

guardians, being brought up to be dutiful to one's elders. And she had only dimly realized that they had taken her in, not in charity but so that they could get their hands on the property she'd inherited. She'd been determined not to let them know what had really happened. But she had been living with the Bellamys for over four years and the lack of any real warmth or fellow feeling had made her withdraw into herself.

Sally had been a surprise, prepared as Emma was for a grim Miss Mason. Emma hadn't known how to react. But the habit of silence and keeping a distance had frozen her feelings, and she'd deliberately kept Sally away. Until recently, Emma had thought that she was there on sufferance, only because of the money, just as she'd been in Sheffield. Sally was much nicer than Mrs Bellamy, of course. But Emma hadn't realized that Sally, too, had her own problems. Not until now.

Emma felt that she'd matured these last few weeks, without realizing it. She had started to look at things from Sally's point of view. Badger's Gill had already done her good. There had been no harsh words, no frigid silences; just the peace of this old house and healing walks in the lovely countryside. Gradually, she had allowed herself to relax. And although she'd kept Sally at arm's length, the warmth of her host's personality had gradually melted the ice in Emma's soul.

When Sally tapped hesitantly on her door, Emma dried her eyes and put on her coat. She stepped on to the landing and smiled at Sally's anxious expression. There was no turning back, Emma took a deep breath and moved into the future. 'Will you have the time to come for a walk with me?'

Emma felt rewarded; the anxiety vanished and Sally's face was lit by a radiant smile. 'We'll have to hurry up, the sun's going down. Shall we go to collect the cows for milking?'

The two girls walked down the green lane towards the river. From a thorn bush, a robin piped his evening song. They could hear the distant cawing of homing rooks and see them dark against the sky. They walked slowly, because Emma was now heavy and awkward. Nothing was said for a while and then Sally turned to Emma. 'Thank you so much for saying what you did this afternoon. It must have been very difficult for you. But it certainly stopped my aunt in her tracks!' She laughed, a clear happy laugh that set Emma smiling.

It was hard to break the habit of over four years, but Emma knew she had to do it. 'Yes, Sally, but it was time for me to stop being so selfish! It must have been difficult for you, dealing with me when you have nobody else to talk to. But I've had plenty of time to think as I've been sewing.'

The cows were waiting at the gate ready to come in and Sally let them through into the lane. 'Come on girls, hurry up! Joe's waiting for you.' Emma stood behind Sally, afraid of closer contact with the cattle. They looked so big! When the cows were plodding up the lane Sally said quietly, 'You've had a dreadful time and I think your, er, reserve has been due to that. I understand now, how you've been feeling.' She closed the gate and rejoined Emma.

'My problem has really been that nobody thinks I should keep the farm going by myself. My father died, you see. And I don't know where he left our money, if there is any. Of course most people think that women are not able to run a farm on their own.'

Emma nodded, but said nothing.

'Your coming here made all the difference, Emma. With your money I was able to hire Joe to work for me and we bought more cows. I was almost desperate just before you came. It was true what people said, the work was too much for me. Too heavy.' She could admit it, now that a solution had been found.

'And is everything now going well, Sally?'

'Well, there are still big problems. The farm is now owned by someone else and he's trying to get rid of me.'

Emma stood still in the lane, wanting a rest as they were walking uphill. Sally still had troubles, that was obvious. But she felt amazed that anything she did could help anybody, even by default. 'I'd like to help you more, if I can. Obviously I can't do much at the moment, although I feel much healthier, since you persuaded me to walk and to eat the right foods. You've done me a lot of good, Sally.'

The next big hurdle was the birth and Emma was afraid. At school, she'd heard horror stories about women in childbirth, although the stories were whispered behind closed doors. No teacher ever mentioned such things, or allowed discussion of the human body and its development. But Sally was a farmer, she would probably know about it. The twilight deepened and the evening air was cold. Emma shivered under her coat.

'Well, we could be friends. Let's eat some of our meals together, and I'd like you to come into the parlour sometimes,' said Sally firmly. 'You can look through my books and – do you like music? I haven't played the piano since Father died, but we used to love music.'

Emma thought that Sally's face changed expression so quickly, it was hard to keep up with her; she went from eagerness to sadness in a moment. It must have been hard for her, tired by gruelling farm work and living alone.

'I used to play and sing when I lived at home. My parents died, too, both together, in a boating accident at Scarborough. But at the Bellamys I was never allowed to speak of them. And of course there was no music in that house.'

Sally shook her head and Emma felt that she understood how barren her life had become.

The cows went into the milking shed, each one to her accustomed place. How did they know where to go? Joe tied them, gently putting a chain around the neck and soon the shed was full of the sound of munching as the cows ate their evening hay. Emma lingered by the door, watching them. There was something soothing about contented cattle. In time, she thought, she might lose her fear of animals.

That evening Emma was happier than she'd been for years, even though the birth was still looming. Sally put some logs on the sitting-room fire and they looked at books and leafed through music. And Emma surprised herself by sitting at the piano and playing a simple piece from memory. It was strange to be a person again, not an outcast. And not to be whipped. Perhaps she'd left that behind, forever.

The weeks went by quickly as the days shortened. The factor called to buy Sally's cheeses and pronounced them excellent, which was a source of pride. The cheese money was put in the Penny Bank.

One morning, Sally came into the kitchen full of determination. 'I would like you to come with me over the green to have a cup of tea with Martha, Mrs Dawson.' She glanced at Emma, to see the effect of this drastic proposal.

Sally had several reasons for the visit. Emma needed a change of scene, since the weather had kept her in the house for a week. And also Martha might be needed to help with the baby, and Emma had only met her very briefly once or twice.

'Thank you, I know you mean well. But I'm very shy, especially...' She looked down self-consciously. 'It's so long since I met anyone.'

'Exactly. It's time you did. Now, Martha's had children and grandchildren and she's a great friend. Get your coat, Emma, we'll go now.' I'm getting very bossy, Sally thought to herself as she pulled on her boots. It must be all the responsibility; just like Mama's schoolteacher ways.

A light powdering of snow had fallen on Thorpe, etching the houses and trees with delicate white. Part of the pond was frozen, but there was still water for the ducks to swim. The village was enjoying a quiet morning as the two crossed over to where Martha and George lived.

'Doesn't Thorpe look pretty in the snow? We skate on the pond when it really freezes over.' Sally remembered skating with Robin in their carefree childhood days.

Sally looked at Emma as they got to the door and saw that the girl was trembling slightly, either from fear or the cold. 'We won't stay long. And George is away delivering turnips, I saw him go down the Ripon road. So there's only Martha here. Don't be shy, lass!'

To Sally's relief, the visit went well. Martha offered sensible advice, from her own experience, about pregnancy and Emma's composure soon came back. In some ways Emma seemed such a child and yet she'd shown amazing maturity, standing up to Aunt Bertha. Sally smiled as she thought about it.

'You'll have spring-cleaned the bedroom, I expect?' Martha peered over her glasses and Sally felt young and inexperienced, faced with one of the greatest of life's emergencies. 'And you've got a rubber sheet and plenty of big jugs for boiled water, and a lot of towels? These days they say you should boil all the towels and such and leave them in a bag, to keep out the infection. Germs, I think they call them.'

Emma's pale face went even whiter and Sally tried to jolly her along. 'It's only a natural process, after all! And with me and Martha to look after you, and the doctor when we need him, there's nothing to worry about. We've got a washstand in the room, of course and we have a little table that the doctor said would be good for the ether apparatus.' In the circumstances Sally didn't like to mention the baby, and Emma seemed indifferent to it, but they had a few baby clothes ready for the new arrival.

Sally began to feel a little less anxious; Emma was not going to be a problem. But she still had the Radfords at the back of her mind and she was forming a plan of attack. There had been no reply to Sally's letter to her landlord and weeks had gone by. 'I'm worried about it,' she confessed to Martha. 'Heaven knows what Sol is telling him. I really think that I must go over to see Mr Radford very soon. If I can tell him what we're doing with the farm face to face, he might see reason. But – I don't like to leave Emma, she's due any day now.'

Martha cleared the teacups and said gently, 'Well, now Emma knows me, I can keep an eye on her. I'll pop in during the day. Isn't that right, lass?'

Emma smiled her thanks. 'Don't worry, Sally, I will be quite safe with Martha calling in.'

'And,' Martha continued, 'George ought to go with you. It's a long way to Radford's and the weather's uncertain. It could snow again and you know what the moor's like: deep drifts, and they don't find you until spring!' Again the grim moorland smile.

'George might be needed to fetch the doctor from Kirkby,' Sally reminded her. 'It's only two miles, but that's a long way in an emergency.' She was quite determined to go the next day. There was very little snow after all, and Jed the horse was quite used to winter conditions. Better to get it over with, before Emma's baby arrived.

Back at the farm, Sally told Joe what she intended to do. He leaned on his shovel, not so shy now and even more likely to give advice. 'My, that's a long way! Nearly to Pateley. It's more than ten mile off, I reckon, where Mr Radford lives.'

'Tell me how to get there, Joe.'

'Nay, miss, weather's none too good. Er – would you like me to drive you?'

Sally shook her red curls. 'Joe, you'll have to milk the cows and if I'm not back in time, feed the sheep and the poultry. Can you pour the milk into the setting pans for me?'

Joe nodded, somewhat reluctantly. Then he put down his shovel and bustled off. Five minutes later, the trap was out in the yard, being given a clean and polish. The brass lamps were buffed. Jed was thoroughly groomed; Jed was a good-looking animal, with a chestnut coat that shone because Joe often slipped him a few extra oats.

The process took a long time; even the harness was treated with neatsfoot oil. Sally had tried to keep the outfit reasonably clean and the harness was always oiled as a safety measure to keep it from cracking, but it obviously wasn't up to Joe's standard.

Seeing all this activity, Sally realized that Joe was right. People judged you by how you looked and a smart pony and trap would imply a tidy farm. And as Joe kept reminding her, 'A tidy farm's a prosperous farm.' She would wear her good coat and gloves and she and Jed would make an early start. It was good to look smart, but as Emma pointed out, it was bound to be cold on the moor. 'I'll wear the old driving cape of Father's and my good coat underneath,' Sally decided.

The long-awaited letter arrived the next day and it made Sally even more determined to pay a visit to her landlord. She only hoped she wouldn't fizz too much when they came face to face.

Dear Madam,

I do not enter into philosophical debates with tenants.

The tone of your first letter, which the second has hardly ameliorated, was astonishing. You forget your place, madam, and your youth.

You obviously have no respect for your elders, or understanding of business conventions, and the deference due to the owner of a property, of which you are – for the moment – the tenant.

I am far too busy to visit Thorpe and will rely on my agent's reports, which as previously stated, are most unfavourable. And so is my estimation of your capabilities.

Refer to my previous letter, the terms of which still stand. I hope this is the end of the matter.

Yours faithfully,
Oliver Radford

In spite of her anger Sally smiled grimly at this letter. Mr Oliver Radford seemed to take a perverse pleasure in writing the most hostile and offensive letter that he possibly could devise, unless it were written with a stark humour. Some of the High Side characters had just that kind of mind. The spiky black writing, jabbed on to the page, drove the point home.

What on earth had she done? Sally wondered, to make this man hate her so much? It would be most interesting to meet Mr Radford and she no longer felt afraid. She felt like telling him what was what, using the longest words she could find. A philosophical debate about women and their capabilities was just what he needed to set him straight.

The next day was cloudy but rather warmer and the snow in Thorpe had melted, although they could still see patches of white on the moorland. Promising to take extreme care, Sally set off as early as she could, Jed trotting proudly along the Kirkby lane as though he knew the errand was important. Sally went through Kirkby and took the moor road, enjoying the unusual feeling of freedom and the sensation of speed. Much as she loved Badger's Gill, it was good to get away for a few hours just for a change.

Snow had drifted on the moor, filling ditches and banking up behind stone walls, and up here the air was colder, but the roads were clear. Low clouds hung over the highest ridges and the November sky looked as though more snow was possible. A horseman came towards her, a familiar shape and Sally felt the familiar flutter when she saw that it was Robin. His saddlebag was stuffed with papers.

'Hello Sal, what are you up to? I'll ride a mile or two with you.' And he turned his horse's head and came alongside.

'I'm off to see the landlord, Robin. To ask him for the tenancy. I really want to stay at

Badger's Gill.'

The young man grinned at her and shook his curly head. 'We must be complete opposites, lass. All you want is to stay at Thorpe, while all I want is to get away! That's why I do the errands for Father, like this one today. Got me out of the village for an hour!'

Sally stared straight ahead between her horse's ears, in shock. 'I never knew that you wanted to leave, Robin. Are you unhappy or something?' He'd always seemed so carefree, it was hard to believe.

'Well, I've been here all my life, except for school. I want to go off and have adventures, see a bit of the world! But I don't talk about it at home. They want me to farm with them for ever. Or of course I could go into law like Father, and advise all the old farmers on their legal problems and how to sue their neighbours. It upsets the family to think that I might leave. That's why I've never mentioned it to you.'

'And what do you really, really want?' She looked at him briefly and slowed the horse down.

'Shall I tell you? Don't say a word, it would upset Ma and Pa. I want to set up a farm of my own in Australia. To achieve something myself, instead of tagging along with the family! The twins will still be here, the folks can manage without me. I'm trying to find out how to go about it. I think you can still get cheap land in Victoria. It's all forest, you have to clear it yourself. And I've a little money of my own that Grandfather left me.'

Sally swallowed. 'And are you planning to take anyone with you? A wife, perhaps?' It was the first time she'd asked him about his future plans.

'Not so fast, my girl! I'm not ready for matrimony yet. And I'm sure the life will be a bit rugged at first. Too rough for a woman. But tell you what, bairn, when I get the farm organized I'll be looking round for someone like you!' He beamed at her.

'Wh-what do you mean?' Jed made his own way up the road, as Sally stared at Robin.

'Oh, you know, somebody who's not frightened of hard work, and likes getting dirty and all that.' Robin waved a hand airily. 'Somebody who doesn't care about pretty dresses and doesn't worry at all about how she looks. That's what I'll need. A worker!'

You don't know me very well young man, thought Sally. The image he had of her was disappointing and she was hurt. But not devastated. Robin was just insensitive, when she thought about it. Marcus, to take an example, would never have said something like that. But it was no use thinking of Marcus either, except as an antidote for yearning after Robin. There would be no future with Robin for her; she could see that even more clearly now. He would probably find a sturdy Australian girl to marry, and if he did come back to look for his old friend Sally it wouldn't be for love, but for convenience.

'Goodbye, Robin!' He turned back to Kirkby and she waved as he left, riding out of her life, it seemed. And this time I mean it, she thought. He's too – what is it? Too practical for me. There is no romance in Robin.

Sally set herself to think of the business in hand. They passed the Drovers' Inn on the top of the moor, a sort of dividing line between Wensleydale and Nidderdale. There were a few horses tied up outside and Jed snorted at them as he passed. They were now in foreign country, on the other side of the hill.

'Now, how shall I talk to Mr Radford? Politely but firmly, I suppose.' Jed cocked an ear as though he were listening and trotted on. 'I'll begin by asking him what he wants from a good tenant and that will give me a clue about what to say. And then I'll ask him whether it matters who farms the place? Surely all that matters is the land and whether the buildings are falling down?'

As she drew nearer to Nidd Grange, the Radford headquarters, Sally began to feel slightly nervous. So much was at stake! And the tone of those letters was so hostile, she couldn't really hope for a good reception. Although if the letters were the expression of a rather sardonic humour after all, he might appreciate a spirited reply. Either way, she would know more when she met this ogre. She reminded herself that she too was a High-Sider, with the fierce Viking ancestry that seemed at times to surface all these centuries later. She could stand up to a Radford!

Sally turned carefully off the main Pateley road and went down a winding track, as Joe had instructed. Far below was the green valley of Nidderdale, with the River Nidd shining here and there and the bulk of the Pennines rising at the far side. The Radford farms were spread out over the nearer hillside, and Sally could see a large stone house with an immense stable yard, gardens, orchards and long barns. Some of the land went down to the river, while the higher slopes merged into the moorland. It was an impressive sight. By the time she rolled into the stable yard Sally was feeling very small indeed, perched up on the trap trying to look adequate, if she couldn't look smart. Jed pulled up and stood quite still, very obedient and on his best behaviour.

A groom appeared and looked up at her appreciatively. 'Tidy outfit, that, miss. What can we do for you?' He held a hand out for the reins and tied them to a rail. The trap cleaning had been a good idea; it had impressed this young lad, for a start, even though it wasn't quite the racy type of trap that the doctor drove and that usually impressed young men. Feeling rather better, Sally smiled at the man.

'I'd like to see Mr Radford, please. He doesn't know me, but it's rather important.'

'Sorry, miss, boss is away in York this week, on business. Young boss is coming over some time, just to keep an eye on us.' He gave a sly grin. 'But, of course, we don't know when.'

NINE

Sally felt her heart drop down to her boots. She was bitterly disappointed; her head drooped and she felt like crying. All this way and he wasn't at home! 'Oh, dear.' She hadn't thought of that possibility.

'There's a farm manager in that office, over there. Mr Hill, he is, you could see him instead. I'll keep an eye on the pony for you.' And he gallantly helped Sally down from the trap.

Walking stiffly after her long cold drive, Sally crossed over to the manager's office and the young groom announced, 'Young lady to see you, sir.'

The manager looked up from accounts, obviously surprised. 'Good day, miss.'

Sally went up to the desk and took a deep breath. This man might be able to help. He would know the best way to impress Oliver Radford. 'Mr Hill? I'm Sally Mason and we farm Badger's Gill at Thorpe. I wrote to Mr Radford about three weeks ago, asking to keep the tenancy. But today I came to ask him myself. To explain that I and my staff' – she'd thought of that one, driving over the moor – 'are quite capable of running the farm properly.'

The manager stroked his beard. 'Badger's Gill? You'll be Robert's daughter, then. I knew your father when we were young. He was a good man, Robert, very conscientious. Come to the fire, you must be cold.'

A good start, he's known Father. Sally moved nearer, grateful for the warmth of the fire. 'Then you'll know the story. I've been asked to leave, about a month after Father died. I believe I saw you at his funeral?'

The man nodded. 'Big turnout, wasn't it? Robert was well-liked and he died before his time.'

'I wonder whether you can help me? Can you persuade Mr Radford to let me keep the farm?' He might do that, for Robert's sake.

'We never made a great deal of money, but we treated the land well, and the stock too. We farmed well, rather than trying to make a quick profit.' The manager was listening attentively, which was encouraging. Sally decided to press on. 'Mr Hill, I am farming well. We always took a pride in Badger's Gill. But I have a feeling that Mr Radford believes otherwise. The agent, Mr Bartram, is always finding fault with me. I gather that he has told Mr Radford that I'm not capable of farming. But it's not true!'

Looking rather regretful, the manager shook his head. 'Miss Mason, you'd be better off marrying a young man with a farm of his own and forgetting about independence.' He smiled in a fatherly way.

Sally's hope evaporated, as she realized that this was another man who thought that a woman's place was in the home, not managing a farm.

Mr Hill seemed to feel sorry for her. 'A bonny lass like you should have the pick of all the young farmers on the High Side! And then you'd have the benefit of a man to look after you, and farm men to do the heavy work.'

Sally smiled dutifully, but stuck to the point. 'I'm afraid I don't know many young farmers. But you will remember that Badger's Gill was ours, once. I'd like to keep it.' And buy it back for my children, if I ever have any, she added to herself. If ever I make enough money, or find out where Father kept his. 'So – what chance do you think I have?'

Mr Hill turned in his seat, rather uneasily. 'Sit down, Miss Mason. I shouldn't keep you standing.' He fiddled with the papers on his desk. Sally waited. 'It's hard to know what to say to you, my dear. I am afraid there's not much chance of changing Mr Radford's mind. There's the old quarrel, for one thing – Radfords and Masons don't agree. But you'll know about that.'

Sally shook her head. 'I realize that this is a problem, but Father never told me any details about it.' The hot fire was making her cheeks burn. 'I know there was a quarrel, but no more.' She knew that Father had resented the way in which the Radfords bought the farm. Mother had never once mentioned the Radfords, a silence that was ominous in itself.

'Oh, dear ... well, there's a matter of a death between them.' The manager avoided her eyes.

'You mean a murder?' Sally looked at him, wanting to know the truth. 'Please tell me. I'm a Mason, I think I've a right to know.'

'Nobody knows for sure. It concerned your grandfather; he's been dead for about ten years, hasn't he? Radfords and Masons were friendly – the two boys, Billy and Rich-

156

ard, grew up together. Billy was Oliver's father, of course.'

There was a pause. So, thought Sally, she'd known that they were friendly, once.

'And then one day when they were in their thirties, with wives and families, they both went off into Foxholes Wood. I think they were taking a short cut to Dallagill, to buy sheep.'

'So what happened?' A murder in the family would take a lot of getting used to. Sally was almost afraid to hear what came next.

'And only one came back. Richard Mason came back. Billy Radford was never seen again.'

Sally said slowly, 'And Radfords blamed Richard Mason? What exactly happened, do you think?'

The manager stood up, as if to end the interview. 'Yes, Radfords were very bitter, still are. Your grandfather, Richard Mason, he swore he hadn't done it. Nothing was ever proved, either way. Richard was a decent man, as far as I ever knew. I remember him as Robert's father of course, a very reserved man. As he might be, after all the fuss.'

Grandfather had been quiet, Sally remembered. He didn't take part in the community's activities. But he went to church, and helped the vicar in little ways.

'But that might be why, when he got the

157

chance, Oliver bought Mason's farm. I'm not sure why he bought it, unless he wanted revenge. So it looks as though he'll not be likely to leave you there.' His tone was final.

Mr Hill opened the door. 'I'm sorry, Miss Mason. None of it's your fault. Your father should've told you years ago. But just to give you an idea of how things are now, I didn't tell Mr Radford that I was going to your father's funeral. He wouldn't have liked that. And I think it best not to tell him that you've visited today.'

'Thank you, Mr Hill,' Sally whispered, and crept back to the trap utterly crushed. She'd had no idea of how bad things were between the two families. What might have happened if Oliver Radford had been at home? Just as well that he wasn't. Sally felt shocked once again. Robin had shocked her earlier, but that didn't seem to matter now. Even so, two shocks in one day were quite enough. Sally wanted to get back home back to her familiar routine as quickly as possible.

The sky had a heavy look, promising snow. The huge buildings and impressive house looked unfriendly. Radford possessions, the enemy stronghold. And now she knew how unfriendly they might be. Sally patted Jed, a symbol of home. Jed was bored and wanted to be off, so he wheeled smartly and trotted off as soon as she untied the reins and climbed on board. Pity there was no one in the yard to see them go.

Clopping down the track to the Pateley road, Sally thought about her father. He'd tried to shield her from this ugly story, she realized. He'd thought that it was all forgotten and his father had surely never spoken of it. And now it had risen up to haunt her. Poor Father! How it must have irked him, to pay rent to Radfords.

'Come on, Jed, we'll soon be home!' she urged, and the horse responded. They reached the main road as the first flakes of snow began to fall. Her nervous excitement, all her hope, had vanished and Sally felt very tired indeed. But she urged on the horse, trying to cover the ground quickly as the snow whirled round them, narrowing their world down to a few yards of moorland. Sally was not afraid of missing the road. She knew that it would take a great deal of snow to cover the track and there were various landmarks like the Drovers' Inn, which would be coming up soon on the left. Once past there, she knew the way quite well in all weathers. She and Jed were cold and wet and both of them wanted to get home.

Tired as she was, Sally's mind was whirring, trying to find a solution to the Radford problem. What if she saw Oliver Radford and made him believe that the old quarrel was nothing to do with the present? She was jerked back to the immediate present with a jolt. A black grouse rose suddenly from the side of the road and rushed across in front of them under the horse's feet. Young Jed reared and Sally, unable to control him, saw his front hooves coming up above his head.

'Whoa, boy! Steady, now!' She stood up and pulled frantically on the reins. The terrified horse then jumped away from the bird into the ditch. The shafts twisted and the trap slowly turned over on its side. In a moment Sally was in the snow, her face in the bank at the far side of the ditch. She hit her head on a stone and passed out.

When Sally came back to consciousness she could hear the horse neighing loudly, obviously frightened, but dimly, from far away. She concentrated with some difficulty. With a splintering sound, Jed kicked and pulled until he was free from the shafts. He cantered down the road a little way and then pulled up, and it sounded as though he started to nibble at the short moorland grass that poked through the snow.

Sally was glad the horse didn't seem to be too badly injured, or so frightened that he would gallop for miles and get lost. A more experienced horse might have shied, but probably would not have reacted by bolting into the ditch. Jed had seen a lot of ground birds, pheasants and partridges, in the lanes near Thorpe; he should have known better!

Confused and with an aching head, Sally tried to struggle free but the trap surrounded her and was too heavy to move. It blocked her from getting away from the bank. She'd been lucky that it didn't fall on top of her ... it was hard to think. Sally drifted off again and when she resurfaced the snow seemed to have stopped. She could hear Jed munching grass not far off. At least if anyone came by they would see the horse. But how many folks were likely to travel on this road on a snowy winter afternoon? Not many. It was very cold and she'd forgotten to put on the driving cape. Sally fumbled around until she found it and managed to drag some of it across her. Martha's words came back to her then, with force. 'And they don't find you until spring.' She tried again to get free, without success.

An hour later Sally was ready to give up. The cold had numbed her until she didn't care any more; all her problems had floated away. Dimly she heard Jed give a whinny, and sounds of another horse approaching. Would it be friend or foe? Sally had heard tales of travellers in trouble being assaulted and robbed on the moor. Some of the more isolated moorlanders were very wild folk, especially at this side of the divide, they always said in Thorpe. Even the carriers who crossed the moors with goods were suspected of evil deeds. She should have let Joe come with her. At that moment Sally was willing to admit that there were times when a man could come in useful. Robbers would hardly attack a man like Joe.

A deep voice said, 'Hello, there's been an accident. Anyone in there?'

'Yes!' Sally's voice was a squeak. Friend or foe, she needed help to survive.

'Are you hurt?' The voice was concerned and sounded familiar.

'Not much, but I can't get out – the trap's too heavy!'

There was a small gap at one side and a face appeared. 'Oh, what a mess!'

'Marcus!' Sally was flooded with relief. To her shame, she started to cry. Marcus had appeared, for the third time in her life. It seemed symbolic to her, light-headed as she was, that of all the people in the world, the Roman soldier had come to find her. Everything was going to be fine.

'Well, it's Bo-Peep! You poor lass! I'll go down to the Drovers' for help. Won't be long, we'll have you out in no time.' Hoof-beats thudded down the road, muffled by the snow. Marcus was going for help. Sally couldn't think of a better rescuer.

It took a couple of gamekeepers and the landlord of the inn, as well as Marcus, to get Sally out and the trap back on the road. A keeper caught the rather subdued Jed and ran his hand down the horse's legs. 'Not much, just a deep scratch or two. No bones broken. We'll put him in the Drovers' stables for now.'

Looking at the damage to the vehicle, Marcus shook his head. 'Not good, but it's mendable. Let's look after you first, young lady. Do you come this way often, all alone in bad weather?' He looked down at her, his deep brown eyes anxious. Sally stumbled and he put an arm round her. 'Now, I know we haven't been formally introduced, and one should never pick up a lady without an introduction. But I also remember very well that we've met! You're the little china shepherdess and I'm a Roman soldier. I'm going to carry you to the inn.' He spoke lightly, perhaps to lessen the shock.

Sally arrived at the Drovers', wet and bedraggled, carried easily by Marcus and weeping weak tears of relief. The Drovers' Inn was used to catering for weary travellers. It was an ancient building with a low, beamed ceiling and stone floors. There was a roaring wood fire in the bar, and a big settle in an inglenook with warm rag rugs at their feet.

Marcus gently took the driving cape from Sally and put it by the fire to dry. He looked down at her with such concern that she blushed and turned away. The intrepid adventurer was in pain, with an aching head.

Her feet and hands ached so badly as the circulation came back that she pleaded to sit away from the fire for a while. They sat at one of the tables and Marcus made Sally drink a small glass of whisky. She began to feel more normal after a while and tried to thank him, but he waved it aside.

'Just rest, Bo-Peep, and get warm. I am so thankful I was here at the right time. I don't use this road more than once a month.'

The landlord produced bowls of thick pea soup and hunks of crusty bread and Sally found she was hungry. Then he left them alone. Marcus ate with her and talked quietly about all manner of subjects; anything except horses and spills. Sally felt that he was doing his best to get her over the shock of the accident, understanding how she felt. She felt herself being ever more drawn to this man, and not just because he'd rescued her.

Marcus had read books that Sally knew and was interested in local history, archaeology and natural science. She realized that she'd missed this kind of conversation since her father died. Their talk was wide ranging, but it never touched on personal matters.

When the grandfather clock struck the hour they both looked up in amazement. 'I suppose you're on business, and I'm holding you up. I'm very sorry,' Sally said.

'My errand was not urgent. I can go there

tomorrow instead,' Marcus said easily. 'The keepers are trying to mend the trap and I'm hoping you'll be home before dark. But I'm not sure you should drive. I think I should drive you home to make sure that you have no more adventures.'

It sounded sensible, but it wouldn't be fair. 'I live at Thorpe, it's a long way for you to drive on a winter day. I'm Sally Mason from Badger's Gill.' Sally pushed back her hair, which had dried and was curling round her face in its usual wayward fashion.

Marcus looked down at her, his face sad. With a rush of feeling, Sally felt like reaching out to comfort him. A moment before he'd been talking wittily, but now he had a haunted look. 'I know who you are, Sally.' He took her hand and his voice was low, and full of emotion. 'I have often thought about you since the day we met. But I wish you were not Miss Mason from Badger's Gill.'

Sally stared at him. 'Why is that?'

'Because my name is Marcus Radford.' The enemy! Marcus was … another shock, on a day of shocks.

The enemy leaned forward and kissed her cheek. 'It seems that we can never be friends, Miss Mason. You won't want to know me now! I can't tell you how much I regret it.' He stood up. 'My father, Oliver, has suggested that I shouldn't see you again.' The strong voice deepened a little. Marcus went out and Sally could hear him asking the men whether the trap was fit to drive.

Sally waited a long time until her heart stopped thumping. When Marcus came back she said, 'As a conversation stopper, that's the best I've heard.'

Marcus laughed then and the tension eased. 'Thank you, Bo-Peep! That's the sort of reaction I'd expect from you. I'm sorry if I sounded melodramatic but the fact is, both our families are very bitter and set against each other. And it matters, in farming families and in communities like ours.'

Sally breathed deeply. 'Marcus, I understand some of the story. Today Mr Hill told me that there was a death, possibly a murder involved. I'm afraid I'd never heard about it before.'

'You met Hill? You've been to Nidd Grange?' Oliver's son was startled.

'To ask for the tenancy.' Sally was too weary to go into details. 'If you spoke to your father about me you'll know that he's told me to leave.'

Marcus shook his head sadly and changed the subject. 'Well, your horse and trap are ready to go, ma'am.' Sally put on her driving cape, which had dried by the fire. As he held open the door for her Marcus said quietly, 'I've paid the bill. It's a gentleman's privilege, you know.'

Sally fired up immediately, fiercely independent. 'I can't let you do that!'

'Imagine that we have been dining in a fashionable restaurant. A lady would never offer to pay the bill in such a place – so why here?' He was laughing at her. 'The lads wouldn't take any pay for the repairs, so I left the price of a drink at the bar for them.'

'I will go to thank them,' said Sally firmly, but she wobbled a little as she walked out.

There was no question of Sally driving home alone across the moor. Marcus simply tied his horse to the back of the trap, handed Sally up and then jumped up and took the reins.

Sally would never forget that drive with Marcus. Sitting close together, but looking at the road ahead they talked easily. And Marcus seemed to want to clear the air and talk about the families and their old quarrel. This time they were on a personal level without any barriers, as they watched the snow clouds piling up in the distance. They were taking their time. Jed's knees were sore and Marcus did not hurry him.

'I'm sorry you had to hear about the old story, Sally. But you'll understand, you're from a family of farmers yourself. It's a blessing and also a curse, but we are closer as families than people who live in towns. Closer to our parents and grandparents, because we work with them and we are their hope for the future. And this means that when they have very strong feelings about anything, we try to please them.' He smiled. 'Or we've been brought up to think as they do.'

Sally agreed. 'I know a few farmers' sons and daughters who stay at home on the farm just to please the old folks! Yes, I worked with my father and mother quite happily. But some of the girls I knew at school couldn't wait to leave home and didn't see much of their parents at all.'

'Exactly. And my father's been good to me, we get on well enough. I run the Colsterdale estate and he has Nidd.'

'You live alone?' Sally wanted to know more about this man.

'With a couple to look after me. I've been away from Nidd for years and have my own way of thinking by now! I don't hate the Masons, Sally dear. Far from it. But when I found out who you were and then asked Father about you, his reaction was extreme. "Keep away!"'

Looking along the battered shafts to Jed's shoulders Sally said, 'But he's never met me.'

'He was probably thinking of Grand-mother. His mother is still alive, in her eighties, and she is the widow of the man who died, you see.'

A little wind got up and whipped round them. Sally shivered and Marcus pulled the cape closely round her with his free arm. Sally was trying to imagine how it would be if a Radford had been involved in the death of her relation.

'But Grandfather Mason was a good man, I believe. None of our family history has anything violent in it. I think the chief fault of the Masons has been a lack of proper interest in making money.'

'Oh, Sally, I'm sure you're from a good family.' Marcus looked down at her with a smile. He added in a lower tone, 'I'm afraid, you see, that I could get too fond of you, my lass, which would cause problems for us both. And these days you can't just gallop off into the future in a haze of romance!' He stopped and looked at her earnestly. Jed, left to himself, wandered into the side of the road and had to be corrected.

'When Father said he didn't want me to see you,' Marcus continued, 'I thought that perhaps you wouldn't care to see me anyway. I'd been thinking about you quite often, but we hardly know each other. It should not be too sad a parting if we don't get any closer. Tell me, what do you think?'

Sally looked up into the dark, eager face. Should she make it easy for him and pretend indifference? I've been thinking about you too, Marcus, but I can't say so. I think I'm falling in love with you. Sally decided to be honest. And she tried to speak lightly to ease the pain. 'What should a modest young woman say? I can't think of anybody I'd rather gallop off with! I wish we didn't have this feud, Marcus.'

'That makes it worse, of course. We both regret it.' The grim look on Marcus's face reminded Sally of that glimpse she'd had of his father.

'I wonder,' said Sally quietly, as they clopped into Thorpe, 'If the truth could ever be known?'

Marcus shook his head. 'My family went through the wood, the police investigated, nothing could be found. And it's fifty years ago, Sally. Any clues would have disappeared long ago.'

'And what did Richard Mason say? My grandfather?'

'He couldn't remember anything. That was the odd part. But there's something else.'

Sally sighed. 'What, another reason to hate each other?'

'I'm not sure.' Marcus spoke slowly, as though unwilling. 'There's something else troubling Father about the Masons, but I don't know what it is.'

They arrived at Badger's Gill and Marcus unyoked and led the horse into the stable. It was getting dark. Joe could be heard in the cowshed, whistling as he worked. Sally went into the loose-box to take off the harness and Marcus followed her to help. She hung the harness up in its place and they looked at each other. Marcus and Sally moved towards each other and she was scooped into a hungry embrace. In her own stable, in the winter twilight Sally Mason had her first real kiss. A gentle, loving kiss – a firm and honest one. Marcus was warm, vital. She knew then, what she wanted: the love of Marcus Radford. But it could never be. Just for a moment, Sally clung to Marcus wordlessly. Then she looked up at him, peering through the darkness of the stable while Jed tried to chew her coat.

'You were right, of course. We'll have to forget about each other.' With a quick change of mood, Sally took Marcus by the hand. 'But just so that you can correct your father's impression of me, please come for a quick look round before you go.'

Marcus was led round the cowshed, where Joe looked up from feeding the cows and smiled. 'Evening, miss, glad to see you're home safe!' Emma came in to collect a jug of milk. She smiled a greeting to them on her way through. The shed was clean, fragrant with the smell of hay and new milk. The farm yard was swept clean and not a straw could be seen on the cobbles. The poultry clucked drowsily from their wooden house. In the evening light the hedges stretched away, neatly cut back and beyond, the winter pastures slept.

'It's a neat little farm, Sally. You look after it well, I can see.' He turned away to lead out his horse. 'I – I certainly do hope to talk to you again one day.' Marcus jumped on his horse and was gone.

TEN

'The baby's on the way!' Sally had run across the green to fetch Martha, feeling almost as scared as Emma herself.

Martha, steady as ever, made her sit down and catch her breath. 'Now don't go getting too excited, it will never do. The mother must be kept calm,' she said quietly. 'It's nine in the morning, 'twill probably take all day. No call to panic.'

'But I've no experience...'

'You've plenty,' Martha assured her. 'Think of all the cows you've helped to calve and the lambs you've seen into the world! There's not a load of difference in the end. Baby comes when it's ready and that's that.'

Emma would not be flattered by the comparison, but ... if cows knew what to do instinctively, maybe humans did, too? 'But she's very young. The doctor said so.' Sally was not convinced.

'Aye, that's true, but she's healthy – you've

172

seen to that. You've done the best for her, Sally. You've given her plenty of raspberry leaf tea. The rest is up to Emma and maybe to God. Now I'll go and find George.'

God and Dr Bishop, thought Sally, as George yoked up and trundled off to Kirkby to tell the doctor. High Side folk thought that Dr Bishop was looked after by God because his patients often actually lived, whereas the drunken doctors before him had managed to kill a lot of people. Including, Sally believed, her poor mother.

The bed was ready, the water was boiled, the towels were in a sterile bag. Emma paced up and down the dining-room, pale as a ghost. 'Keep moving, that's right,' advised Martha. 'Now, Sally, why don't you go and do your morning jobs? Feed the hens and such? I'll stay here with Emma.'

It was early December; all the animals were on winter rations and feeding was a much bigger job than it was in summer. Thorpe winters were long and cattle were in the sheds for most of the time. Sally put some turnips through the chopper to help Joe, gave some hay to the sheep and scattered grain for the fowls, but she was thinking about Emma as she worked and what she was going through. It was one thing to undergo this ordeal of childbirth and to be rewarded by a healthy baby, a little new-comer to the family and someone to love.

Sally could imagine how the dream of a child of one's own would carry a woman through the nine months of discomfort, the pain of birthing and even the indignity of having a doctor there.

Emma, poor girl, had nothing to look forward to. She had not mentioned the baby, so perhaps she was reconciled to its loss. And then, the father was a man she had hated and the baby would remind her of him and his cruelty. Sally now remembered that it would fall to herself to take the baby away. How would Emma feel when it came to the parting? They would all be relieved when it was over. They'd prepared the minimum of clothes for the little creature. The rule laid down by the Bellamys was that the baby should be taken from the mother immediately after birth. But Martha, when she heard of this had said firmly that first it must be fed by the mother. 'There's special things in the first milk that a baby needs,' she told Emma.

Sally, thinking once more of cows, agreed. Was it so bad, she wondered, to compare human beings with animals? 'We are all animals, after all!'

It was a difficult birth as the doctor had foreseen. He came as soon as he heard that Emma's pains had started and set up the ether apparatus with Martha's help. 'Done this before?' he asked Martha.

'Of course, doctor!' Martha was quite composed. 'I used to work in the hospital at Ripon before I was married. Not exactly a nurse, just to clean up the wards and help with the patients. And the ether, sometimes in the middle of the night.'

Dr Bishop looked relieved, Sally thought. And she was very glad that she didn't have to take the responsibility. Martha had told her once that too much ether could kill the patient and too little would leave her in pain. Sally's role, they told her, was to hold Emma's hand, to give her something to push against if she needed it and to try to keep her calm, because a nervous woman had a harder time of it. The muscles needed to relax, the canal had to dilate to let the baby through. But she was so young and so small...

It was a strange day. The cold winter winds blew round the old stone house and Sally kept up the fires, including one in the big bedroom where Emma lay. The minutes ticked away, became hours, but nothing much happened except that Emma's pain increased. Sally was once more impressed by Emma's courage. Her body was immature, but she seemed to have the mind and will of an older woman. She'll be a force to be reckoned with in a few years' time, Sally thought. A determined woman with great self-control.

At long last as the evening shadows fell,

the baby appeared. Martha bathed it expertly while Sally helped the doctor with Emma.

'She did well. She's a brave girl!' The doctor was approving and Sally was pleased that Emma woke in time to hear it. She'd only had the ether in the end, to make the doctor's job easier.

'Emma has a lot of character,' agreed Sally.

Emma was propped up in bed, still rather limp and the little boy was placed in her arms. Martha showed her how to give him the breast. And Sally felt like crying as she saw Emma gently kiss the baby's head. The maternal instinct was there, in spite of the recent ordeal and in spite of the horror of the baby's conception. Nature had triumphed over reason.

Downstairs in the kitchen, Sally turned to Martha with a worried expression. 'Letting her hold the baby may have been a mistake, after all. She'll want to keep it.' Perhaps the Bellamys had been right. Sally felt maternal herself when she held the little scrap. How would his mother feel?

'I know.' Martha, too, was sad. 'Oh Sally, what devils men are to use a young girl like this! But I suppose least said, soonest mended. Let's have a cup of tea.'

If you carry a baby inside you all those months, there must be a strong bond. It's natural for Emma to grieve, Sally thought. We must give her time to recover. A telegram had been sent to the people who were to adopt the baby, telling them to meet Sally at Ripon station the next day. That night Sally sat with Emma, both of them watching the sleeping baby. And both had tears in their eyes.

'I'd better go to bed, and you should sleep, Emma. It's been a very hard day for you.' And she put her arm around the girl's shoulders.

Emma gave Sally a tired smile. 'It's over, thank goodness. But, I never expected to love him. I don't want him to go!'

George drove Sally to Ripon the next day in her own trap, now repaired by the Thorpe carpenter. It was a subdued parting. Emma gave the little mite a last feed, remarking that he was a good feeder. He would thrive with his adopted family if he went on as he'd begun. She wrapped him warmly against the cold air and turned away, weeping.

Sally held the baby to her inside her cloak as they clopped down the road, feeling almost as sad as his mother. How hard life was! There was some consolation in the fact that the servant who had come to collect the baby arrived in a first class railway carriage and was a pleasant middle-aged woman. 'I've had bairns of my own!' she said, taking him gently from Sally. 'I'll be his nurse. Madam is so looking forward to having him! She's been longing for a little one and she can't have children, you see.'

It looked as though he would be welcomed, and going to a well-off family at that. As he was handed over to the woman the little thing grasped at Sally's hand. He was far too young to have any idea of what was happening, but it was as though he knew. Sally saw two porters watching them. 'Another High Side bairn goes down road!' one said. This must have happened before.

As they watched the Leeds train roll out of the station, carrying the little boy to a new life, George looked at Sally. 'Now lass, don't upset yourself. It's all for the best, you know.' He shook the reins and they turned for home with heavy hearts.

Sally herself felt that her arms were empty on that cold return journey without the little warm body to hold. How easily one could get attached to a small child and want to care for him, to protect him. It was only natural, of course. She wiped away a tear and George coughed discreetly, keeping his eyes fixed straight ahead between the horse's ears. 'Don't take on, lass.' He grinned. 'You'll have bairns of your own before too long! And then you'll have your hands full!'

For a few days after the birth Emma kept

to her room, as the doctor had dictated. She was sad and exhausted, and needed time to recover. Sally had thought hard about what might happen next and she planned an outing to Studley Park, for when Emma was well enough to go out. The Bellamys would expect her to go back to Sheffield, but there was no hurry. Sally found herself dreading the day when she would lose her paying guest, now her ally.

They had written to tell the Bellamys of the birth and were surprised when a packet from them came almost immediately. Sally took the letter with the Sheffield postmark up to Emma with her breakfast tray. She looked at the patient critically. 'You're looking better, Emma, not quite so pale. But do you feel like reading this letter? It's from Sheffield, the Bellamys I suppose.' It was quite possible that it contained another sermon about her wicked ways. And that was the last thing that Emma needed just now.

Emma drank some tea and held out her hand. 'They can't get any worse, can they?' She opened the letter and Sally turned to go. She picked up a jug of water from the side table and went out on to the landing. Then Emma called her back. Her face was even whiter than usual and she was shaking. 'Oh Sally, they've turned me out! They don't want me to go back – ever! And they've sent some money, saying – saying–' and the girl broke down, sobbing. She held out the letter. 'Read it!'

Sally went hot with rage when she read what Mrs Bellamy had said. It was to the effect that they had decided to end their guardianship of Emma, feeling it was better for her to make her own way from now on: 'We had been hoping that your infirmity might eventually prove to be a tumour, and that you would be proved to have been innocent. But now we know that our worst fears have been realized and that you had indeed sunk to the depths of lust and depravity.'

Sally's hands shook as she held the letter. The words seemed to scorch into her brain: 'You betrayed our trust in you and dragged our name in the dirt. Your behaviour can never be forgiven and so we have decided to end the connection. You are no longer welcome in this house.'

The enclosed money was all that was left of her father's estate. The valuables, her mother's jewellery, had been placed in the bank for safe-keeping. They did not want to hear from Emma again: 'Any further communication should be through our solicitors. Their address is enclosed and they will be your legal guardians until you come of age. They will contact you and also advise you of where the jewellery has been stored. The rest of your belongings will be sent by rail or given to charity. We want no trace of you to be left in our home.'

It was the coldest piece of writing that Sally had ever seen. And it was deceptive.

'What do you think, Emma love?'

Emma swallowed and struggled for words. 'I am quite sure that my parent's estate was worth much more than this. They have sent me ... let me see ... three hundred pounds. But my father owned property, shops in Sheffield and so on.' Her voice was getting stronger. 'I think I will need to ask someone about this.'

'Robin's father, Mr Scott, knows about law. We can ask him to help, you know.' Sally thought that while Emma was concentrating on the money side of the story she wouldn't hurt so much. How could she love people who treated her so cruelly? It was probably a good thing that she was not returning to Sheffield, Sally thought. She might be so angry that it would be easier for her. But as time went by Sally could see that Emma was deeply hurt, although she never mentioned the Bellamys again.

This was the start of a decline in Emma's spirits. The baby was gone, the Bellamys were out of reach and she was quite alone in the world, with no idea what to do next. At least they had given some structure to her life; now there was none.

'Don't let her run about too much for a

while,' Dr Bishop had told Sally firmly. 'She's got some healing to do.' But Emma showed no intention of running, or walking either. Emma listened politely to what was said and was just as friendly, but she was quieter, sadder than before.

'Low spirits are quite common, after a baby,' Martha advised. 'And in this case it was more like a bereavement.'

Sally found it was impossible to talk about the future. When she mentioned future plans, Emma shrank back into herself. With something like her old manner she said quietly, 'There's enough money to pay for my keep for quite a while. If you don't mind my staying here, that is.'

On Christmas Day, Sally and Emma were both invited to the Scotts' and Robin did his cheerful best to make Emma smile. Sally flew through the farm chores, singing as she went. They all went to church in the morning and then back for a huge midday dinner. The log fire burned brightly, the twins were bouncing as usual and everybody had a glass of sherry before dinner.

'It reminds me of when I lived at home,' Emma volunteered. It reminded Sally too of happy days when she was young. As they were leaving Robin whispered to Sally, 'I'll come over to see you both soon. I want to tell you about Australia – it's so exciting!'

Sally looked at him like an elder sister. 'I

suppose you've got to tell somebody. But, isn't it time your family was told about it?'

'Not yet!' hissed Robin. 'There's a lot more to find out!'

At one time Sally would have been thrilled that Robin was coming to visit them. But since the day on the moor her feelings had changed. She felt much older than he was somehow: still affectionate, but only as an old friend. She thought she must be in love with Marcus, but that was hopeless too. Better to forget about love and get on with farming.

One cold evening Sally came in from the farmyard, planning to wash and then to prepare their supper. There were no lamps lit in the house and the kitchen fire was low. This was odd; Emma usually lit the lamps at dusk and kept the fires burning. Perhaps she was ill?

'Emma! Emma!' Sally went through the house, but Emma was not there. And then she noticed that the girl's boots and coat were missing. Emma must have gone for a walk. But it was nearly dark and the girl never stayed out in the dark, frightened of losing her way. With relief, Sally heard the dog barking. Emma must be coming in. But it was Robin, clattering into the yard on his horse, coming to talk over his plans with them. When he heard that Emma was missing he immediately offered to look for her.

'She's maybe lost her way. Let's take a couple of lanterns and go down the lane.'

Robin stabled his horse quickly while Sally collected two lanterns. She put on the old grey shawl against the cold and they set off down the green lane, calling as they went.

'Poor little lass, she's not used to the country. She's bound to be scared.' Robin seemed quite worried about Emma.

A dark thought came to Sally's mind and she couldn't get rid of it. Emma had been so low in spirits ... what if she'd decided to end her life? She thought back quickly. The last time she'd seen the girl was about three o'clock that afternoon. She'd had time to go a long way since three.

Hackfall was deep and dangerous, a ravine through which the Ure flowed on its way down to Ripon. It would be lethal at night. Please God, let Emma not die there before she had started to live. On they went and the night got darker as the path led them down to the river.

They reached the oak wood, leafless now, the branches stark in the lantern light, beckoning like skinny fingers. Sally shuddered. Hackfall looked different at night, more sinister.

'There's a moon tonight, see it coming up yonder?' said Robin cheerfully. They could hear the roar of the waterfalls in the distance as they drew nearer to the river. 'Surely she wouldn't go to the river?' Robin sounded suddenly scared.

Sally knew suddenly with great certainty that Emma had gone to the river. And she was afraid of what they might find there. A black pit seemed to open up as she imagined how bleak the girl's mind and soul must be. Bleak enough to feel that life held nothing for her but pain and misery. When Emma was safe again, Sally vowed she would make sure the girl knew she was needed, that she had a place at Thorpe if she wanted it or help with finding work somewhere else. There were all sorts of things they could do together. When Emma was safe ... but now it might be too late. She'd had a long head start.

As they went, stumbling over tree roots, Sally felt she'd been too slow. Instead of waiting for Emma to recover she should have started to talk to her about future plans, to prevent a lapse into despair. But the girl had seemed so strong and in some ways she was so reticent even now.

Brambles were tearing at them but Sally hardly felt the scratches. Her anger was rising, anger at a world that would make life so hard for a young girl. With Sally, anger was energy and she strode along, even overtaking Robin's fast pace. There was a path down to the water. Sally scrambled down and just as she did so, the moon peeped over the top of the ridge above. She could hear Robin following her down the steep track. Something white caught Sally's attention in the river far below, shining in the moonlight. Emma lay in a shallow pool in the river bed, under the water. The river lapped over her but her face was clear of the water. She looked young and peaceful, lying there. 'She's dead.' Robin pronounced.

Nothing more was said. Sally held her lantern up high, while Robin pulled Emma clear and on to the bank. He turned her limp body over, and water gushed from her mouth.

'I think she's breathing!' Sally had caught a faint movement in her chest. Robin moved Emma's arms energetically up and down, in and out and in a minute or two she coughed up more water and took a deep, shuddering breath. It took many minutes before Emma's breathing became regular. She was extremely cold and had to be taken home quickly.

'But we can't carry her up that track!' Sally looked in despair at the looming steep side of the valley. It seemed almost impossible now that they'd come down that way. They could never get back. At the top was Thorpe and safety.

Robin clucked impatiently. 'Sally, use your head, woman. We can make a seat with our hands and carry her along the level track, out on to the Masham road, the way the visitors come in to see the follies.'

Sally nodded. She knew the way. Hack Fall was a local beauty spot and the owners had built paths for visitors, with curious little buildings along the way. It would be a long way round, but it was the best way to get Emma home.

They left the lanterns near a big stone, Robin promising to collect them soon. Trusting to the moonlight they carried Emma between them. She was small and light, but after a while they had to stop to rest several times before the road was reached. Then Sally stayed with Emma while Robin trotted back to Badger's Gill to collect Jed and the trap and at last they got Emma home. She was cold, bruised and sick, but she was alive.

'Of course, you fell in by accident,' Sally said quite firmly as she tucked the girl up in bed with three hot water bottles and some bread and milk.

'No, Sally.' Emma lay with closed eyes. 'I am sorry to cause you so much trouble... I wanted to die, you see.'

'To everybody else this was an accident! And please Emma, I hope you'll stay and work with me. I have so many plans for the things we can do together!'

'Dear Sally, thank you.'

Emma didn't want a doctor, so Sally gave her salve for the bruises and asked the herb woman for some treatment for damaged lungs. The girl was quite ill for a few days, feverish and restless. But gradually she improved and Sally told her how tough she was.

Robin seemed to take Emma's case as a personal challenge and visited nearly every day. She lay on the sofa in the parlour and Robin teased her and told her stories about Australia, and one day Sally heard her laughing.

'She's a tough little thing,' Robin said admiringly to Sally. 'And she'll be very pretty when the bruises fade!' Oh Robin, thought Sally, you would have made me feel jealous once. By mid-January Emma was quite recovered, and in much better spirits than Sally had ever seen her. Robin still visited them both, explaining that all was in order since they could chaperone each other.

Emma had her duties in the house and helped Sally in whatever ways she could. Sally taught her bread-making and how to make Fat Rascals, the rich local scones full of currants. With Robin, Emma had duties of a different kind. He would bring her articles and books about Australia and then test her knowledge. Sally was quite critical, thinking that Robin was determined to see only all that was good in Australia, and disregard the rest. The summers even in Victoria were apparently hot and dusty and it was a long way to the nearest town for supplies, when you were out in 'the bush'.

Emma seemed unusually interested, even in the rigours of Australian life. A girl from a big town would surely find the life even more rugged, as Robin had called it, than someone who'd been brought up on a farm. Sally began to wonder whether Emma was getting fond of Robin; she rather hoped not. It was quite possible that his charm would influence her, but that in the end he would be just as detached as he had been with Sally herself. A slender little town girl who was afraid of animals would never meet the prescription for Robin's future wife. Robin was likely to sail off to Melbourne without a backward glance. He would leave behind him a grieving family; Sally hoped that he wouldn't also leave Emma with a broken heart. Emma was mending nicely at present and Sally felt an almost ferocious concern for her happiness.

ELEVEN

'Ma's got another guest for you. What do you think?' Robin asked, one day in February. 'She says it will be good for the business. You'd better see her about it!'

'Thank you Robin, I will.' Sally was arranging snowdrops in a vase. Another guest would be a good idea – of the right type, of course. That night Sally had a talk to Emma as they sat by the fire. Emma was sewing and she put down her work and listened with great attention, as Sally explained her plan. 'I thought of a sort of partnership for you and me. To run Badger's Gill and make a profit!'

A glimmer of a smile lit Emma's small face. 'But you're a farmer, Sally. I'm still scared of cows!'

'There's the house as the guesthouse. You could help a lot with that. We could take another resident and maybe some walkers and holiday people in the summer. Mrs Scott says that walkers like good farm food, a clean bed and pleasant company ... we can manage all that.'

'So – you're saying that I can earn a place here and work with you? And I needn't look for employment?'

'Exactly. And I won't be on my own any more. We'll both support each other! Mrs Scott has somebody else for us; I'll go to see her tomorrow.'

'Well, call me your assistant!' Emma looked very young, her eyes round as she looked across at Sally. 'I am far too young to be a partner, even though I'm nearly seventeen!'

Already Sally was planning the necessary arrangements. 'If you don't mind a smaller bedroom Emma, we could put the new guest in the main bedroom.'

It was good to have a new idea to think about. They worked on the house, moving furniture and changing things round as much as they could. Sally felt reasonably happy when she was busy, which was most of the time. But when she went to bed at night the image of Marcus often entered her mind. Since the afternoon of the accident and the time spent in his company, Sally had felt the pain of love without any hope for the future. So this was what happened when you fell in love. And it had happened so quickly! This was what inspired those sad pieces of music: she felt she could play them better now.

Wryly, Sally realized that what she had felt for Robin was nothing like this. She desperately wanted to see Marcus Radford, to talk it all out, to work out some solution so that they could get to know each other better. But she understood, because she was from the High Side too, the depth of bitterness that quarrels could leave behind, lasting for many years. Sally believed that he was thinking of her position as well as his own. Her heart was in Thorpe; she would never want to leave and start a new life elsewhere. There was no way out of the situation.

The pain was made worse by a small parcel that arrived in the post about ten days after the accident. Sally opened it in the privacy of her bedroom. Carefully wrapped in many layers of paper was a small Dresden china shepherdess complete with crook, with a tiny lamb at her side. There was a scrap of paper tucked under her arm. It said: 'For Bo-Peep.' That was all. The little figure was soon wet with Sally's tears. How long was it going to take her to forget this man? Sometimes she wished that she'd never met the Roman soldier.

'Welcome to Badger's Gill!' At Emma's suggestion, remembering her own arrival at the farm, a rather formal reception committee consisting of Emma and Sally was waiting to greet the new guest. They wore businesslike black dresses and white aprons, and with little white caps Sally felt that they looked most professional, even though they were both too slightly built to look really imposing. Aunt Bertha was much better at that.

Looking at Emma, Sally felt a glow of almost maternal pride. Her light brown hair shining with health and her complexion clear, Emma was a different person from the downtrodden little orphan who'd come to Badger's Gill. The guesthouse too was entering another phase, with some new curtains and chair covers and a rug or two to brighten the old house. A little spare money made a lot of difference.

Sally knew that the new guest's health was failing and hoped he would not be too fractious and difficult. As the slim young man with fair hair came up the path, a stray shaft of sunshine lit the afternoon and he smiled. 'What a lovely place!' It was a good start. Would he, like Emma, find recovery in the quiet fields of Thorpe?

Sally reviewed what she knew about the stranger. Simon Drury was a young man from a family of West Riding mill owners. At the age of twenty, four years ago, he had developed a heart defect after a fever and was no longer able to work. His doctor had suggested that the air of Bradford was not good for him and that his health might improve if he went to the country. His mother knew someone who knew the Scotts, and Mrs Scott had recommended Badger's Gill.

Sally was relieved that he wouldn't need nursing. 'He has no infection and no bandages,' his mother had written rather tartly, when explaining her son's requirements. 'He is perfectly normal apart from excessive fatigue. He needs a quiet life, with no excitement.'

'That should be easy enough. It sounds just like Thorpe,' Sally commented as she read the letter to Emma. 'Thorpe's only excitement is the annual Sunday School treat.'

However, Mrs Drury recognized that looking after her son was a responsibility and the pay was accordingly generous and delivered monthly in advance. The question was how he should be treated: as a house guest or a lodger?

'You need to allow us some privacy. And we don't yet know what he'll be like. Let's start off formally and see how we get on.' Emma had smiled her new smile. 'You've got me for company now, you know,' she said.

'Yes, but what about him? You know how lonely it was all by yourself in the dining-room!' Sally had felt sorry for this poor sick lad even before they met.

The first evening they all ate together round the big dining-table, with everybody at their most polite. 'And what sort of farming do you practise, Miss Mason?' The fair head turned attentively towards his host.

'It's a mixed farm, Mr Drury. Thorpe is on a ridge, with the moors above us and the Ure valley down below. We have both flat and hilly land.' Sally stopped, afraid she was boring him.

'I see. So you'll have sheep, cattle, poultry, maybe a few pigs and some crops as well. I don't know much about country life,' and he smiled apologetically, 'but I love country scenes. Village greens, ponds, old buildings ... that kind of thing.'

'Are you an artist?' Emma asked curiously.

'I'd like to be. I studied art in Bradford for a time, when it became clear that I couldn't join the firm. My father's business, that is. Drury & Sons are woollen manufacturers, as you may know.'

Sally cleared the soup plates, wishing she knew more about the industrial West Riding. The Masons had always considered it a place to avoid.

'Art will be a very good occupation for you while you stay here, Mr Drury. In summer artists often come to paint our local landscapes.' Sally was glad he'd have something to do; the way Mr Drury's eyes followed her round the room was disconcerting. She hoped he didn't have ambitions to be a portrait painter. She could never sit still for more than five minutes.

'There's plenty of room in here for an easel and painting materials.' Emma looked round the dining-room. 'We could cover the carpet in case you make a mess!'

The young man agreed. 'Although I plan to make sketches, at first. And as the weather improves I may be able to work outside.'

A new routine was established, with Emma helping to cook and serve the guest's meals. It was a quiet time of year on the farm and in the garden, with everything waiting for the spring. With Joe's help, Sally was managing to get through her farm work quite well. The new guest seemed to feel the cold, and 'as the day lengthens, so the cold strengthens,' as Martha quoted from her stock of old sayings. Simon needed a fire in his bedroom as well as in the dining-room where he sat during the day.

Simon was in the big master bedroom which looked out across the village green. He soon found that he could sit at the window and sketch the scene below him. He was quite talented and Sally admired his work. 'I'll do a proper drawing of your farmhouse when the weather's warmer,' he promised eagerly.

Sometimes Simon ate with his hosts because it seemed lonely for him, dining in state at the big table. He said that he liked music. 'Would you play for me?' He looked at Sally wistfully one evening.

'Yes, if you wish.' So, that night they gathered in the panelled parlour, with its books and music, both of which interested the guest.

'Have you read this one, Mr Drury?' Sally asked, handing him a book of travels.

'No, but I'd love to borrow it if I may. Travel appeals to me, perhaps because I'm not allowed to go very far these days.' He looked up at Sally from his chair with sad grey eyes that seemed to be pleading for something. After a moment he said, 'Would you mind, will you please call me Simon?'

Emma frowned a little, but Sally's warm nature took over. 'Of course, so long as you remember that I'm Sally!'

Emma got out the music and Sally played a slow Chopin nocturne. Perhaps it was a mistake; Simon looked more tragic than ever as the lovely notes floated through the house. Sally wondered how ill he was and whether he had a hope of recovery. It must be very hard for him, living such a restricted life.

Musical evenings soon became a feature of life at Badger's Gill and Sally enjoyed them. Robin continued his visits and the four young people had some pleasant hours around the piano. Sally still wondered whether Emma was the attraction for her old friend; he seemed much more animated these days, but it might be the prospect of Australia, which was growing nearer. Robin teased Emma and talked to her, but it seemed to Sally that with her he was no different; still smiling, detached, the elder brother, just as he was with Sally herself. This of course was what Emma needed.

One evening Robin and Emma went out to make some tea, and Simon was left with Sally. The young man sighed and stretched. 'How I wish I were healthy like the rest of you! I feel so tired all the time.'

'But perhaps you'll improve with country

air.' Sally took her usual optimistic view.

'I feel I am improving a little with your company, Sally. You're such a happy person, with no cares! Nothing ever seems to worry you!'

Simon gazed at her and Sally wondered if he had drunk rather too much sherry before dinner. The doctor had prescribed a little sherry and Simon was very careful to follow medical advice. It was embarrassing to be gazed at and Sally jumped up. 'Early to bed for you, Mr Drury! Nurse's orders!' And she went into the kitchen. At least, she thought as she carried the tea tray in, my 'cares' are well hidden. Nobody in her world knew about Marcus; although Emma and Joe had seen him on the evening when he'd taken her home, they didn't know he was other than a kind stranger.

One day Sally took Simon with her in the trap for a short trip to some of the lower villages, delivering eggs to the shops. He seemed to enjoy the change of scene, well wrapped up against the cold. They both admired the patterns of bare twigs against the winter sky and the long, slanting shadows of a winter afternoon. 'I would like to sketch the old church,' he said as they passed the Kirkby church with its Norman door. 'One day, when the weather is warmer!' Simon was a pleasant companion and most appreciative of the countryside that Sally loved.

'Have you lived here all your life?' he asked, as they turned for home.

'Masons have farmed Badger's Gill for a very long time. How many generations are there in two centuries?' Sally laughed as she urged Jed to go a little faster. 'Yes, it's my home and I can't imagine living anywhere else. But...' Better not tell him about her problems with the tenancy.

Simon looked at her with a smile. 'You must feel very secure, living and working on your family's farm. Women are beginning to take part in more professions these days, and why not? You'll be a pioneer, a modern woman farmer!'

Honesty compelled Sally then to tell the truth. 'But it's not my farm, unfortunately. I'm a tenant because the farm had to be sold.'

The young man looked at her keenly. 'And so I suppose you'll be planning to buy it back again as soon as you can.'

This lad seemed to have an interest in business. What a pity he couldn't work with his father in the woollen mill. 'As soon as I can. Now Simon, you can see Ripon Cathedral from here, if you look carefully!' Sally had never intended to discuss her business affairs with paying guests. But just as in the case of Emma, the guest had gradually turned into a human being with a personality that could not be ignored. Perhaps

Emma was right and Simon should have been left to languish as a figurehead: Mr Drury, in the dining-room, The Paying Guest, neatly compartmentalized. But it was too late now; he had become part of the family.

'Thank you, Sally, I so enjoyed the ride and your company.' Simon stood aside to let Sally go into the house first. 'Please may I be invited again?'

That was the trouble. Once you allowed the professional relationship to turn into something else there was no going back. Sally liked Simon, but she was slightly uncomfortable at times. He seemed to take rather too close an interest in her. But then he asked questions of everyone and listened carefully to the answers. He was in a new environment, contrasting completely with his industrial home and he was trying to understand it. I must be imagining things, Sally told herself. I'd better make some butter and get down to Ripon for a change of scene.

There was less milk in winter since the cows tended to calve in spring, but Sally was sometimes able to make enough butter to make the trip to market worthwhile. She decided to take Emma with her on these winter trips. It was part of her secret plan to help the poor lass to mix in company again.

It was a fortunate coincidence that Mr Marcus Radford had urgent business in

Ripon nearly every Thursday that winter. He wondered himself sometimes how it was managed but there he was, striding through the market every week and scanning the crowds for any sign of copper-coloured hair. And he was rewarded on those occasions when the butter had to be sold.

Sally found that she was more cheerful as the winter went on. The whole world was brighter, because she sometimes saw Marcus and she knew that he was making an effort to see her.

'Your butter sells faster than any!' Emma remarked brightly one cold day. And it was true; the old customers had come back and Sally's butter was appreciated by the Ripon housewives for tasting as it should and lasting a long time. A quick sale meant that the girls had just a little time to spare to look round the town, before they plodded back to Thorpe and the evening chores. And when Marcus joined them he was very happy to show Emma the historical side of the little city, with its ancient cathedral.

'It's important to see you,' he said quietly to Sally, one day when Emma went on ahead. In spite of the feud, the attraction was still there and they both felt it. Sally agreed. She thought about Marcus more often than she should perhaps, but time with him was precious, even time in public and walking in the town.

'Let's go down Kirkgate, Emma would like that!' Sally said one day. They only had a short time; they had to get Jed and the trap back to Thorpe before dark. So they strode out briskly, talking as they went, admiring the ancient buildings.

Afterwards Sally would think of those times in Ripon as the happiest of the winter, as she and Marcus talked easily about history and gardens, and anything that came into their heads. Because Emma was there it was not possible to discuss the problems of the Radford-Mason quarrel, or even their own feelings. But this liberated them, Sally thought. They came to appreciate each other on an everyday level and put the future to the back of their minds.

'I sometimes think,' said Sally dreamily, as they walked back to the trap in the fading light, 'that living in the present is best!'

And Marcus, smiling at her, agreed. 'I wouldn't be anywhere else.'

And then Sally said for Emma's benefit, 'Those folks who lived in the little medieval town must have had a hard time, I always think'

'But they didn't know anything else.' Emma was practical, as always. 'So they probably didn't find it was hard.'

Thick snow fell in February and Thorpe was cut off for a while from the outside world.

Trips to Ripon stopped; even the carrier stayed at home. The snow muffled the usual village sounds, wrapping the cottages in silence, even muting the Sunday church bell. There was always plenty of food in the larders to last through the winter and the villagers were used to being self-sufficient. But normal work was impossible, so the young lads turned to digging tracks along the street, down to the pond. Thorpe pond was frozen hard and it was time for skating.

'Can you skate, Emma?' Sally asked her helper. 'We've an old pair of my skates that might fit you.'

Emma said she'd never tried and looked rather doubtful.

Most of the village went to the pond that night. The blacksmith gave candles which were arranged round the pond in jars, giving a pretty effect. Young people skated, laughed and teased each other while the older folks looked on. Someone played a mouth organ and Martha cooked hot chestnuts over a fire. It was a sort of impromptu village festival, all the better because Thorpe was isolated by the snowdrifts. Only Thorpe people were there and that was a good thing, Sally told Emma. 'Kirkby hasn't got a pond and Kirkby folk would be here for the skating if they could, getting in the way!'

Being cut off was a sort of relief for Sally. She knew that there was no hope of seeing

Marcus until the roads were clear; she could settle down and stop being restless. There was still no word about the tenancy but with her usual optimism, she decided that no news was good news.

'You can watch from the window, it's too cold outside. It's quite a pretty scene!' Sally told Simon, as she made up the fire in his room before she went down herself to skate on the pond.

'You look charming tonight, Sally. How I love the colour of your hair!' Simon was gazing at her again, speaking softly in his educated voice with only a hint of the West Riding accent that was so different from the Thorpe dialect.

'Goodness me, you artists do make personal comments! Have you plenty to read?' Sally asked him in a matter-of-fact way, blushing slightly. 'We'll be back in time for supper.'

Sally and Emma made their way over the green and Robin spotted them from the far side of the pond. 'Come on, Sal, we always skate together!' Robin grabbed her and off they went, holding hands as they circled the ice, going faster and faster as they gained momentum. They were laughing, Sally was breathless and just for a minute or two she felt happy, caught up in the moment.

Emma watched from the bank but was afraid to go on the ice. 'Next time I'll try it,' she promised.

Robin and Sally glided towards her and one on each side supported Emma on to the ice. 'Come on Emma, trust us!' Sally wanted the girl to enjoy skating as much as she did. She managed a few yards with their support, but then Emma fell down and Robin picked her up and took her to the bank. 'That's enough, you'll be bruised, poor lass. I'll take you home.'

'No, please go round again with Sally. You skate so well together! I'll have a chestnut with Martha.' Emma went off and Robin took Sally's arm again. This time the pair went over to where there were fewer skaters and tried some more complicated figures on the ice.

'We're pretty good, considering we've had no practice since last winter!' Robin said as he caught Sally round the waist and took off again, looping and swerving, dodging in and out of the beginners.

'You're showing off,' laughed Sally.

All too soon, it was time to take off their skates. Laughing and talking they crossed the green to Badger's Gill. Emma put the kettle on the range for supper and Robin sliced a big teacake his mother had made. Sally ran lightly upstairs to see what Simon would like to eat and knocked on his door. There was no reply.

'Simon!' Sally called. Perhaps he was

asleep? But the room was silent. Heart thumping, Sally walked into the room. Simon was slumped in the chair by the open window, cold and unconscious. His lips were blue. Terrified, Sally flew downstairs to tell the others, and they raced upstairs with her.

'I'll go for the doctor!' Robin's reaction was immediate. 'Cover him with a blanket, he feels cold.'

It was a long wait until the doctor arrived. Sally sat in a chair beside Simon, watching his shallow breathing and wondering if there was anything else she could do for him. After about half an hour Emma brought Sally a cup of tea and as she drank it, she saw a movement of Simon's head. Gradually he opened his eyes and looked at her. 'That was a bad one.'

He must have had attacks like this before, Sally thought. Perhaps we shouldn't leave him alone for too long. She felt guilty now, for having fun on the ice. 'Oh Simon, I wish I could help you! What caused this, do you, think?'

'You don't really want to know.' The grey eyes closed again. 'Do you?'

'Yes, I do. So we know how we can look after you better.' Sally turned towards him.

Simon sighed, reached out and took her hand. 'You caused it. Skating with Robin down there, happy, carefree ... and me up here peering out at you like an old man.' He shook his head. 'I was jealous, Sally, and got upset, and I'm not allowed to get upset.'

'Poor lad!' Sally's eyes filled with tears of sympathy.

'I might as well tell you what the problem is. I'm head over heels in love with you, Sally, my dearest. So now you know.' Simon lay back, exhausted.

The door opened suddenly and the doctor bustled in. Sally was thankful for the diversion and went downstairs, her thoughts whirling. Was Simon really in love with her or was it just a case of his condition? This complicated the situation considerably. She didn't want to lose a valuable paying guest who was also a pleasant enough companion. But Simon might not wish to stay.

'Sally, we might not be able to keep him if he's really ill.' Emma was evidently worried about the threat to their livelihood as well as being concerned for Simon.

What if he were really in love with her? If she rejected him it might make his health worse. But in all honesty, Sally couldn't pretend to a love that she didn't feel. She knew now just how love felt, knew that this gentle regard she had for Simon was nowhere near the real thing.

The doctor came down and was given water to wash his hands. He looked grave. 'Absolute rest for a week in bed I'm afraid,' he pronounced. He was a locum, deputizing for their usual Dr Bishop. 'I have given him a dose of opium to make him sleep – he seems agitated. And now,' he lowered his voice and drew Sally aside, 'I have advised the young man to make a will, I said I would ask you to make the necessary arrangements. He may live for another fifty years of course. But I have my doubts.'

TWELVE

'Well, if it isn't young Mr Radford! Come your ways in, sir! What will you have to drink?' Sol Bartram's fat face creased into a smile as he waddled forward eagerly.

Marcus Radford had meant to go back to Thorpe before now, but work and the snow had prevented the journey. Thorpe had been on his mind for weeks ... and now it was nearly spring. Stooping to go through the inn door, he took off his gloves and went to the fire. He'd better have lunch before doing business.

'I'm here instead of my father. He has a few concerns about the Thorpe farms and wants to know your views. It will soon be Lady Day.' He glanced out of the window at the cold March sunshine. 'But he can't spare the time to come over here himself.' This was more or less true; Marcus had offered to go to Thorpe on behalf of Oliver the last time they had met. To his surprise his father had been pleased to let Marcus visit that part of their estates. He'd refused in fact to go to Badger's Gill to see for himself the state of the farm.

'I really don't want to meet the woman!' Oliver had seemed quite agitated. 'And as I said before, I would rather you kept away from Masons too. But I'll leave it to your judgement as to what to do about the tenancy. I probably shouldn't, but you're old enough now to take some of the responsibility. You know my views.'

Marcus was actually wondering what the old boy's thinking was. Did he secretly want Sally to stay on the farm, or did he want her to leave? It was odd that he'd left the decision to Marcus.

Sitting in the bar with a mug of the Crown's home brewed beer, Marcus reflected that Sol Bartram was not the man he would have chosen as their agent in Thorpe if he'd had the responsibility years ago, when Sol had wormed his way into the job. In the weeks since he had rescued Sally from the snowdrift on the moor, Marcus had thought carefully about the situation. It was, he told himself, weak of him to give up too easily. His memories of the girl had a sort of radiance and they all increased his admiration for her approach to life, reinforced by the meetings in Ripon. Sally hadn't complained after the accident, where other women would have had hysterics. She'd been bruised and trapped for some time, but she made light of her injuries. She worked hard, she sold butter to make the farm pay and the customers loved her. The young lady was obviously running the farm very well and Marcus had told his father so. The brief twilight tour of the farmyard had been enough for his experienced eye to see that Sally and her 'staff' knew what they were doing.

And then their kiss in the stable had told him that she responded to his warmth until she remembered that he was a Radford. It always came back, in the end, to the problem of the feud. Marcus sighed and attacked his pork pie. Could that problem ever be solved?

Sol came back to clear his plate away and Marcus asked him to sit down. 'How are things in this part of the world?' He started with an open question to see what would come up.

The agent lit his pipe, sending clouds of acrid smoke to the stained ceiling. 'Well, Mr Marcus, the Camp Hill tenant's a good lad. Seems to be framing well. But he wants to see you, needs a shed repaired. And old

Brownlee over at Biggin, he's talking about retiring.'

Marcus leaned back on the settle and waited.

'But I have to say that Badger's Gill's run down. Getting worse every day. A young lass can't run a farm of course, we all know that. I told yer father, she'll have to go.'

'What's wrong at Badger's Gill?' Marcus was non-committal.

'Why, everything! Sheep's out in village, walls down, weeds everywhere. Cattle starving, so she'll surely not manage to pay rent. It's a bad job.' He shook his head sadly. 'Best thing for her and you is to clear her out.'

Marcus looked at the fire, thinking. Should he call Sol a liar or go along with the fiction? Sally's cattle were sleek and well-fed. He looked up and saw the man was watching him closely. 'Who've you told about this?'

Sol laughed. 'It's common knowledge, round here!'

'I see.' Marcus looked hard at the agent. 'And what do you suggest we do with the farm if the tenant leaves next month?'

A crafty expression crossed Sol's face. 'I can take it off your hands if you like, to oblige. Save you looking for somebody else. With my experience place'll soon improve. I could buy stock off her, save her the trouble of a farm sale. Won't be worth much I can tell you.'

'Thank you, Sol.' Marcus looked at the man with distaste. His motive was obvious; he'd thought that Sally would be easy to push over and that his argument about women farmers would clinch the matter. But Marcus didn't intend to make an enemy of the man. Not yet. 'I think,' he said slowly, 'That we'd better leave Badger's Gill as it is for the time being. My father can come over and inspect.' He saw Sol wince at this. 'We will give the tenant another year to see how she goes.'

'You'll rue the day, mark my words!' Sol was openly disappointed. 'But it's up to you, boss. Thought you'd be glad to see the back of Masons!'

This gave Marcus an opening. 'I suppose you'd be too young to remember what happened between Radfords and Masons? I've never really understood.' He made his voice casual.

'Nay, my old father had some newspaper cuttings, but wife threw them out years ago. I understood that young Mason murdered yer grandfather and then denied it. He got away with it, too!'

'Nobody seems to know what really happened,' Marcus murmured as indifferently as he could. It was time to change the subject and talk about grain prices, but Sol

212

had given Marcus a slender clue. If there had been a newspaper report of the death he might be able to find it in the archives at the *Clarion*. He would visit the newspaper offices the next time he was in Ripon.

He was tempted to visit Sally while he was in Thorpe, tell her she was to keep the tenancy and see her face light up. But that would be a mistake. Marcus didn't want her to know that he'd had anything to do with that decision. Their relationship, if they ever got so far, would be one of equality. A modern idea and no doubt one that Oliver would laugh at. The other reason for avoiding Badger's Gill was that he wanted to find out more about the 'murder' before he saw Sally again.

Leaving the Crown, Marcus deliberately turned his back on the Ripon end of the village where Sally lived. But he was looking out for a redheaded young lady until he was half way to Masham.

Marcus left the newspaper offices the next week feeling distinctly weary after hours of dusty searching through old yellowed papers of fifty years ago. He pulled back his aching shoulders out of habit and strode down towards the town centre. Too much time had gone by and he wanted to see Sally before she left the market.

At least the time hadn't been entirely

wasted, he thought as he shouldered through the market crowd. In the end the big bound folders had yielded a few paragraphs about the presumed death of William Radford, Billy, to his neighbours. Marcus had copied them out, rather than rely on memory.

The newspaper reported the mysterious disappearance of Mr Radford, a well-respected farmer in the prime of life. One thing that Marcus gleaned was from the tone of the piece: there was no breath of blame attached to the other victim, Richard Mason, who had been 'fortunate to survive'. Mr Mason had been interviewed, no doubt reluctantly, but he had agreed to talk to the *Clarion*. He said that he had been extremely ill after the event and that 'everything was blue'. He could remember nothing of what happened except that he had found himself alone at night several miles from home, three days after they had gone into the wood.

Where had they been for those missing three days? And what did 'blue' mean? The journalist must have written it down without understanding it. Was it metaphorical, meaning that he was sad? And why was he ill?

The redhead was visible to someone who was looking for her, half way across the square. And Emma, the young helper, was with her. As Marcus got nearer he saw that Sally was selling her last pound of butter. The tall man strode straight up and was greeted with a radiant smile. Sally was prettier than ever, he thought.

'Hoped I might find you here ... I've been reading old newspapers...' And he told her briefly what he had discovered. 'Nothing definite, but at least I could see that Mason wasn't blamed, publicly at least.'

'Thank you, Marcus. I wish we could find out more!' Sally felt happy to know that the mystery meant so much to Marcus. Their occasional Thursday meetings were no doubt noticed by the gossips and the curious, but no comments reached Sally. If the three of them walked across the square or down to the cathedral, talking all the time, they were not so noticeable as if Marcus and Sally were alone together.

Leaving Sally, Marcus collected his horse and headed out of Ripon. But half a mile out of the town he had a thought that made him turn back. Although he had been warned never to ask Grandmother about the death, he would go to see her. Serious investigators – Sherlock Holmes came to mind – went over a story many times, picking up different pieces of the puzzle until they could make a pattern. He would do the same, treading softly so as not to upset the old lady.

Grandmother Radford lived quietly in a small house in Ripon, attended by an ancient maid. The family called to see her as a duty but Marcus had not been there for some time, he thought guiltily as he tied his horse to the rail.

The maid met him at the door with the usual grim face and led him into the parlour, which was extremely hot. Grandmother had large fires winter and summer. Sweating, Marcus sat upright on a slippery sofa, eating seed cake which he disliked and drinking scalding hot tea. I am suffering for my sins, he thought wryly. There was small talk and the old lady questioned him closely about the family. His brother Tom was studying in Edinburgh and he had to report on the lad's progress. Next, Grandmother wanted to know all about Oliver's doings. She was always more interested in Oliver than in anybody else.

'My father was a very good horseman I believe, when he was young?'

A spate of stories about his father followed. 'You boys were never as good as Oliver! Left without a father, he was determined to succeed in everything he did.' She smoothed her black dress with wrinkled hands.

Marcus knew that Billy's brother, Walter, had taken over the farms and run them until Oliver was old enough to take over. Walter had no children and so Oliver was the sole heir. A convenient arrangement, which seemed to have worked well enough.

'But he had a good uncle, had he not?'

'Of course, his uncle was there. My chief worry for Oliver was always his health. He did too much. I was so afraid that he had inherited his father's weak heart, but time has shown that this was not the case.'

The old girl is still sharp, Marcus thought. 'I didn't know we had heart problems in the family! What exactly was the trouble?'

Grandmother sat upright, shoulders back, staring at him and suddenly Marcus had a thought. I look just like her. Oh, dear, how grim I must look!

'No trouble.' She was scornful. 'Radfords are very healthy! Billy was perfectly able to live a normal life. But he was told by doctors that his heartbeat was slow and it could have developed into an illness. He was warned not to over-exert himself and fortunately we had plenty of labourers, so that was not necessary.'

Marcus leaned forward. 'Grandmother, I hate to ask you this. But – do you remember anything about Grandfather's death?'

The old lady stood up with the aid of her stick and turned to the fireplace, looking away from Marcus. Her voice was a hoarse whisper. 'We never discuss it. You are very wrong to ask.' She swung round to glare at

217

her grandson. 'But yes, I know that he was murdered. By Richard Mason, who should have been hanged. That man robbed me of my husband, my youth and my happiness. I shall never forget.'

After that, it was back to small talk again until the old lady recovered. After about quarter of an hour Marcus decided that it was time to leave, and pecked Grandmother on the cheek as he went out.

'Tell your father to come to see me!'

Grandmother always left Marcus with a feeling of coldness. His other grandmother had been warm and cuddled him, but that was long ago. She was dead, as was his dear mother. And he was a grown man ... but a little affection, a little less acid, would have been welcome. However, his grandmother might have given him another tiny clue: the weak heart. It might mean nothing. Marcus jogged home in the moonlight, thinking about the events of fifty years ago. There were only two more things he could do and nothing made sense as yet. He could visit the wood where Billy Radford disappeared. And he could talk to his father. He was due to see Oliver that week and had intended to ride over to Nidd Grange. But on the table waiting for him at home was an invitation, in the familiar spiky writing: 'Time you got out and stopped moping. We've been invited to Mrs Russell's, on Masham Square. Be there at 5 p.m. on Thursday for dinner. And wear a clean shirt. O.R.'

Clean shirt indeed! Marcus knew that he didn't dress so well as Oliver, who always looked elegant and was measured by the best tailors for expensive tweeds. But Marcus was extremely clean and neat, the difference was that he preferred plain unobtrusive clothes.

Marcus was in Masham on time. The two men stabled their horses at the King's Head, not far along the street from Mrs Russell's house and Marcus decided to book a room at the inn for the night rather than face another long ride home. To his surprise so did Oliver. 'Not so young as I was,' the older man admitted.

Mrs Russell had been a friend of his mother's and Marcus knew her quite well. She was a widow in comfortable circumstances, he supposed. Her husband had been a substantial farmer, but there were no sons and after his death the farm had been sold. Mrs Russell's house was stone built and double fronted, with lighted windows looking on to the square. As the men approached a maid drew the heavy curtains, but not before Marcus had seen the dining-room ablaze with candles, silver and polished wood.

'Come in, Mr Radford! And Marcus dear! Come to the fire, it's a cold night. Now, can

Maggie fetch you a glass of sherry?' Mrs Russell was plump and pleasant, and her daughter Maggie, in her late twenties, had obviously tried to make the best of herself with an elaborate hairstyle and an expensive dress a little too small for her. Marcus amused himself by trying to imagine how Sally would look in a dress like that. It was dark green and would have suited Sally's colouring and her slim little figure.

Meanwhile, Oliver and Mrs Russell shared the local news. Marcus tried to enter into the spirit of the thing, but it was difficult. Maggie Russell asked Marcus whether he hunted – no – and whether he was a cricketer – no. He admitted to being interested in local history but Maggie could find nothing to say on the subject. She was looking round rather desperately, trying to find a suitable topic of conversation when dinner was served.

Marcus had to sit next to Miss Russell but as there were only four of them, the conversation was general. It was sustained very well by Oliver, who appeared to be enjoying himself. Time went by, measured every fifteen minutes by the silvery chimes of the mantelpiece clock. Making an effort, Marcus told them news of Colsterdale, but as little happened in his secluded retreat that was soon exhausted. The fish was excellent and beef followed, after a long interval. Marcus tried not to wriggle on his hard dining chair. Time went by, very slowly.

After dinner they went into the parlour and Oliver suggested music. Marcus had played several instruments at school and was a good pianist, but he rarely played on occasions like this. But starved of music as he was, he agreed to perform for them on the Russells' new piano.

Marcus played a few chords, appreciating the beautiful tone. What should he play? For Oliver, 'The Last Rose of Summer' and a few other drawing-room pieces, as he called them. To finish the recital, Marcus played for Sally. He imagined she was sitting beside him. All his hopes, his sadness for what might have been, he found in the music. There was silence when he finished; the others did not know what to say. Then Maggie obliged by playing in her turn and Marcus was allowed to think his own thoughts for a while. He wondered how soon he would be able to find the time to visit Foxholes Wood and whether fifty years after the event, he would be able to find information that had eluded all the people who had searched the wood at the time.

Miss Russell delivered a rather plaintive Scottish song about calling sheep, which she hoped they would like. Meanwhile Marcus reminded himself that unless the mystery of his grandfather's death was solved, and by a

Radford at that, there was little hope of ending the feud.

'You look sad, Mr Marcus,' Maggie remarked as she rose from the piano.

'It was a sad song, was it not? Very affecting.'

Walking back to the King's Head Oliver said how much he had enjoyed the evening. 'But you were rather quiet, I thought. You should get out more, meet new people. You've been up in that dale by yourself too long. But you can still play the piano, my lad.' He laughed.

It was too late to ask questions that night, but the next morning the Radfords breakfasted together in the dining-room at the King's Head beside a cheerful fire. This might be the best time to ask about the incident, Marcus thought, waiting until his father had enjoyed a plate of ham and eggs and several cups of coffee.

Before Marcus could speak Oliver took the initiative. 'I've been meaning to talk to you for some time, Marcus. Now listen to me. Your old father knows what's good for you. Don't you think it's high time you got married and had some children? Think of posterity, and carrying on the Radford name. I know you were upset when Elizabeth died, but life must go on, you know.'

Marcus busied himself with buttering his toast, while Oliver went on eagerly. 'Your brother won't settle down, not for a long time yet. It's up to you and in my opinion, you could do worse than Miss Russell. What did you think of her?'

Marcus felt his heart sink. So there was a hidden agenda to last night's dinner. He was to be married off to a plump farmer's daughter, just to please the family. And even worse, if he hadn't met Sally he might have obliged! He could hardly say so, but Marcus had thought that Miss Russell was good-natured, reasonably pretty and monumentally boring. But her chief sin, he was quite aware, was that she was not Sally Mason. Oliver was waiting for a reply.

'Oh, Father,' Marcus said wearily. 'How about you? Why don't you marry Mrs Russell? You've been on your own for five years now.'

Oliver grinned, pouring coffee. 'I might do that,' he said cheerfully. 'You never know. We get on quite well.'

Well! That was rather unexpected. But Marcus kept his mind on his task 'Speaking of posterity and family, have you any old records of the family? As you know, I'm interested in local history, and there could be something interesting...' Marcus tailed off, conscious that his father was looking at him hard.

'Marcus, I am surprised at you. If you are speaking of the murder, no I have not, and

I'll thank you not to go dragging up the past! Your grandmother told me that you'd mentioned it to her and that is something we never do. I have told you to keep away from the Masons and that should be enough!'

Marcus waited a few moments and poured another cup of coffee. He looked round quickly, but they were still alone in the big dining-room.

'Father, you seem agitated. The Masons worry you more than one would expect. Is there another problem that you haven't told me about? I realize that it must have been a terrible shock at the time, but ... it's a long time ago. There must be something more recent?'

Oliver fiddled with his napkin and seemed at a loss for words. Then he said abruptly, 'Well, you are right. There are things that one does not discuss.' His mouth shut tight.

Well, Marcus thought, I got nowhere with that. But it was important to press on.

'While we're on the subject, you sent me to see Bartram and I told him to give Miss Mason another year at Badger's Gill. I hope you agree.' He spoke firmly.

His father stood up. 'Very well, it was your decision. I am indifferent. And now I will call the waiter. My horse was to be ready for eight.' And he strode to the door.

That night, the owner of Nidd Estates

224

wrote yet another letter to his recalcitrant tenant at Thorpe.

Madam,
It has been recommended to me that you should be granted a Lease At Will for the next year for Badger's Gill Farm, rent to be paid quarterly as before. This is entirely against my better judgement, I would like you to know, but I have agreed.

My agent will be checking to see that you comply with his requirements with regard to walls, fences and gates and maintain a proper crop rotation. I trust that your understanding of farming is sufficient for you to appreciate what is necessary, although I am not very optimistic on this point.

I should be grateful if you would refrain from further correspondence, which is tiresome in the extreme, and deal exclusively with my agent in Thorpe.

Oliver Radford

A small, ironic smile twisted Oliver's mouth as he blotted the letter. Was he enjoying this acrimonious correspondence? He rather thought he was. And he knew she'd still write back. She was nearly as bad as he was.

THIRTEEN

Marcus went straight home from Masham, saying goodbye to Oliver as they left the square, and the big horse made good time. He had decided to go round all their Colsterdale farms in turn to check that the lambing was going well. After that, he'd go to Foxholes Wood. He was committed to trying to solve the old mystery and wanted to start as soon as he could. But bad news was waiting for the young farmer in his own kitchen.

'Oh Mr Marcus, thank the Lord you're back! We didn't know what to do! Poor Daniel's tumbled down a mine shaft and bust a lot of bones, and there's five hundred ewes to lamb over at Slapestones!' Jeanie Brown twisted her hands in her apron, much distressed.

Marcus snapped back into the present and took the cup of tea she offered him. 'Where is he now, Jeanie? He was lucky to get out alive. The poor lad might not know all the shafts on the moor, it's his first lambing time with us. Did anybody show him the maps?'

'Aye, that's what Jesse said. Bob from next door saw him and fished him out. He likely didn't know it used to be all lead mining up there. They took him down to Ripon hospital in a cart and there he's to stay for a while they say, poor lad. His mother's that worried ... but what's to become of the sheep?'

'I will go up to Slapestones and keep an eye on the sheep. We've no shepherd that can be spared at the moment.' Damn, thought Marcus, frowning as he drank the tea. That means I won't get a chance to visit the wood for another month or so. Jeanie was still watching him and after a while, Marcus said, 'What's the matter, Jeanie?'

'Well, I'm sure I hope you don't mind, but my Jesse went up there last night, to check ewes of course and he's to light fires and make up a bed for you. Nobody's lived at Slapestones for years, as you know. Daniel lodged at next farm. And I've cooked up some pies and things for you to take.'

'Thank you Jeanie, that was most thoughtful. Could you pack me up some candles and two oil lamps? With that, a cheese and some bread I can last for a week or two.'

After that Marcus was caught up in the familiar routine, learned in childhood. Radfords were progressive farmers and controlled as much as they could of the processes which earned their living. But we can't predict the weather, Marcus thought grimly as he rode up to the isolated farm. If there was late snow he could be stuck here

227

for weeks.

Slapestones made his own home look positively urban. Up here, Marcus thought as he looked round, there's only the sheep for company and a few curlews and grouse. The system involved keeping the lambing ewes together in a paddock near the farmhouse and checking them as often as possible, in case one of them needed help. The Radford shepherds were expert in delivering lambs and 'mothering them up' if the ewe was not sure what to do next. There were stone buildings ready for use in very bad weather, or for sick animals.

Every lamb saved was a victory. All the Radford workers knew that every lamb saved would help to pay their wages. Records were kept so that shepherds could compete with each other in the percentage of lambs reared successfully for each flock. It was years since Marcus had needed to attend ewes himself, but he had a reputation to keep up. His records would be carefully watched by every worker on the estate. After that there was no time for thinking about anything other than sheep. Nights were broken by the need to go round the flock three or four times, and sometimes it was hard to get to sleep again, although Marcus was very tired after the first week. He could hear their incessant bleating, day and night.

If Marcus's conscious mind was fully occupied by sheep, at another level he was thinking of Sally. One night in one of his shallow naps he dreamed about her. In the dream he was trying to save her from falling off a precipice, but she was slipping away from him.

It would have been so pleasant to find some business in Ripon on Thursday and to see Sally and Emma for an hour or so. He desperately wanted to see her again, to wander with Sally and Emma through Ripon's old streets. Surely it was a modest enough ambition? Living up here on top of the moors made you get back to essentials. Marcus decided the next day that as soon as the lambing was over and he could send a labourer to tend the ewes, he would go to see Sally. But first, he reminded himself, he must go to the wood.

Snow did not fall but there was rain: constant, bitter, cold rain, driving in on the wind from the North Sea. Marcus spent most of his time damp if not wet, and always had clothes drying before the fire. He imagined that down in Thorpe Sally would be working in the same weather. Her sheep would be lambing too and the cows would be cold and miserable in the fields. She'd be keeping them in the shed for most of the time, and struggling in the mud. Winter was exhausting for everybody on the land.

A few Slapestones lambs were lost, chilled

by the rain before they could be warmed by their mother's milk. A few were taken by foxes. Some of the weaker ones were bedded down with their mothers in the barns and needed extra attention to ensure their survival.

No wonder there's no family at Slapestones, Marcus said to himself. Father could never get any of the men to live here permanently. The climate up here is twice as bad as it is lower down the hill. The constant rain was depressing and Marcus found himself descending into a settled gloom. Catching sight of himself in a mirror one day he was shocked by the stern, black-bearded stranger looking back at him.

It was nearly a month before the young shepherd Daniel came limping back and Marcus could go home. Four weeks of broken sleep, hurried meals and damp depression. The moors with their wide expansive views, so lovely in the summer, shrank in the rain to a few yards of sodden heather. Marcus was glad to leave, to get back to the lower land where spring was softening the harsh winter landscape. 'I'll send up another man to help you,' he said as he rode out of the yard. 'It's miserable here by yourself!'

After two or three days of warmth, good food and sleep, Marcus felt more like himself again. But some of the depression remained: he could not rid himself of the feeling of hopelessness. He found his thoughts always returning to Sally. It was hard to imagine that the Mason feud would ever be settled; it was all too long ago to find out the truth. And even if he did, the truth might not be palatable. After his time on the moor any dark, tragic thing seemed possible. Sally seemed to be forever out of reach.

Just at that time Marcus had a letter from an old friend who had been working in London and who came back to Kirkby several times a year on holiday. 'Come over and see me when you can!' The letter was cheerful, invigorating. It would be good to see Harry again. He was a medical specialist and full of interesting stories and good jokes. And Kirkby was quite close to Foxholes Wood. He could take a ride through the wood, just to confirm to himself that there was nothing left to see.

A pleasant April day did a little to lighten the mood as Marcus rode down from Colsterdale to Kirkby. Spring had come earlier to Kirkby and the gardens and orchards were in blossom. The air was full of the sound of birds and the sun was warmer, once Marcus dropped below the moor wind.

It was disappointing to find that Harry was not at home. Marcus settled himself on a garden bench to wait for his friend, planning to ride through the wood on his way home. Kirkby was quiet that day; Marcus could hear sounds of sawing from the carpenter's shop and the bleating of lambs. There was nobody on the street, not a soul that he could ask about Harry's whereabouts.

Hearing the creaking of a horse and trap, Marcus looked out over the garden wall. And there, trotting down the street, was the young horse Jed and his owner, Sally Mason. The red-gold hair was covered by a straw hat, but he'd know that trim little figure anywhere as well as that ungainly young horse, the one that turned her over up on the moor. Marcus saw with a sudden shock that Sally was not alone. Beside her was a handsome, fair young man, talking earnestly and looking at her with a turn of the head that showed great interest.

Marcus turned away, sick at heart. While he'd been trapped on the moorland, some other man had stepped in. He should have expected it: Sally was too lovely, too vital to be left alone for long. He'd known from the start that there was no one in the world quite like Sally. And now more than ever, it was impossible. Time had taken her away. Why should this girl mean so much to him? Someone else sat beside her now where Marcus should be! He watched hungrily as the trap passed out of sight. For a long time the tall man sat in his friend's garden. Harry did not appear and eventually when his horse stamped impatiently Marcus pulled himself together, mounted and rode off. He had no heart for anything else; he would go home.

Marcus couldn't blame Sally. She had not heard from him for weeks and life has to on. While he was on the sodden moor, Sally had been making new friends. Marcus was surprised at himself. At twenty-eight he had not expected to be so devastated. It wasn't jealousy so much as utter misery, like a physical pain. The dream of her slipping away came back to him with a new reality.

Sally had done the rounds with her eggs that day and Simon had come with her for the ride. They both enjoyed the spring weather and Simon planned to make a quick sketch of the Kirkby church, as they passed it on the way back to Thorpe.

It was not easy, but Sally was keeping the young man at arms' length without upsetting him too much. She tried not to be alone with him in the house and out in the trap there were plenty of distractions.

One day when she was making up the fire in the dining-room they'd had a private conversation of the sort she had dreaded.

'I want to talk to you Sally, but there never seems to be a chance.' The young man's voice was low and urgent.

Sally sat down beside him; now for it, she

thought. We'd better get it over.

'I told you back in the winter that I love you.' The grey eyes were clear and honest as they looked at her. 'And the more I get to know you the deeper it is. Unfortunately I can't ask you to marry me. My health makes that impossible, it would be unfair to you. But – can you love me a little, Sally? You are so kind to me. I would be so happy with your love!' Simon sat back in the chair and waited.

What can I honestly say? Sally thought furiously. Simon was civilized and cultivated. He was a perfect house guest and most thoughtful. She was fond of Simon; he was far more than the commercial undertaking that Emma had once recommended. But he was not Marcus Radford. That was the problem.

Sally was bound in some deep way to Marcus, even though there were skeletons in family cupboards, even though she hadn't seen him for weeks. Did that mean he had found it all too hard? And even though he'd not asked her to marry him. But whatever happened, Sally knew that a commitment to someone else would be a betrayal of her own deepest feelings. 'To thine own self be true...' her mother had quoted and Sally had always remembered. She couldn't give Simon what he wanted, the committed love of a woman to a man, and be true to herself.

'Yes, Simon dear. I do love you, as the brother I never had. And I admire you, you know – the brave way you manage your illness, with no complaints. We all enjoy your company and we're very fond of you. You're one of the family at Badger's Gill. Will you be my brother?'

Simon moved towards her and kissed Sally gently on the cheek. 'Any kind of love you can give me, I'm grateful for. Maybe brotherly love is the best kind for me! But how I wish things were different!' He couldn't quite hide his disappointment. He took Sally's hand and she felt his tremble slightly.

Love hurts, Sally thought bitterly. I know it and I can't help it, Simon. It was time to look on the bright side. 'Let's try to be as happy as we can. Let's enjoy each day, Simon. Come out with me in the trap and do some more drawing.' Sally had turned away to hide her tears.

Jed pulled up smartly at the gate, and Simon slipped into the churchyard with his pad and pencil and a small stool. 'I'll wait here,' called Sally. Jed was rather young to be left in the street on his own. She slipped the reins over his head and led him into the yard of the Queen's Head on the opposite side of the road. There she tied him to a rail and then sat on a low wall, enjoying the sunshine. Simon was out of sight. Ten minutes went by, fifteen ... through the open window of a nearby house Sally could hear a piano. Scales, exercises at first, and then the pianist played some wistful drifting notes that seemed in perfect harmony with the drowsy afternoon. She listened in a dream, the music carrying her away until she heard a horse approaching quietly down the main street. The rider turned into Church Street and Sally saw that it was Marcus.

At first she hardly recognized him. His eyes were on the ground, he looked sterner, older. But – it was Marcus! Sally felt her whole being light up with joy. She stepped out into the road and held out a hand, in case he had not seen her. Marcus stopped motionless and looked down at Sally. There was no answering smile of greeting. Just a lifeless 'Good day'. Then he sighed and squared his shoulders in the old way and looked straight ahead.

'Marcus! What's wrong?' Sally held out her arms to him, there in the middle of the road. He must be ill!

'Oh, Sally!' It came out like a groan.

'Get down off that horse!' The red-gold hair fell over her face as Sally took off her straw hat, and she pushed it back impatiently. 'Please!' It was a command.

Stiffly, Marcus climbed down and followed Sally into the inn yard. Her arms went out towards him and then dropped back, as she looked up into the unhappy face.

'Whatever is the matter, my dear Roman soldier?'

She saw Marcus relax a little. In the middle of the yard they stood close together, almost touching. Sally could feel the tension between them. His horse pushed its head forward, seemingly wanting to be included and Sally patted its nose, laughing 'Back, Odin!'

Marcus smiled too. But then he drew back, shaking his head. 'Sally, you've found someone else, I know. I saw you going by with a young man... I don't blame you, it's all so difficult and I've been away. It's too late in any case.' His voice was low and infinitely sad. 'I can't see a way out. You should be happy with someone else.' A labourer went by leading a carthorse and looked at them curiously.

Sally felt her volatile nature begin to fizz and tried to hold it down. 'Simon is not Someone Else! He is my paying guest – a commercial transaction. I am his house-keeper, if you like. And he's an artist. He's drawing the church, you see, and I'm waiting like a good employee should, for him to finish.'

Marcus looked down at her and she thought how handsome his dark face was, and how miserable. 'He's in love with you. You passed me earlier, I was in a garden. I could see it from the way he was looking at you. But that's a good thing if you like him, he might be able to look after you. And you'd better forget about me. We have no future, you and I. There's no news about the murder and my father is still implacable.' Marcus paused and Sally said nothing to help him. She was still fizzing inside. His father had written another rude letter, but left her on the farm for a further year. That wasn't entirely implacable! And then, what if they hadn't met by chance today? Was he just going to ignore her for the rest of their lives?

'It's no good, we'll have to give up and we both know it. Let's not pretend any more, Sally.'

This didn't sound in the least like the Marcus she knew. What had happened to the man who was so decisive and strong? He must have had a change of heart, somehow. But it wasn't fair! Sally's redheaded nature asserted itself and her eyes sparkled with anger. 'You are impossible!'

Marcus drew back, shocked.

'I haven't seen you for so long, and I wonder where you are. You meet us in Ripon a few times and then we never see you again!' She paused to draw breath. Better not let him know how disappointed she'd been. Jogging down to Ripon in the trap as soon as the snow cleared, hoping and wondering ... and for weeks now, no Marcus.

'I've been away lambing, on the moor.' He didn't sound very convincing.

'And then we meet by sheer chance and you decide my future for me, just like that in the middle of Kirkby! It's NOT GOOD ENOUGH!' Sally's voice was low, but extremely forceful. She was almost dancing in the road by now, thoroughly irate.

At last the stern face became more human, the amused quirk of the mouth came back. Marcus laughed. 'If you could just see yourself, Miss Mason! So, I'm not allowed to give up. I am trying to do the right thing!' He was equally forceful. 'I don't want you to waste your time on me when I can't sort things out. Youth is soon overed with, as they say round here. How can I keep you hanging on, waiting for a solution to the old mystery?' The smile faded and Marcus let out a huge sigh. 'I blame myself, of course. And lately I must admit that things have looked very black.'

Sally was aware that the piano music was still floating out into the street, weaving silver threads of enchantment in the air. If only they could live in a fairytale with a happy ending! Slowly her anger subsided. Who was she to order Mr Radford of Radford Estates off his horse? With a quick change of mood Sally drew him into the side of the yard beside the trap, where they would be less conspicuous. 'I'm sorry, Marcus. I shouldn't get angry with you, I know. I admit that I've been feeling the same way, that this family feud thing is very serious and makes it difficult for both our families.'

Marcus nodded. 'I suppose it depends on whether I can find out more, to lay the ghosts to rest. There must be some way!' But he didn't sound hopeful. 'If we can prove it wasn't a murder, my family might be easier to persuade to meet you. I think they must have jumped to conclusions, at the time.'

They stared at each other and Sally realized in that moment how much she loved this man. She wanted to spend the rest of her life with him. They should have children together ... but she was too proud to throw herself into his arms. She had been quite forward enough already. Thank goodness nobody they knew had seen them together! Sally Mason, a young single woman living alone, apart from her guests, had to be very careful of her reputation. Marcus was prepared to give her up, she reminded herself bitterly. Well, she could be independent too.

Marcus' horse scraped its foot impatiently and was ignored. Jed in the trap was chewing at his bit. Somewhere, a blackbird was singing its evening song. Marcus stood silent, looking at Sally. Head up, shoulders back, he was evidently struggling to be his old self again.

'Where were you, Marcus, all last month?' All this time, Sally thought, I've been agonizing over you and wondering whether I would see you again.

'As I just said, I had to work as a shepherd. One of our men was injured. I couldn't get away. And it rained, of course.'

She believed him this time. Perhaps it was time to normalize the conversation, to be civilized. 'My little flock have all lambed, very good lambs too, just as you said. And Mr Radford said I could rent the farm for another year, but after that I was to get out! A year's grace is better than nothing.' She looked up at him. My chief worry has been about you, but I'm not going to tell you that.

'Good. I'm glad to hear it.'

The sun was beginning to go down behind the row of cottages opposite the church and Marcus picked up his reins. 'I must go now, dear Sally. I want to get to the wood before dark, just to ride through there again and see whether there is anything unusual to be seen...' Marcus looked at her with eyes full of love. But Sally didn't want to have false hope.

'That is not really likely, after all this time.' Sally wished she felt as cool as she sounded.

He slipped the reins into place and put his foot in the stirrup. A whisk of the horse's tail and they were gone.

There was no possibility of solving the problem. How could there be anything in Foxholes Wood, fifty years later? Perhaps the feud was just an excuse to back out of the friendship, if they had such a thing. Perhaps Marcus rather fancied her but had no intentions of getting too involved with a poverty-stricken tenant farmer, a woman who did rough farm work for a living. He was a gentleman, he would find a polite way to back out of any relationship. Sally patted Jed, trying not to cry. She felt that the situation was now clear. Even when he'd thought that Simon was her new man he'd said it was a good thing! Swallowing hard, she went over the road to find Simon. It was hard to appear normal, to pretend that nothing had happened when her heart was aching so much. But Simon was bent over his drawing, completely absorbed.

'That's a good drawing!' Sally said sincerely. She had done enough drawing herself to know that his technique was good.

'The light's going, I'll have to stop. Goodness, I've kept you waiting so long! Did you find someone to talk to? I thought I heard voices.' Simon packed up his papers.

'Yes, thank you, the time went quickly. I was talking to – a farmer.' Sally led the way to the trap. 'We'd better trot off home, it's milking time.'

FOURTEEN

'Have you seen Simon? I took him some tea but he's not there!' Emma's eyes were round as she came into the kitchen. 'He went to post a letter, didn't he?' She looked at the kitchen clock. 'But that was over an hour ago!'

Sally stopped kneading bread and wiped her face with a floury hand. 'Where can he be?'

'One of us had better go to look for him. The other day he came for a walk down the lane but he couldn't go far. The post office is maybe too far for him, right at the top of the village.' Emma sighed. 'He's so short of breath, Sally. I offered to post the letter for him, but he insisted – he wanted to go to the shop.'

Poor lad was probably feeling a bit cut off from everything, shut away in the country, Sally thought sadly. He led such a restricted life. It was about four o'clock, time for a cup of tea and a scone and nearly milking time. Emma had a newly baked scone on the tray for Simon, beside the tea. 'I'll go in two minutes, once this bread is set to rise.'

The afternoon sun, stronger now, was

slanting through the ancient trees on the green as Sally sped up the street. There was nobody about to disturb the afternoon quiet, even the ducks were bobbing on the pond, quietly contemplating. Sally rushed into the post office, which was also the village store. 'Mrs Hollis, have you seen Mr Drury? My guest?' Everybody knew by now that Sally Mason took paying guests.

Mrs Hollis looked up in surprise. 'Nay, lass, he went off ages ago! Should've been home well before now. Wanted to buy some sweets for Miss Mason. Wanted to know whether you like mint humbugs, acid drops or barley sugar.' She smiled knowingly. 'Thinks Miss Mason is wonderful, I can tell! He wanted chocolates but we've none.'

It was impossible not to blush. Sally shook her head, thanked the woman and ran out. What next? Where else could she look? She walked home more decorously, thinking about Simon. Since the winter they had gradually become real friends, she thought. In one way she was worried; she was being drawn in all the time to a closer relationship. And it would not do. Marcus was lost to her, but she couldn't love another man in that way.

As she walked, a cold dread began to creep over her. What if Simon too was feeling desperate? She realized now that Emma had nearly drowned because she, Sally, hadn't seen the danger signs in time. Could Simon be suicidal? It was possible that he too had slid into depression; after all he had little to be happy about. They needed help, if they were to find him. Passing the Scotts' house, Sally turned in on impulse. She would ask Robin for help if he was at home. Robin was good in an emergency. But help was not needed after all, for there at the Scotts' kitchen table, drinking tea and laughing at some joke, was Simon. He looked very pale in spite of the laughter, Sally thought. I won't be too hard on him. He probably needed a rest.

'We were worried about you, thought we'd lost you!' Sally kept her tone light.

Simon jumped up immediately. 'I am so sorry! I didn't think of that.' He took out a watch. 'Heavens! No wonder you were worried. I won't do it again, Sally. I promise you.' He gave her a look of contrite devotion and Sally thought she saw Robin hide a smile.

'Have you time for a cup of tea?' Robin's mother was already pouring the strong black tea into a cup for her and Sally collapsed on to a chair, feeling suddenly rather tired.

'Well, Sal, you are careless! You used to misplace your sheep and now it's the guests you lose!' Robin's hearty laugh sounded rather hollow to Sally. He seemed to lack feeling, somehow. Couldn't he see that both Emma and Simon deserved sympathy?

'I really came in to see Mr Scott about a will.' Simon was still apologetic. 'But he's not home yet. Perhaps he could come down to see me one day when he's not busy?' He looked at Mrs Scott.

'I'm sure he'll be happy to visit you on the next rainy day! He saves the legal work for when he can't work outdoors.' Mrs Scott looked slightly embarrassed as she looked across the table at Sally. 'I happened to ask Simon what he did in the family business, before he came here. He says he was in the financial department, he's an accountant.'

Sally was embarrassed in her turn; she should have known that. But she hadn't liked to question him on his previous life, afraid of making him sad.

Mrs Scott seemed to be waiting for something and Sally realized what it was. The Scotts had been very keen for her to keep accounts. 'I wonder whether you'd like to help me to set up some farm accounts, Simon? You would be starting from scratch, I'm afraid. But only if you feel up to it.' Sally looked at her guest carefully to judge his reaction.

A huge smile lit up Simon's face. 'I should love to do that for you, Sally. I didn't like to offer, accounts are your private business, of course. But if you agree it would give me something useful to do. I feel so useless, sometimes.'

Susan Scott smiled approvingly. 'That was my idea, too. It will help Sally to run the farm more efficiently – not that you're inefficient, dear! I didn't mean that.'

'You will know just how efficient you are!' Robin laughed. 'If you have time, Simon, I can show you how to keep cattle and sheep records. I bet you didn't have those in the woollen mill.'

It would mean more time with Simon, alone. That was probably not a good thing, Sally decided as they went down the village street. But it couldn't be helped and it was time that Badger's Gill had some records, apart from notes on scraps of paper. Simon seemed very happy, but he was soon in trouble. Walking home down the familiar gentle slope to Badger's Gill, Sally noticed how breathless he'd become. Tactfully she stopped by the pond to watch the ducks and he sank down gratefully on a wooden seat.

'It will be wonderful to work with you more closely and to be of some help to you.' The young man gave her one of his devoted looks. 'I so admire your courage, dear Sally, in running the business alone.'

'I didn't have much choice!' Sally looked across the green at her beloved farm. 'It was either that or go to live with Aunt Bertha! Now what do you think of the farm from this angle? Should you like to sketch it from here?'

After a few minutes, Simon stood up slowly and offered Sally his arm. 'I can manage to walk home now, with your help.' He suddenly grinned and looked much more boyish. 'And I do hope you like barley sugar, Sally. I've bought you a large bag!'

The world of Thorpe was turning greener as April gave way to May and Sally thought she'd never seen such beautiful apple blossom as there was in the orchard that year. The cows were happy in their deep grass and as the calves were born, there was more and more milk for making butter and cheese. It was a busy time and the young farmer had little leisure time. Sometimes in the middle of the night, Sally would wake and think about Marcus and the life that might have been. But there had never been hope with Marcus. He was a Radford after all and she had her Mason pride. Aunt Bertha didn't matter, but Sally loved Uncle Samuel and he would be devastated by any friendship with a Radford. The thing that had upset him most was the way in which Oliver Radford had bought Badger's Gill, just to wield power over the Masons. Technically Samuel had lost his share of the farm since it had paid for his education, but he felt the injury almost as much as Robert did. And, when it came to the crunch, so did Sally.

Marcus's father bore them ill will; Marcus had admitted it himself. And their meeting in Kirkby had shown her that Oliver's son could be moody. Sally told herself that she was better off without Marcus Radford. And then she thought of his quiet voice, his smile and the kindness he'd shown to her. He was most lovable. This thought made Sally miserable; Sally Mason just didn't seem to have any luck But then she would remember Simon and his precarious future. 'I'm lucky to be Sally Mason!' she told herself. 'Healthy at least, if not wealthy or wise!'

One rainy day in May, Mr Scott appeared with a sheaf of papers and sat down with Simon in the dining-room. 'I've come to do your will,' he announced solemnly. The two men were there for most of the afternoon. At about four, Sally decided to interrupt them with the tea tray, judging that Simon would probably have had enough and be needing a rest. She noticed his pallor as soon as she went into the room, and the weary droop of his head.

'Please join us, Sally!' Simon begged and so she sat with them, although she'd intended to go off to collect the cows for milking. They talked about farming for a while and Simon asked questions that showed he was taking his recording duties seriously.

Sally described how Joe had taken on much of the heavy work, the difference it had made and how well he justified the expense of a worker. 'Joe's wages are the one thing I won't cut back, if cuts are needed!' Sally was becoming aware that attention to expenditure was an important part of success.

Mr Scott was at her father's big desk and Simon sat at the dining-table. The older man looked round the room. 'Just the same as I always remember it!' He ran his fingers over the desk, as if appreciating the fine craftsmanship. 'Nice piece of oak, this desk. Did you know that there were only two made to this design, by Abbots of Ripon? Robert had one and I bought the other one.' He smiled. 'And of course they both have the secret drawer.'

Sally stared at him. 'What secret drawer?'

'I'm sure Robert told you – didn't he?' Mr Scott bent over the desk, moved his hands and a compartment slid open. 'So clever! You can't see the join from the top.'

Sally looked down into the desk, which was now deeper inside than before. The first thing she saw was a letter addressed to herself in her father's handwriting. There were bank books and other papers ... this was where Father kept his records. And she'd never known!

'Please show me how to open it, Mr Scott.'

Sally had no intention of reading the papers just then. This revelation had given her a shock and she needed time to get over it. She opened and closed the desk several times until she could do it smoothly. This was another thing that Father would have shown her if only he'd had more time.

Holding out his empty cup for the tray, Robin's father said comfortably, 'Susan said I was to tell you that some walkers would like to book in for a week, if you can take them. She's got the details.'

Some walkers? How many? Sally felt her head spinning. But then Emma was keen to do more and there were two spare bedrooms they could use.

'I think we can manage that, Mr Scott,' Sally found herself saying. She picked up the tray. 'I'd better tell Emma to stand by!'

As soon as milking was over later that day, Sally raided the desk, feeling almost guilty. She took the papers up to her bedroom. Now for it ... but the letter was the most important, the last message from her father.

It had been written about a year before, when his lungs were getting worse and Robert Mason had faced the fact that they might give out at any time. He didn't know how long he had left but to be on the safe side he wrote down all the things that Sally would need to know. There were details of insurance, some pedigree records for their cattle and bank records. Sally found that they had three bank accounts, all at different banks in Ripon. None of the bank accounts seemed to hold more than a hundred pounds, although there would now be a year's interest to add to the totals. And the letter contained an apology, in a loving paragraph that made her cry.

You are a wonderful daughter, Sally, and a loyal and hardworking assistant. I only wish I could leave you more, so that one day the farm might be yours. But the money we have earned in the last few years has not been enough for me to save. I am hoping to live for a few more years, so perhaps by the time you read this the bank records will be much better!
I love you, Sally.

Your devoted father,
Robert Mason

The last item she found was the farm lease from Radford Estates. It was a Tenancy For Life, in the name of Robert Mason only. Her father's life. And it left her with no legal arrangement at all. Sally knew from talking to Mr Scott that in the absence of a legal lease, the landlord could evict the tenant with due notice: in her case, a quarter's notice, since the rent was payable quarterly.

Oliver had the law on his side. There had just been a faint hope that Sally's name was on the lease, but now that hope was gone.

Marcus Radford was a disappointed man, although he couldn't say what he had expected to find in Foxholes Wood. After he met Sally in Kirkby his depression deepened until he was weighed down by a settled melancholy. The ride through the gloomy wood did nothing to help. The evening sun was slanting through the trees as Marcus rode the well-trodden grassy track. This was a short cut to Dallagill, a tiny village in a hidden valley and people still rode this way at times. This was the track his grandfather had taken with his friend Mason, those were the same trees they had ridden under, now fifty years older. Some of the younger ash and elm would have grown up since then.

There were no forks in the trail, no other tracks to follow. So he plodded slowly on, watching and listening as the sun sank and the world under the trees grew slowly darker. Was it stupid of him to worry about a feud so much that he was giving up the girl he loved? It was more than the feud and his grandmother's wishes, of course. There was something else gnawing away at his father. And although he didn't always agree with 'the old boy', as he thought of Oliver, Marcus was deeply attached to him. That was the problem.

It was a relief to see daylight at the edge of the wood and to get out into the sweet air of early evening. Marcus sat motionless on his horse for a while. He'd been through the wood and was none the wiser. Rooks were cawing their way home against a pink sky; distant sheep bleated to their lambs. The High Side was at peace, but was still keeping its secret.

Why not go to see his father? Much nearer in time to the tragedy than Marcus himself, he might just be willing to reveal something this time that would provide a clue. Partly on impulse, Marcus turned his horse's head to the moor road. He hadn't been to Nidd Grange for weeks. By the time he reached the Drovers' Inn Marcus saw that the moon was rising. It was a perfect night for riding; he could stay at Nidd for the night and go back to Colsterdale tomorrow.

Turning over the old story in his mind, Marcus tried to imagine himself into the scene. The two friends rode into the wood together, just as he had done. In the middle of a summer's day, with no sinister twilight. Just suppose for a moment that Richard Mason had red hair and a volatile nature. A vivid image of Sally, dancing with impatience, came to him. Did she inherit that red hair from a volatile grandfather? This was not a comfortable thought. Reluctantly,

Marcus took the story further in his mind. Suppose that the two friends had argued and in a hot temper, Mason had struck Radford. He might have been injured or killed by a freak blow to the temple. Here, the story broke down.

Sally might be hasty and rather excitable but she was full of a shining integrity. And any person of integrity would, in the situation as he'd imagined it, try to get help immediately. A grandfather of Sally's would surely have admitted what had happened and faced up to the consequences. Any man of sense in fact would have owned up. Wouldn't that be better than facing a lifetime of evasion, of deceit and isolation? Richard Mason must have endured a lonely life as an outcast in his own community. High-Siders never forgot or forgave; his grandmother was an example of that. Marcus sighed and rode on through the moonlit landscape. Now he was at the top of the moor and could see the valley glimmering below and the faint lamplight in the windows of Nidd Grange.

'It's good to see you, lad. But I'm afraid you're too late for dinner – there's none left!' Oliver came forward to greet his son in the hall, looking pleased. 'Fancy a game of chess?'

I feel like a pawn on the losing side, Marcus thought. 'I'd like a bite of bread and cheese and a drink!' He pulled off his riding gloves.

Oliver's housekeeper soon bustled in with a tray of food that contained much more than bread and cheese and drew up a small table for him by the fire. Although it was early May, the evenings still held a chill.

'Would you care for a whisky?' Oliver looked over the hearthrug at him. 'We haven't had a drink together for a long time and there's the bottle you gave me at Christmas.'

His father poured generous measures of the old malt and Marcus added plenty of water to his own glass. He wanted to be able to think clearly. Father was in a good mood, more mellow and relaxed than usual. Evidently the farms were in good order, the farm servants were behaving well and nobody's pig had died. When things went wrong, Oliver could be very gloomy.

Reporting progress for Colsterdale, Marcus was pleased that he had good news to offer. 'More lambs than last year. Daniel's on the mend and as you'll know, the wool prices are set to rise.'

Oliver almost smiled. 'Ah. You do well, my boy. I always thought we could produce more lambs over there.'

When the tray was taken away, Marcus picked up the whisky bottle. 'Will ye tak another wee dram?'

Oliver laughed. 'You sound like Tom when he comes down from Edinburgh. Have you heard from him lately?' They talked about Marcus's younger brother for a while, and Oliver leaned back in his big leather chair, content.

'Father, I have to ask a favour. I must try once more, there is so much at stake. Would you please tell me about the past? I wonder what happened to you personally, fifty years ago, that has had such a lasting effect on you? That makes you still hate the Masons?

Oliver closed his eyes, looking suddenly older, and waved a hand. 'Not fifty ... but over thirty years ago it was. My world turned upside down,' he said hoarsely. 'But why should I bore you with the story?'

Marcus waited, looking into the fire.

Oliver sat up again. 'You might as well know, I suppose ... you'll be the first. I have never talked about it. And it was all over long before you were born. Before I met your mother.' He sighed.

Marcus sat very still.

'I fell in love you see, with the most beautiful woman in the world. Louisa Benson was a lovely girl and from a good family. She had a sweet disposition, too. I was young and headstrong, and rather serious I suppose ... perhaps not light-hearted enough. But that girl meant everything to me. I couldn't live without her.' There was a silence and Oliver took a sip of his whisky. 'In a way, I didn't. The daft lad in me died and I was harder, more ruthless after that. Good for business, I suppose.' The handsome face looked stern, even in repose.

'Of course I loved your mother, though in a calmer sort of way. We were happy together, you know that. We were a happy enough family until she died.'

'We were,' said Marcus gently. He still missed his calm, practical mother.

'I think she helped me to survive.' Having started, Oliver seemed keen to revisit the past. 'I was very bitter and she helped me over that, your mother did.'

Marcus was aware of a deep sympathy. Father was human after all, and had been just as passionate as he himself. And just as unlucky.

'Louisa had lovely copper-coloured hair and a creamy skin. And she could be fiery, too!'

'Oh, dear. She sounds dangerous!' Marcus thought of Sally.

'I never told anyone – it seemed disrespectful to your mother. And of course we don't talk about emotions. Not until we've had enough whisky, that is!'

After a while Marcus ventured again. 'What happened to Louisa, Father? Did she die?'

Oliver shifted in his chair. 'She married

Robert Mason. I had never told her of my feelings, of course. I was hoping to, but there was never a chance. I didn't know she had any other attachment, until their engagement was announced. And then it was too late. So she never knew.' Oliver sighed.

So the beautiful Louisa was Sally's mother.

'There was no love lost between us and the Masons, of course, ever since the murder.' He persisted in calling it a murder. 'But for me that was the last straw. I hated him.'

Things begin to fit into place, thought Marcus. Oliver hated the Masons because Robert had stolen his best girl ... a girl with red hair. So Sally got her glorious hair from her mother and not her grandfather. And so the theory of the crime of redheaded passion that Marcus had invented earlier didn't hold up. Marcus took a deep breath. 'Now I understand. That's why you don't want to meet Sally Mason. And you won't go near Badger's Gill!'

'That's why. So don't push me, Marcus!' Oliver looked tired, but there might never be another chance to talk like this. Marcus went resolutely on to the sticking point for the Mason family, the reason for their own reciprocal hatred.

'So then when you had the chance, you bought the Mason's farm out of revenge? So you had a hold over them?'

His father shook his head with a wry smile. 'Don't be dramatic, lad. It was good business, the right price. It's good land you know, better than this.' He paused. 'And there was another reason. I did it to help Louisa.'

Marcus was bewildered. 'To help?'

'They were in terrible trouble financially – almost in the poorhouse. It was bad luck mostly, although I must say they weren't too hard-nosed in their dealings. Farmers should be hard-nosed to survive! Cattle plague took all their stock and that's sheer bad luck. But there was nobody would buy their farm and lease it back to them. They couldn't afford to wait, and Watson never got a bid. So I bought it.' Oliver laughed. 'Folks thought I did it for revenge. I didn't mind so long as nobody knew the truth. It's not good to be thought too soft, not on the High Side.'

Suddenly the story had taken another turn. 'You were watching over her still, and she didn't know it!' Or perhaps she did. Sally had told him that her father and uncle were bitter about the Radfords, but her mother had never uttered a word against them.

'Don't get too romantic, Marcus. I told you it was a good deal.'

The two men sat in silence for a while and the fire burned low. Then Marcus roused himself. 'I'd better go to bed. But, just one more thing, Father, and I won't mention the business again. If the Masons wanted to buy back the farm, would you sell it?'

Oliver stood up with his arm on the mantelpiece. 'They wouldn't be able to afford it, Marcus. It's worth too much these days. They'd never raise the cash.'

FIFTEEN

Two battered leather suitcases stood in the hall and Emma circled them warily, feeling apprehensive. Visitors were coming, which meant change. But Emma liked things just as they were and didn't want anything to change. The carrier had delivered the luggage, but no people appeared. 'They're walking up from Ripon,' Sally explained. 'They'll be here before dark. Would you like to make them a gooseberry pie?'

While the pie was in the oven with some scones, Sally made a fruit cake. Walkers were likely to be hungry and would expect good farmhouse fare. They could have the traditional ham and egg 'high tea' this evening. Martha had told her what to expect. They had decided that Simon could eat at a separate table, just like hotel dining-rooms.

He could then talk to them or not, as he wished. He seemed to be looking forward to seeing new faces.

Emma ran upstairs and checked over the two spare bedrooms, now to be used by the walkers. Simon's parents had stayed twice and some of his friends had come to see him, giving Emma more practice with guests and adding a little to the income since they all insisted on paying. They had all loved Badger's Gill, which gave both Sally and Emma more confidence.

Everything was in order, she noted with satisfaction. Emma herself had sewn pretty new bedcovers and pillowslips. The ancient furniture was polished with beeswax to a high gloss, because Emma loved to polish. Her love of order, once so set on rules, had transferred itself to housekeeping and Emma had found that she was good at it. The marble washstands were set with jug and basin, with towels, sponges and soap to hand.

There was one problem, a thought that kept bringing back the shameful memories of the past and Mr Steele. One of the rooms was next to her own and round the corner from the other rooms. Emma went downstairs again, slowly. 'Sally, do you think – is it possible to have a lock put on my door?'

With the cake halfway to the oven, Sally paused. 'All the bedroom doors can be locked. There's a pin on the sneck. Haven't you noticed?'

What on earth was a sneck? 'I don't quite understand, Sally. Sorry.'

'It's I should say sorry, lass. That's a dialect word we use up here, for a latch!' Sally laughed and they both went up on to the wide landing at the top of the stairs. The downstairs doors were solid panelled affairs, with big brass knobs. Emma knew them well, because she polished the knobs. But upstairs were old-fashioned latches, painted black. A small pin on a chain could be slipped into place and the latch couldn't be raised.

'But why worry about a lock, suddenly?' Sally asked.

Emma felt uncomfortable. 'It's just the visitors...'

'Don't worry, Emma, love. They'll be decent gentlemen, I am sure. Just like Simon and his folks. You didn't worry when Simon came, did you?'

Sally was looking at her keenly and Emma blushed. 'No, I didn't. He was an invalid! But these guests are tough walkers and they–' she couldn't finish. They were temporary, passing through, just like that other man.

Sally sat down on the big oak chest on the landing and drew Emma down beside her. 'These gentlemen will be just like Robin. Now Emma, you feel quite happy with Robin, don't you?'

It was true; Emma felt safe with Robin, secure, somehow. He was light-hearted, but also reliable and he seemed to understand how she felt about most things, without her having to explain. She nodded. 'Of course I do, Sally. He's our friend!' She decided to be brave and plunged on. 'Is Robin your particular friend, Sally? I've sometimes wondered whether you and he were ... but I shouldn't ask. I'm sorry.'

A loud rap on the front door made them both jump. They straightened their black dresses and prepared to meet the guests. As they went down, Sally put a hand over Emma's for a moment, on the banister. 'No, Emma. I'm quite fond of the lad, but I'm not in love with him. Now, let's put our caps on.'

Emma went into the kitchen as Sally greeted the guests. She could be introduced later. And she wondered as she put the kettle on the fire, why she felt suddenly lighter, and happy that Sally wasn't excessively fond of Robin.

There was a buzz of talk in the hall and a laugh or two. Then the walkers clattered upstairs to wash off the dust of the road, saying how hungry they were. They seemed to be pleased with their rooms, thank goodness; Sally had carried up the cases before they arrived.

Emma's first look at the strangers was in

the dining-room, where two clean rosy faces, with plastered-down wet hair, turned expectantly towards her. 'Food! Thank you so much!' Both lads were more interested in their supper than in the waitress, which suited Emma very well. Neither of the young men looked in the least like Mr Steele. She gave them plates of ham and eggs and stood before them with her hands folded, in the proper serving attitude.

'I was to ask whether there is anything that you don't like to eat?' she asked.

Simon came into the dining-room just behind her and sat at his little table. He bowed in the direction of the guests and said easily 'Good evening, and welcome to Badger's Gill. I can recommend all the dishes that Miss Mason provides; the food here is excellent.'

'So it is!' The taller of the two men looked up briefly from his plate. 'Especially when you haven't eaten since breakfast!'

Emma observed that the men were quite young, in their early twenties and they wore old, shabby tweeds. They both looked tanned and fit. She heard them introduce themselves to Simon. 'We've come by train from Leeds and we plan to walk every day this week. Walking is a nice change from our usual work We're teachers, of course.'

Simon smiled and reached for the salt. 'So it must be half term, I gather. I am Simon

Drury, a guest here, and this is Miss Wake-
ield, the assistant housekeeper.'

Emma blushed. What a grand title!

One of the guests looked across, apologetically. 'So sorry, I thought you were a
maid! How do you do, Mr Drury, Miss
Wakefield.'

'How do you do.' The other smiled at
Emma appreciatively. 'You took early prom-
otion, then!'

I'm seventeen, Emma thought. And a
good enough housekeeper, too. She smiled
slightly, and took away the tray.

The walkers required an early breakfast,
much earlier than Simon's, but that was
easy. The household was always up early.
They were out all day and only returned for
supper. And presumably they slept well after
their days in the open air, for nothing was
heard during the night. Emma began to
relax about halfway through the week.
These guests were no trouble at all. She told
them about the walk down to the river and
the next day they walked all the way to
Masham along the riverbank, had lunch at
the King's Head and walked back in time
for supper.

By the end of the week, Emma quite liked
the visitors and chatted to them easily. She
was proud of this; it meant that she was
normal, after all. Perhaps she would get over
her fear of men in time. She hadn't very

much experience of talking to strange men and she had no brothers. But as Sally had pointed out, she enjoyed the company of Simon and Robin. They proved that men could be respectful and kind-hearted.

When they left, the walkers thanked Sally and Emma for their wonderful hospitality and promised to come again. The visit had been a success. It was agreed between them that Sally would accept more bookings from walkers, if any came. She said as much to Mrs Hollis at the post office, who was likely to be asked about accommodation. She said that strangers often passed through in summer, and she would recommend Badger's Gill.

In the middle of June there was a spell of fine weather and Sally realized that the hay should be cut. There were two hay meadows and she decided that they would harvest one before cutting the other.

''Twill give us time to get it properly, and split the risk if the weather turns,' agreed Joe wisely. He was in charge of sharpening the scythes and George would be the other mower.

When Robin heard of the plans, he had another idea. 'Pa bought a horse mower and it's very fast. Much easier than scythes! Would you like me to cut the grass? I could do it tomorrow and help you to harvest it, too. Ours has already been done; it's Pa's idea to cut the grass while it's still green. Takes more drying, though!'

Robin went off to get permission from his father, which he said was a mere formality, as a stranger came up the path. Bravely, Emma went to the door. Taking off his hat, the young man revealed a brown face and dark eyes. He smiled pleasantly as he said, 'The lady at the post office recommended your guest house, Miss Mason. Could I have a bed for a night or two? My name is Toby Jackson.'

'I will ask Miss Mason, Mr Jackson. I am the assistant housekeeper.' Emma turned and marched inside.

Sally invited the man in with her usual friendly smile and showed him to a room. He had no luggage apart from a small pack on his back. His purpose in taking the holiday was to experience country life and he hoped that Miss Mason would allow him to walk over the farm.

'I am afraid we're very busy this week, Mr Jackson. It's haytime, we cut the first meadow tomorrow. But I'll see what can be done.'

Mr Jackson ate hungrily, as the others had done, while talking to Simon about art. The two had much in common, both being amateur artists. Simon enjoyed the change of company but from the start, Emma felt uneasy about Mr Jackson. Unlike the first two young men, he looked at her a lot, which made her blush and he teased her: 'What will the assistant housekeeper do today?' he enquired at breakfast. 'May I call you Emma? You are a very pretty girl, young Emma.' His eyes roved over her figure in a most disconcerting way. Simon was engrossed in the *Yorkshire Post* and didn't notice. The table was cleared quickly and Emma escaped into the kitchen. She was thankful when she saw Mr Jackson go off down the village with his pack.

At supper that night, Mr Jackson was even more familiar and Simon did notice this time. He frowned and asked him politely to leave Emma alone. 'She is very shy, Mr Jackson, and doesn't like to be teased.'

'Nonsense! All young girls like to flirt a little. I mean no harm, Mr Drury!'

During the day, the meadow had been cut with the Scotts' new horse-drawn machine and Robin came in for a drink and a bite to eat before going home.

'What do you think to that?' he asked proudly, wiping the hayseeds from his sweaty face. Joe and George were the most impressed because of the hard work it had saved them.

'By, it's a grand outfit!' Joe beamed at Robin.

Sally was keen to plan the next stage. She explained the process to Emma, who remembered the first time she saw Sally the year before, bringing in the hay. 'We leave it in the sun for a day or two and then we turn the grass with hay forks – you know, the two-pronged ones in the barn? And hope for a breeze, and no rain. Then when the grass is nearly dry, we rake it into little mounds called haycocks. That makes it safer from the rain. We lead it when it's cured – bring it into the hay barn, that is.'

'You'll need plenty of helpers, Sal. Why doesn't Emma have a go?' Robin helped himself to a second scone. 'These fat rascals are good, who made 'em?'

'Emma made them, Robin ... but Emma might not like to help with the hay. It's hard work, very hot. She's not used to farm work, as we are.'

Sally was trying to look after her, as always. But Emma thought that it would be good to help Sally, when she needed it the most. 'I'd like to help, if you think I would be any good,' she said diffidently.

In two days, the grass was judged ready to turn and the haymakers took to the field. Martha volunteered to bring out their refreshment, which was all-important and much anticipated. So both Sally and Emma were free to work in the hayfield.

Emma was decked out in a large straw bonnet and advised to wear long sleeves against the sunburn. Feeling rather scared, she took the long hay fork. What had she let herself in for?

Robin was beside Emma and he showed her how to flip the swathe of grass over, to show the damp underside. 'And then, you can let it fall gently, like this...' and the breeze blew through the grass, as it fell lightly to earth. 'Every little helps, Emma. Every forkful you move is one less for someone else! So don't try to rush, just work at your own pace.'

The fork seemed heavy and soon Emma's hands were sore. But she persevered and after a while found a rhythm and began to feel that she could cope. Robin and Sally, Joe and George, were all doing the same thing, moving steadily across the field, leaving a trail of light green grass behind each fork.

After a couple of hours, it was time for the mid-morning break. Emma was slower than the others and her row was the last to be turned, but she was proud of the fact that she could keep going.

'Have some bait!' Joe said. There were many different names for the mid-morning snack. Emma sat thankfully on the ground, happy to drink cold tea and eat a scone. It was wonderful to sit down, even on the hard ground.

Robin came over to inspect Emma's hands. 'You need some salve on those blisters!' He gave her a pair of gloves to protect her hands. 'You're going very well, lass!' That was high praise.

All too soon, the workers took to the field again and this time it was harder for Emma. Her muscles and back ached and she fell further behind. She envied Sally for being able to move so easily and quickly across the field. After half an hour of steady work, Emma stopped to wipe her brow and noticed that the hay was turning colour, from light green to a deeper colour, as it dried in the sun. The scent of drying grass was sweet, holding the faint perfume of the meadow flowers. Clover, milkmaids, ladies' bedstraw were all mixed with the grass, in the gradual curing of the hay. Although the work was hard, Emma enjoyed the experience; the hayfield was framed with tall hedges, beyond which they could see a patchwork of fields and woods. From the distant workers came the faint sound of talking and laughter. It was a happy, peaceful scene.

The peace of the morning was soon broken, however. Emma saw a figure striding over the field to join them and her heart sank. It was Mr Jackson, evidently still eager to join in country life. She didn't think that he would appreciate the hard work of the hayfield, but if he wanted to join them he would have to sweat a little.

Sally gave the guest a fork and he took up

his position in the swathe next to Emma. 'So glad to join the merry peasants!' Emma thought there was something wolfish in his smile. Sally glanced at Emma and smiled; they had often discussed the patronizing way in which city people spoke of country folk.

Things went along quietly for a while and Mr Jackson concentrated on his task, managing the fork quite well. Perhaps her fears were groundless, Emma thought. But she found it impossible to work fast enough to draw away from him.

Gradually the other workers moved over the ridge and down the other side, lost to view. Only the amateurs, Emma and Toby Jackson, trailed behind, still going up the hill. Jackson looked up, saw the situation and grinned at Emma. 'This is what you've been waiting for! Dairymaids always like a bit of fun!' Jackson dropped his fork and came over to Emma. He grabbed her round the waist, threw her bonnet in the hedge and planted a kiss on her lips before she could resist.

Outraged, she fought back. Her boot came up and she kicked him hard in the shin.

Mr Jackson was amazed. 'What, don't you want a kiss? Oh, I see, playing hard to get! What fun! Of course, your sort do, it adds to the excitement!'

The man was pawing at her dress, trying

to unfasten the buttons. Emma hit him with a fist and he stopped for a moment. 'Don't be silly dear, we don't want an audience! Now, come here, and I'll teach you a few things, Miss Emma.'

'You stupid man, go away!' Emma's fury overcame her fear, and she kicked out again as hard as she could. 'Just because we live in the country, don't think we are simpletons!' She felt the panic rising, just as it had with Mr Steele. Jackson stared at her, still holding her as she struggled. 'I like to see a pretty girl in a rage! It becomes you, my dear!' He stood back a little, maintaining a grip with one hand on her dress.

'Do you not understand? You can't treat women like this!' Emma still held the hay fork in one hand. Should she use it?

Jackson laughed. 'I really thought that a bit of play was part of country life! Larks in the hayloft and all that! What's wrong with you modern girls?' He moved towards her again. With a ferocity that surprised herself, Emma jabbed the man in the leg with her hayfork. In pain, he yelled and let her go.

Robin had come back to look for Emma and saw what was happening. He charged over the hill at full speed and headed straight towards them, yelling as he came, waving his fork in a dangerous manner. 'Leave her alone! She's my girl. Stop, or I'll kill you!'

Jackson moved back 'These women, they lead you on and on a hot day, it's hard to resist! And then they pretend to be virtuous.' He leered at Emma. 'Hot little thing, isn't it? She loved it really, but she won't admit it!'

Emma was crimson with shame and rage. He lips were bruised and she felt soiled. She turned her back on Robin, picking up her bonnet from the hedge.

'Go away! Right now! And take yourself out of Thorpe and never come back!' Robin was quietly ferocious. 'Or I promise, I will break your neck!'

The man took himself off, muttering about ungrateful peasants who didn't know what was good for them.

Robin turned to Emma, who was buttoning up her dress, hot and dishevelled. What if Robin believed that she had led Jackson on? But Robin was his usual cheerful self, now that the threat was over. 'Come on, Emma. I should never have left you alone with him, it's my fault. This isn't the way we usually conduct our haymaking! Come over the hill and join the others. The beast didn't hurt you, did he? I saw you jab him, I hope it hurt!'

Emma was trying to take herself in hand. She felt shaky, but triumphant. She had not been a passive victim, she'd fought back. 'Thank you, Robin. The fork came in handy.

I never did like that man! But oh dear, I hope you didn't believe what he said about me!' Emma faltered and looked down in shame.

A quiet voice spoke in her ear. 'Nobody would believe that man, Emma!' Strong young arms went very gently around her, and Robin said softly, 'You've been treated so badly!' Automatically Emma tried to pull away, but Robin held her. 'Dear Emma, you have to know the difference. He was an enemy, but now you're with a friend. I really care about you. Do you not feel it?' His sun-tanned face, with brown eyes earnest behind his glasses, was close to hers.

'Robin, oh, yes ... I do. But – but – I am still afraid of men.' Emma made herself relax just a little in his arms. She began to feel safer.

Robin laughed. 'I'm not surprised! There are some horrible characters about. But I'm not any man, I'm Robin. You feel safe with me and I want to protect you. What shall we do now, lass? Do you want to go home?' He stroked her hair.

Emma stood up straight, as she had done to defend the Rules. 'We have hay to make for Sally and I want to help. Let's get on with the work, Robin.'

'Well done.' Robin approved and picked up their hayforks again.

'And ... lad!' She tried to speak lightly. 'I

care about you too, but I'm not sure that we can either of us forget my past, and be normal!' Emma felt near to tears. How could she have any sort of relationship with a man without remembering the hurt and the shame of the episode at Sheffield? And then, there was the tragedy of the little child she was not allowed to keep. She was a fallen woman, now. A bad alliance for a respectable family, and not even any sort of dowry, since her parents' fortune had disappeared.

Robin gave one of his carefree laughs. 'I shall be very happy to help you! But we can talk about that later.'

Robin and Emma picked up their forks and went back to turning the hay. As they worked, Robin talked quietly about the harvest, giving her time to recover. Just before they joined the others, he stopped and looked at Emma. 'I believe that with time, you'll feel as normal as anybody else. All you need is time.'

'I hope you're right, Robin.' Emma's muscles were screaming in protest, she had a torn dress and was exhausted, but she had never been so happy before as she was in the hayfield, that day.

SIXTEEN

'Simon, come with us as the last load goes in. We've something to celebrate, a really good harvest!' Sally bounced into the dining-room, where Simon was finishing a sketch. He looked up and there was something sad about the way he smiled at her that touched her heart.

'I'll bring the sketch pad,' he said quietly.

It was hard to know how she felt about Simon, Sally thought, as she walked with him out to the barn. He was so attentive, so loving to her and so vulnerable, too. She felt almost maternal towards him and her attachment to him was growing. But it was nothing at all like her feeling for Marcus, the Roman soldier. Marcus was a distant figure to her now, out of reach. She tried not to think of him, although her heart beat faster whenever a tall horseman rode by. Her loyalty was to the Masons, she reminded herself and to her beloved guest. Simon was part of the family now and Simon needed her thought and her care; she was pleased that she could give it to him.

In the last few weeks, Sally had seen the deterioration in her guest's health and the effort he made to conceal his weakness. Simon was brave, but he was fighting a losing battle. On her last visit, his mother had told Emma that she thought Simon was improving. 'He loves Thorpe so much, it must be doing him good!' And Emma had agreed, but quietly, while Simon had smiled and said nothing.

It was a warm evening and the sun was going down behind the moors, leaving a clear sky. 'How lovely the smell of fresh hay is! But harvesting must be very hard work, especially for you and Emma. I wish I could help you.' He brushed the fair hair out of his eyes.

'The fresh air will do you good. Now, let's bring out a stool for the artist to sit on.' Sally was determined to be bracing.

The soft light of dusk fell into the open fronted barn, where the last load of hay was being stacked. George was on the stack, because it was such a skilled job. Nobody wanted the embarrassment of a haystack that fell down through bad stacking. Traditionally, Sally should have been stacking as the official owner, but she was forking from the cart, throwing the hay over to Robin, who threw it up to George on high.

Simon was soon sketching, trying to record an impression of the busy scene. 'This is going to be a painting!' He seemed quite excited. 'Oils or watercolour, I'm not quite sure.' The workers paused for a rest and Simon made Robin pose with his fork for a sketch. 'You move too fast for me, just stand still for a moment, please.'

Robin looked over at Sally. 'Now, Sal, you've got some good hay in the barn! Next, I suggest that we go straight on and cut the second meadow!' He looked at Simon. 'Can I move now?'

There was a general groan at this; the others wanted a break from the gruelling field work, before starting again. But it all depended on the weather.

'What do you think of the weather, Joe?' Sally turned to her helper.

Joe shook his head. 'We've had a good run with this field, but I reckon weather's due for a change. We don't want wet hay, 'twill moulder and make the cattle cough.'

'And make us cough too,' Sally reminded him, thinking of her father's damaged lungs.

Robin moved impatiently. 'With our new machine, it can be cut so fast we'll have it made and home before the rain comes! Let's get on with it. I have a reason – Pa's promised to cut Salter's hay up at Bramley and I want to finish yours first, Sal.'

Reluctantly, Sally agreed that the meadow could be cut the next day. But as Robin cut the hay as fast as the horse would go, Sally wondered whether they were doing the right thing. The weather was dull, but fine. There was no breeze and no sparkle in the air, and for two days the hay lay limp and lifeless. Robin seemed to be there every two hours or so, looking at the hay and willing it to dry. 'I feel responsible!' he said to Emma.

Simon worked hard at his painting of the farmyard scene. The sketch was transferred to canvas, and he worked in oils. 'I want to catch the atmosphere: the evening light and the carts and the urgency of the harvest,' he explained to Sally.

On the third day they all turned the hay, working down the rows as before. Sally began to hope that the hay would be made before the rain, but George shook his head. And he was right, rain fell in the night and the crop was soaked. All that hard physical work had been for nothing, thought Sally, looking at her calloused hands.

A week later it was dry enough and the hay from the second field was taken into the barn, very different from the fragrant, dark green hay they had made earlier. 'We'd better keep it separate,' Sally decided. They stacked the hay where the breeze could blow through the barn, but it smelled warm when they had finished.

'It will finish curing in the stack.' Robin was optimistic as usual, and full of urgency.

This time, it was a quiet group of hay-makers who gathered in the kitchen for a cup of tea when all was finished, just before evening milking. Sally wanted to move the Motley Flock to the hayfield so that they could eat up any bits that were left behind.

'May I come with you?' asked Robin. Rather surprised, Sally agreed and they went down the green lane to fetch the sheep. 'I want to talk to you, Sally.' Robin looked more serious than usual.

'About Australia, I suppose?' Sally watched the sheep as they clustered round her.

'Well, in a way. I want your advice. About Emma, and whether you think I'd better leave her alone for a year or two, or talk to her now about the future. She's young I suppose, but she's growing up fast.'

Sally stopped in the lane, and stared at him. 'Robin, are you – do you want to take her with you to Australia? Oh, my!' She must have been blind, or too bound up with her own emotions, to notice the interest Robin had been taking in Emma in the months since she'd been rescued from the river. Suddenly, she could see it. And Emma had asked her whether Robin was her particular friend...

'I don't think so, it would be too rough for a little lass like Emma. But if I go, Ma wants me to try it just for a year or two, and then come home. She says the only folks who settle there are the ones who can't afford land in England.'

So Robin had told his family at last. Sally

was still trying to recover from the shock he'd given her. Little Emma, who'd been almost like a daughter to her, thinking of getting married!

'If you want my advice, I think you and Emma should talk to each other and work things out. If she wants more time – and you know, she had a terrible ordeal in Sheffield – your trip to Australia could give her breathing space.' Sally wished she felt as calm as she sounded.

Robin nodded. 'We've had very little time together, as you know. But our evenings round your piano have been wonderful.'

'But if you want to marry Emma and your family can get over the social stigma, why not do it now, and take one of the Scott farms? She's a wonderful housekeeper, and you should both be happy!'

Wincing, Robin opened the gate to let in the sheep. 'Well, yes, but she has a history, of course, through no fault of her own, poor mite. My folks are a bit worried about that. But if we leave it for a few years, that should really be history, don't you think? Or we could go up to Durham; Pa has a farm or two up there. And nobody there would know anything about Emma's past.'

As they left the sheep happily nibbling the wisps of hay, Sally looked at Robin. 'Seventeen isn't really too young, you know! But I'll be sorry to lose Emma.' She hesitated. 'I probably shouldn't say this, it's not my business. But your father might have a talk to Emma one day, about her parents' property. The Bellamys seem to have taken it over, but of course she has no proof. No deeds, or anything like that.'

'Pa might talk to her solicitor, for a start,' Robin said thoughtfully. 'I don't think it would do any harm for Pa to know she came from a good family!'

Sally smiled at him. 'Of course not! But even better, it would give Emma confidence to have an income of her own. She's been quietly worried about the future, you know.'

Back in the farmyard, the cows were swinging into the milking shed, and there leaning on the gate was Sol Bartram. Sally's heart sunk.

'Hay's a bit near, innit?' He sniffed at a handful and threw it down. 'Led too soon, that's what I say. Evening, Mr Scott.'

Robin was about to speak when the bull ran past him, having decided not to go into the shed with the cows. He left them to turn the animal into the shed, and Sally moved away. But Sol followed her.

'And I must say, you're a forward piece!' He leered at Sally.

'What do you mean, Mr Bartram?' Sally could feel her temper rising.

'Having a disagreement with young Mr Radford, in the middle of Kirkby the other day! Stopping his horse in the middle of the street – what did you have in mind? You can't do owt round here without being seen, you know!'

Sally, her face fiery, walked abruptly into the milking shed, leaving Sol in the yard. When she looked out later, he had gone.

The next day, the smell of warm hay hung over the farmyard and the second crop turned a light brown. During the night, Sally woke, smelling smoke. She looked out and could see flames coming from the hay shed. She had heard that damp hay could heat up until it caught fire, but it was hard to imagine. The hay had been warm, but not hot when they went to bed. She was horrified. This was her precious winter feed for the animals. Trying not to panic, Sally went across the landing and called Emma. Whispering so as not to wake Simon, she asked the girl to go across the green to fetch George and then dressed hurriedly. Where were all the buckets? Some in the scullery, some on the stone slab outside the dairy. There was a big pump in the yard and a trough for watering the stock.

First of all, Sally primed the pump, filled the stone trough and found as many buckets as she could. Then she found the beaters, and tried to stamp out the flames. The haystack was burning at one end, which was strange if this was a case of spontaneous combustion. The middle of the stack would be the hottest, wouldn't it?

Soon Sally was joined by Emma, with Martha and George, and they formed a chain to pass buckets of water across the yard to the fire, working as fast as they could. By the eerie glow from the flames, they could see each other scrambling about. Moll, the old dog, set up a panic barking, but no animal was in danger. In summer, the cattle always slept in the fields.

After a few minutes, the water started to take effect. The flames gradually lessened and thick smoke hid the fire from view. Turning, Sally found Simon beside her in the gloom. 'You shouldn't be here!' she called. 'Simon, please go back to the house!' Exertion like this could kill him, weak as he was. Simon coughed and passed her a bucket of water. 'I want to help you all, Sally.'

'Go and fetch a lantern, then! We'll soon be in the dark when the fire dies right down.'

The young man brought out two lanterns and hung them in the yard near the water pump, which improved the operation considerably. Then he joined the bucket chain again. The buckets of water got heavier as the night wore on, but eventually the fire fighters could see that they were winning. Simon worked beside Sally, passing buckets with the rest, his face pale, but with a look of joy. 'I've always wanted to get out here and help you when you needed me, girl,' he whispered to Sally as he passed her a bucket. 'This is my dream come true.'

'I do appreciate it, Simon,' Sally panted, as she passed him the next time. 'But I wish you wouldn't. It could be bad for your heart.'

'Bugger my heart, to quote Joe!' Simon was unrepentant. 'Just for once, I'm a real man!' In fact, Simon was a great asset; the more hands the better, in a fire. Sally and Emma, George and Martha were doing their best, but there was no time to run for more help. Joe lived at the other end of the village, too far away. So Simon took his place in the chain, knowing that he was needed.

It took them two hours to put out the fire and when they gathered in the kitchen for a drink of tea, George's face was grim. 'Hay was a bit damp, but not that damp.' He passed a weary hand over his brow. 'I doubt it would have gone up on its own.' There was a silence as George took a deep swig of tea. 'That fire was deliberately lit. I found a tin of paraffin on the ground outside the barn. And I'll wager that Joe wouldn't have left it lying about.'

They all knew that the methodical Joe was obsessively tidy about the farmyard and especially careful with lamps and oil. There had been cases of stable fires over the years. They'd heard of a recent one, when a lamp fell into a pile of straw at Kirkby. After that fire, Joe had warned Sally several times of the danger and made her take all lamps out of farm buildings after work was finished.

George went out and returned with the container. It could have been bought at the village shop, Sally realized, because she had seen them there. But at Badger's Gill they always bought oil in larger amounts. This tin did not belong to Sally. She remembered Sol Bartram jeering in the yard the night before and shuddered. 'Sol was here at milking time.' She looked at the others.

Martha shook her head. 'I always said he wanted this farm. He's trying to force you out lass, by one means or another!'

George spoke slowly as he said, 'If I could prove that Sol Bartram torched this here hay, I'd–'

Martha interrupted him quickly. 'You'd tell PC Brown, that's what you'd do!'

George subsided. 'Aye, and that would be the end of it. Masterly inactivity, that's what doctor says PC Brown is good for.'

What can you do against hatred like that, thought Sally. You can lock up your house maybe, but nobody can lock up a farm. For the first time, Sally wondered whether Sol had waged a long campaign against the Masons. Some of the misfortunes that occurred in her father's time could have been deliberate. It was a chilling thought.

There was no rejoicing at Badger's Gill the next day. They had beaten the fire and saved most of the mediocre second crop. But Simon had collapsed. Sally felt guilty, although she knew she'd done her best to keep him away from the fire. And Simon had worked beside them as one of the team and he had been happy. It was what he had wanted. But what had it done to his precarious health?

He'd been there when they had the tea, sitting in the corner of the kitchen. They were all tired, so nobody noticed how quiet Simon was. And the suggestions of arson had shocked them all, distracting their attention. George and Martha went home and Sally walked with them to the gate. 'How can I thank you?'

'Say nowt, you'd do the same for us. You're our fire insurance now!' George joked grimly. They all knew that George's house had an old 'Sun Alliance' fire mark on the wall, but that it was no use waiting for a fire engine to plod up the hills from Ripon. Villagers had to help each other, just as they always had.

Emma carried water to the bedrooms for them all to wash in. Coming back to the kitchen, she found that Simon was slumped in his chair, with one hand clutching his chest. 'Help me upstairs, Emma,' he mumbled. 'The pain is quite bad.' It was the first time he had mentioned the pain, although Sally could sometimes tell when it came. The doctor had explained that heart pains and probably headaches were a part of the condition.

It took Sally and Emma some time to get Simon to bed. Sally wanted to call the doctor immediately, but Simon asked her to wait until morning. He dutifully swallowed his medicine and a glass of water and said he would sleep. The next morning, Simon was too weak to get out of bed. The doctor tried to conceal his impatience; his orders had been disregarded. Absolute rest and no visitors was the prescription. But Sally thought she should send for his mother.

'You can't tell with heart patients,' the doctor told her. 'Most unpredictable. He might recover from this bout, let's hope so.' He couldn't be sure whether Simon had made his condition worse by helping to put out the fire. Emma volunteered to send a telegram to Simon's parents and sped up the street to the post office.

With his pale gold hair and almost transparent skin, Simon looked fragile, propped up on pillows. Sally sat beside him, holding his hand and trying not to cry. If only she'd taken more time to insist he kept away from the fire!

Simon had something on his mind. 'Would you bring up my painting from downstairs, Sally dear?'

'Of course!' And Sally went down to the dining-room, where the painting of the hay scene was propped on an easel. To her surprise, it was finished. He must have put in many hours in the couple of weeks since the drawing was done. They were all there, Sally and George, Martha in the background, and Robin with fork poised. Emma was carrying a jug of water. And in the bottom corner there was a small figure on a stool, painting the scene: the artist himself, included in the group as part of the team, just as he wanted to be.

'You're in there too – like the artists in their medieval paintings!' Sally was absorbed in the picture.

Simon looked at his work with satisfaction. 'That's about as near as I've ever been to getting it right. I'm so glad you like it, my darling. Now, how about a frame? Is there anyone in Thorpe that can make a picture frame?'

Sally knew that Mr Dean, the local joiner could frame pictures. And Simon wanted to see him right away and to choose the wood. 'There's no hurry, lad. Wait till you feel better,' Sally advised.

The young man shook his head. 'Immediately, if not sooner,' he said, quoting one of their jokes. 'It's for you, Sally. I want to give you your farm. Something to keep for the rest of your life.'

Sally had no words. She leaned across the bed and kissed him on the cheek.

'Now, I wonder whether the frame should be gilt? A gilt frame sets off a painting very well.' Simon lay back, evidently exhausted. 'There is symbolism in every painting, you know,' he said obscurely.

Mr Dean was happy to oblige and came straight away with Sally to measure up the painting. He might have a frame to suit, and in any case, he had some gold paint. It was lucky that he could do the job straight away. Carrying it out carefully, Mr Dean admired the painting. 'Why, that's young Robin Scott! Very lifelike, Mr Drury.'

Simon could not eat and drank only water. He asked Sally to brush his hair, because it hurt him to raise an arm above his head.

While Joe cleared up the debris from the fire and Emma kept the household going, Sally stayed with Simon. There was little said, because Sally knew how tired he felt. She went to close the bedroom curtains, but Simon stopped her. 'Let the sunshine in!'

Sally brought a fragrant bunch of sweet peas in a vase and set it on the table where he could see it. The delicate scent filled the room and the colours of the flowers glowed in the sunlight. Simon smiled his thanks. The afternoon wore on, with no change in Simon's condition. At times he slipped into an uneasy sleep. Sally heard Joe calling the cows in for milking and the clatter of milking pails from the shed. Emma brought her a cup of tea, glancing at the sleeping Simon. 'Can I bring him anything?' Sally shook her head.

Simon woke from a sleep and Sally saw he was watching her. 'I'd like to tell you something.' His voice was low, but clear. For a moment Sally thought he might be beginning to recover. 'Emma talked to me one day, about her life. Does that surprise you?'

'It does, in a way. She doesn't usually talk to anyone, but she feels safe with you, Simon.'

There was a faint smile. The grey eyes were fixed once more on Sally's face. 'She was saying how incredibly lucky we both are, that fate has led us to Badger's Gill.'

'It's I who is lucky, to have such dear friends sent to me by fate!' Sally replied.

'But we were both in need of – your sort of care. And we came as paying guests, but it was much more than a business transaction right from the start.' The pleasant voice was growing weaker. 'Sally, you not only saved Emma's life, you gave her a life and a future. You are so generous, so loving. You've made a difference to me. I want you to be happy, my dearest. To be loved by someone you love – oh, I've imagined your little red-haired children! Thank you, Sally, for everything.'

There was quiet in the room after that.

Mr Dean came back at five with the painting in a gilt frame. He explained that he'd looked through a few old frames in his shed, eventually finding this one that fitted perfectly. Sally was amazed. The finished painting, in its frame, looked even better than she had first thought.

When the joiner had gone, Simon gazed at the painting for a long time. Then he took Sally's hand and placed it on the frame. 'Dear Sally, keep this and remember me. It's a token of my gratitude, for making me happy. You have given me independence from my family, something every man needs, eventually. And a home, a place of peace and friendship. And – just a little love?' He looked into her eyes. 'You know how much I love you.'

'Oh, Simon. I don't deserve such praise. Yes, I give you love.'

With a visible effort, he held out his arms to Sally. And she, sensing his need, sat on the bed beside him and cradled him in her arms. Sighing, he nestled into her shoulder like a tired child. 'I want to be with you.'

For a long time Sally held him, loving him like a child in need of security. Gradually, his breathing ceased. Gently Simon seemed to float away from her, until she knew that he was gone, to where there was no more pain.

SEVENTEEN

'I know what it is; it's the Mason girl that's bothering you. Well, take it from me, lad, it'd never work.' Oliver looked at his son and Marcus detected a rough sympathy. They were dining together once again at Nidd Grange and Marcus had tried unsuccessfully to pretend a cheerfulness he did not feel. No matter how he tried, Marcus could not imagine a future for himself and Sally. There was her paying guest, for one thing, getting in the way, charming her no doubt with his good looks. Why would a young man stay at Thorpe? He should be out earning a living, thought Marcus, who did not approve of the idle rich. The Radfords were reasonably rich but they were never idle. And even if she didn't love the lodger, Sally was a fiercely independent Mason and Marcus was still a Radford – and not ashamed of it. There was a wide chasm between the families. Could a bridge ever be built?

Oliver was still watching him and Marcus felt obliged to reply. 'You think so, Father?' He wasn't going to admit that he agreed.

'Look at it like this, Marcus. Imagine telling your son that one of his great-grandfathers had murdered another one! Think of that now. Or even worse, somebody else telling him the story!'

Marcus said nothing. His father had guessed how he felt, but that didn't help at all.

Oliver sat back in his chair. 'Tell you what, I'll give you plenty to think about to take your mind off things. You can sort out Greystones at Dallagill for me; it's in a mess. My fault, I know. But you can handle it. It's up to you, lad!'

His father had recently taken over one of their farms when a tenancy fell vacant, but the manager he'd chosen was not up to the job. The manager had left and someone was urgently needed to supervise the foreman, so that they could catch up on the work before winter. Marcus sighed, but he agreed.

The ploy worked, up to a point. In spite of himself, Marcus started to make notes and plan and Oliver kept thinking of new tasks for him. 'We could sell most of the Greystones cattle, they're not up to much, and start again. You've a good eye for a beast, you can restock the farm for me.'

Even as Marcus swung into the saddle in the stable yard, Oliver had another distracting thought for him. 'And while you're doing the rounds, keep an ear open for any news of poachers. We've lost a lot of pheasant lately.

There was a rumour of a gang last year, selling them in Leeds.'

Oliver was fond of a little shooting and he kept a gamekeeper to control vermin and organize the shoots for himself and his friends. Some of the game was sold to pay the man's wages, so losses were not welcome. It was often a case of outwitting the men who wanted to steal the game. 'But don't take any risks, mind,' warned his father as Marcus rode off to Greystones, the new plan in his pocket. 'You don't want to get yourself hit on the head!'

The wood was gloomy under a dark, threatening sky. Marcus had used this path often in the last few weeks and today his mind was still on the problems of the farm in Dallagill and how he could solve them. The urgent priority was to trim the flock's neglected feet. A thousand sheep multiplied by four represented four thousand little hooves to be inspected, cleaned, trimmed and dipped in bluestone.

The path through Foxholes Wood was the quickest way to get to the farm. At first he'd thought about the murder every time he went through, but in the absence of any word of Sally or any new information, the mystery had crept to the back of his mind. You can get used to anything, Marcus thought wryly when he realized that he'd got used to Foxholes Wood.

Haytime had given way to harvest, it was nearly the end of summer. Marcus still thought about Sally and she was the first thing he saw in his mind's eye, when he woke in the morning. But every day, his thoughts came back to the barriers between them. You couldn't live your whole life with divided loyalties. He wished he could forget the lass and take up with someone else. Miss Russell of Masham? Perish the thought! He'd do a lot to please Oliver, but not marry Miss Russell.

Thunder rolled around the wood and a gusty wind blew through the trees. He'd have to hurry to get to the farm before the rain came. 'Well, at least we've got the oats in safely, that's one blessing ... what's that?' Marcus pulled up his horse when he saw a gleam of white by the side of the track. It was a newly broken branch. And through the gap behind it, Marcus could see something that had been hidden from him before, a faint path winding off through the trees. He pulled out his watch. He could spare an hour, no more. But he remembered Oliver's mention of poaching. This wood was the perfect place for poachers to hide.

Following the path was not easy on a horse and Marcus soon dismounted, leading Odin, his favourite bay, who followed meekly behind. This was a footpath, not a bridle path, and so faint that he almost lost it in the gloom. Strange that he'd never noticed it before, when he'd been searching for clues to the mystery. A few large rain drops spattered on the leaves and a flash of lightning made the horse tremble. It would have been easier to leave Odin behind, but the horse might bolt if he became really frightened. So Marcus pressed on, leading Odin, trying to reassure him with comforting words.

Was he in danger? It depended, he thought, on what sort of poachers they were, supposing he came across them. The local lads who pinched a pheasant or two for a lark were likely to know who he was and try to bluff their way out of it. They were the boys who crept up on roosting pheasants in the dark and grabbed them from behind. Or sometimes they put out raisins soaked in rum, if they could afford it and then captured the poor intoxicated birds as they staggered about. There were many ways of catching pheasants and Marcus knew some of them.

The birds were low fliers and often quite tame, having been raised by gamekeepers and then released in the woods. But the dangerous face of poaching was a different story. There were organized gangs from the towns, likely to be armed, who made money from selling game belonging to other people. They faced a jail sentence if they were caught and they were not going to give up easily.

The rain came suddenly, in sheets. Peering

through the gloom, Marcus could just make out the outline of a stone building. He tied Odin to a tree and went to see whether they could shelter from the storm. There was a cottage in front of him, old, neglected, crumbling. No sign of life.

It might offer shelter, but it looked as though the roof would leak. It must have been abandoned years ago, by the way that trees had grown up in the neglected little garden. But when Marcus lifted the latch and pushed open the door it swung easily, without a creak. There was light inside.

Marcus found himself in a big kitchen. A man was by the fire, an old man, big but bent with age, his thin features expressing shock and extreme displeasure. He looked up from stirring a black pot. 'Who the hell are you? What are you doing here?'

They were natural enough questions in the circumstances. Marcus himself was taken aback and the voice was totally unexpected in this wild spot. It was deep, educated, a voice of authority. It reminded Marcus forcibly of his headmaster, long ago at school. 'I'm sorry, sir. I was looking for shelter from the storm and I didn't know you were here. It looked like a ruin.' He wiped the water from his face and brushed off his coat.

'Timmy! Sam! Come here!' The big man wasted no time on pleasantries. 'What shall we do with him?'

Two young men came into the kitchen from another room. Three to one it is now, Marcus thought.

The old man straightened slowly and bent his deep-set eyes on Marcus. The lads gazed at him unflinchingly. They were gypsy-brown, with wild hair and beards and Marcus could not place them. A blinding flash of lightning lit up the room, followed immediately by a crack of thunder. Marcus stood there in silence, standing straight, waiting for them to make the next move. He looked into the old man's eyes but could read nothing.

'String him up by his heels until he squeals?' the dark lad suggested helpfully.

'Slice him up and pop him in the pot?' The other young man waved a knife.

Marcus looked round, but nobody was smiling. Outside the rain beat down harder than ever. His wet coat was beginning to steam in the heat from the fire. These two were not professional poachers, Marcus decided as he looked again at the young men. And the old man looked and sounded just like an academic. He was too old for poaching, in any case.

'I'm looking for poachers,' Marcus said conversationally.

'Aha!' The one with the knife flourished it like a cutlass and then laughed. 'I know you, Mr Radford. You won't remember me, or

Tim here. We come from Foxholes Farm up the back yonder. We're Barkers, Tim and Sam. Anybody who poaches game in this wood will catch it from us!'

'I remember two little lads at Foxholes. My word, haven't you grown!' Marcus felt he needed to get the upper hand.

The old man came forward. 'Mr Radford. Well, well. My name's Vernon.'

'He's Professor Vernon, you might have heard of him.' Tim Barker seemed proud of his friend.

'Not the medical Professor Vernon? I have indeed.' Marcus was impressed, having heard of the professor from his friend Harry, who'd studied medicine at Leeds. 'I believe you have saved a lot of lives, sir.' Harry had studied under this man, who had the reputation of a tyrant but was revered for his kindness to the poor and his immense knowledge of the heart and blood circulation.

The old man coughed and looked away. 'Long time ago. I'm retired, more or less. Would you like to stay and eat? The boys have made a good rabbit stew and we were just about to taste it. Take your coat off Radford, it will dry out by the fire.' The professor was rather more gracious now that he had accepted a reason for the visit.

Sitting at the table, Marcus looked round the room. Although from the outside the cottage had looked decayed, almost derelict, inside it was clean and neat. There was a clinical orderliness about the rows of bottled plums on the shelves and the kitchen table was scrubbed to whiteness. Bunches of dried herbs hung from the ceiling.

'Very good stew, thank you!' Marcus found that he was hungry. The stew contained potatoes, carrots and peas, and large chunks of meat in a thick gravy.

Tim passed him a hunk of bread. 'Sourdough, the professor makes it – just like the pioneers in America. You keep some of the dough and add it to the next batch.'

Marcus looked at the young men. 'I suppose this is your land, Barkers' land. But why is this place so well hidden? I've never spotted the path before and I come this way fairly often.' Marcus was still trying to work out what they were all doing there, in the middle of a wood.

'This cottage and the few acres round it belong to the professor.' Tim looked up briefly. 'He's our neighbour – been here for a long time.' There was a silence, while Sam handed round mugs of strong black tea.

'I've been using this place as a sort of retreat since I was a young man. Very private, to get away from the stresses of my work.' The professor looked into the fire. 'And the Barkers are good to me. They supply food and keep an eye on the place when I'm not

303

here. These lads are very helpful, although you wouldn't think it from their appearance.'

Marcus looked at him thoughtfully. 'And so you've kept it hidden, all these years?'

'I have, and I'd be grateful if you would keep quiet about it!' There was a gleam in the old man's eye.

The Barker boys went off as soon as the rain stopped and Marcus stood up to leave at the same time, remembering his duties at Greystones. Valuable time had already been lost. But as the lads went out Marcus also remembered that the professor said he'd been coming here for a long time. Could he know something about the murder? He hesitated, wondering what to say.

'They're good lads, the young Barkers.' The professor watched them go off, smiling. 'But their mother doesn't approve of me, which is why they like to come here. Rebellious youth!' He stood for a moment, looking undecided.

Marcus made for the door and the Professor appeared to make up his mind. 'Can you spare a few more minutes, Radford? I feel we should have a talk.' He looked suddenly very old and rather frail. He sat down in a chair near the fire and looked into the fire in silence for a while. He seemed to be struggling as if not knowing how to begin.

Marcus too kept silent, waiting for what came next. When nothing more was said, he ventured a question. 'Would you be able to help to clear up an old mystery, connected with this wood?'

The professor swung round to face him. 'I knew it would happen, some time or other. You're a Radford. You want to know what happened to your grandfather, it would be. Yes, I know something about it. I haven't long to go now, and I've been thinking that the truth should be told.'

Marcus sat very still. 'What is the truth, Professor?'

The deep voice dropped lower. 'I killed him.' There was silence, except for the drip of the rain from the roof.

After a while, the old man seemed to pull himself together. 'My defence is that I did not intend to kill him. I conducted experiments in those days, for the good of mankind you might say. Yes, some of my discoveries have saved lives, as you remarked earlier. Radford died ... I couldn't save him. But I learned from him.'

'Would you like to tell me how it came about? I am desperately interested, Professor. There's a lot at stake, for me.' Marcus found he was leaning forward.

Vernon leaned back in his chair, considering. 'It must be fifty years ago. I was quite young. But how does it affect you, now?'

It was time to tell the truth. 'Billy Radford's companion, Richard Mason, survived.

You'll know that. And he was blamed for the disappearance of his friend. The two families were bitterly divided. And,' Marcus plunged on, 'I want to marry a Mason.'

'Ah. The toils of love.' The professor looked amused.

How could he be so detached? 'Well, whatever happened, why did you not come forward and admit it? How could you live with the guilt?' Marcus kept his voice level.

'I don't believe in guilt. I'm a pagan, you see. Pagans believe in life!' The old voice had a ring to it. 'In trying to preserve life in others, I caused the death of young Radford. In a way he helped me to help others. But he had a defective heart ... congenital. How's your heart, young man?'

Almost broken, thought Marcus wryly. 'Normal, I believe. But how do you know?'

'I performed a post-mortem examination, of course. Found great restriction of the heart, which was why my treatment killed him.'

'But you didn't report the death – evidently it was accidental – and free Mason from blame!' Marcus felt revulsion. This man was inhuman.

'The pagan way. My life, my survival. It was of course most irregular to experiment on people like that. To confess would probably have ruined my career, but it wouldn't bring the man back to life. So I made sure that Mason could remember nothing. He was heavily drugged for three days, you see.'

'And then?'

'I took off for a while, put some distance between me and Foxholes. I put the body down a mineshaft on Pateley moor, there are plenty round there as you'll know, and went off on Radford's horse to Liverpool. It was the long vacation. And nobody knew I'd been here.' He looked at Marcus. 'I owe you a horse, young man.'

Marcus let out a long sigh. 'You have freed us from the old quarrel, Professor.' His analytical mind took over. 'Would you like to tell me precisely what happened?'

The other man stood up stiffly and put another piece of wood on the fire. 'I think we need a cup of coffee, after all this. Well, I was working at the time with two drugs that could be grown here, in the wood. Aconite and foxglove, to give them their common names.'

'But aconite's monkshood, isn't it? A deadly poison?'

'Of course. Many useful medicines are also poisons, Radford.' The professor paused with the kettle in his hand. 'Both drugs affect the heart, which was my specialization, you see. Foxglove is also the antidote to aconite, but it's slow to act. Oh, it's been known for centuries, but I felt there was more to be learned and I grew the plants here. I tried them on animals, with varied results. And then I decided to experiment on people ... and I met the two young men as they rode through the wood. It was near to the summer solstice, I recall.'

Again, Marcus caught the gleam of fire in the old man's eyes. He was trying to imagine the scene: Mason and Radford, on their way to buy sheep, met this man in the wood. Why would they agree to take his potions? But then, he'd just eaten the rabbit stew! He could easily have been poisoned, himself.

'It was a warm day and I'd made some nettle beer. I invited them into the cottage. And to be honest, I then asked them if they would take part in an experiment, which I described as harmless.' The professor shook his head. 'Radford might still be alive, if he'd had a normal heart. How was I to know that I'd picked the wrong man?'

My grandfather, dying here from poison, thought Marcus ... he'd wanted the truth, but it was ugly.

'And so,' the professor continued, 'I decided to change my outlook. The death affected me, shocked me. I made up my mind that Radford's memory would be honoured by my career. Instead of going for fame and fortune, I decided to be a true pagan, truly life affirming. I worked for nothing if patients couldn't pay. And I put my utmost into research, worked with the top men in the field. We've moved a long way in the last fifty years.' He gestured at the kettle, but Marcus shook his head.

'You haven't described what actually happened.'

The professor looked at him. 'You wouldn't understand the medical terms. But simply, I dosed them with aconite and observed the effects and then gave them foxglove, which among other things makes the patient see the world coloured blue.'

Here was the proof Marcus had been looking for. The newspaper report had mentioned that Mason said, 'everything was blue'. He had been recovering from the dose ... after missing three days. 'So my grandfather was badly affected?'

'He went into a coma. I was horrified by what I'd done. No guilt, I have no time for guilt. But I am pleased that you came here, Radford. It's too late to vindicate Mason; I believe he died some years ago. But it is important for you to know the truth.' The professor leaned back wearily.

Marcus wondered how many other people had unwittingly died in the name of science. And he felt a deep gratitude for the knowledge that Radford and Mason had both been victims. There was no need after all for a feud between the families. Mason had suffered for the rest of his life for a crime he did not commit, but reproaches were useless now and the less said, the better. He sighed and stood up; it was time to go back to the normal world.

'You can go now Radford, I wish to sleep. And you can tell your family what you have learned, on condition that it goes no further. And the Mason lady, of course.'

Marcus picked up his coat and went outside, glad to be in the fresh air. After the storm the sky had a clean, swept look and the wet leaves of the wood glistened in the sun. Odin was still tied to his tree, none the worse and fairly dry. He seemed to be as glad as Marcus was to creep back to the track and then to go swiftly out of the wood and back into the everyday farming world again.

Marcus didn't know what to think. The professor's story had cleared Richard Mason from blame, putting at rest the nagging feeling that he and Sally would always have that shadow between them. But there were many problems left. The fair young man, for one, he'd probably got himself engaged to Sally by now. And the fact that she was so devoted to her farm that she'd probably never want to leave it.

As he rode up to Greystones Marcus wondered how his father would take the news. But for the next week he was not able to share the secret with anyone, although he thought about it a great deal. He was tied up with work, first at Greystones and then at his base in Colsterdale and was not able to see Oliver. Surely, he thought, Father won't want to carry on the feud after this? The Masons are not homicidal liars after all. Richard, with his life blighted, was almost as much of a victim as poor Billy. There was of course still the old boy's reluctance to meet Sally. But even so, as the days went by and he was able to digest the strange story, Marcus found himself feeling more hopeful. If only Sally were still free!

One day his friend Harry came up to see him and Marcus questioned him about what poisonous plants may be grown in cottage gardens and their possible effect on the heart.

'Many an old herb woman could tell you, my boy. But who d'you want to poison?' Harry laughed.

Marcus said hurriedly that it was an academic interest, some detective story he'd read. And he led the conversation round to aconite and foxglove, and what he heard confirmed the professor's statements.

'You've got foxgloves growing wild round here beside every stone wall! Can't avoid 'em! I believe the gypsies use them to make a potion to liven up their parties, but I wouldn't fancy it myself.'

'And is it used in medicine?'

'As digitalin, yes. It's very useful. Increases

muscle activity, contracts arteries, raises blood pressure. It was scientifically established long before my time of course. That prof I used to quote to you was involved in the later research.'

Marcus decided not to mention the fact that he'd met the prof himself. 'I wonder whether the foxglove plant would poison sheep? We sometimes have mysterious deaths, when there's not much grass about.'

The two friends enjoyed a walk over the moor and a good dinner and Marcus began to feel more normal than he'd felt all summer. He went whistling into the kitchen one day and Jeanie remarked on it. 'Got our spirits back again, have we? That's the way, Mr Marcus! No good being old and grumpy before your time!'

'Who says I've been grumpy?' Marcus demanded irritably, and then laughed. 'Well, we've been busy ever since winter, haven't we? And it will soon be winter again!'

That was the core feeling on the High Side, the reason that few people were light-hearted. Winter always came again; the brief summer was full of toil before another winter. But sometimes in autumn there were golden days when the pressure eased a little and folks could enjoy the fairs and shows, and find a little joy in life, after all. There was plenty of good food, fruits and vegetables in the gardens. Marcus believed that a good diet affected people's spirits considerably. But then, so did a little hope for the future.

The chance to move things along came quite soon, when Marcus was asked to visit his father at the end of the week. He would stay at Nidd overnight and have another talk to Oliver.

EIGHTEEN

Sally Mason and Emma Wakefield attended Simon's funeral in their best black, travelling by train to Bradford, apprehensive about meeting his parents again. Sally wished passionately that she had sent for them earlier. She knew what it was like when someone you loved died without saying goodbye, and they had arrived too late.

It was a relief to find that although they were sad, the Drury family had been prepared for this. 'In one way, I feel guilty, because we gave you the responsibility,' Mrs Drury said to Sally. 'But we did it for Simon, of course. He wanted to feel more independent but then, he couldn't travel, or live on his own. Your farm was the best solution and he was happy. That's what matters.'

Sally was surprised at the depth of her

grieving for Simon. He'd only been at the farm for a few months after all, but he was a part of their lives, and the house seemed empty without him. Whenever she saw a beautiful tree or a typical country scene, Sally found herself thinking of Simon and how he would have enjoyed the late summer days. For a while, Sally almost lost her enthusiasm for the farm but with an effort, she decided to do something different. This year, they would compete in the Kirkby Agricultural Show.

'It's about time Badger's Gill showed some stock again!' George chided her one day, when he delivered a load of turnips for winter feed. 'Your pa was always keen, sometimes he won a prize. And your ma used to do well with the butter, remember. Is there 'owt worthwhile in that cowshed of yours?'

Sally was sure that George was just trying to cheer her up, but she went in with him to where Joe was tying up the cows for evening milking.

'Aye, of course we have some good home bred stuff. That there cow,' Joe indicated Primrose with a nod of his head, 'she's a real winner. It's just my opinion, of course. And she's that quiet, I could walk her to Kirkby for the show. Let's have a go, miss. Enter her for any class you like.' Joe was as loyal to Badger's Gill as if he'd worked there all his life.

Primrose was a Shorthorn, a roan cow with a sunny disposition and a huge appetite. When Emma heard the talk about the show, she asked to see this potentially prize-winning animal. 'What's so special about Primrose?' she asked, standing at a respectful distance. Emma was still not sure about cows, Sally noticed.

'Just look at her from the side, she's a perfect wedge shape!' Emma could see the potential now that Joe pointed it out. Primrose had horns with an outward, even curve; she had smooth, silky skin with a dappled effect of white and brown. Her head was small which she carried proudly and she had large, clear eyes.

'A picture of a cow,' was George's verdict. 'But then, we don't know what she'll be up against.'

'She'll need teaching to walk round on a halter. I'll do that,' Joe offered promptly. 'I'll make a new halter for the lass.'

Sally was surprised how the prospect of the show brightened them up, made them keen to succeed. Competition must be good for you, she decided. But she wasn't too hopeful; there were many experienced breeders in the large parish of Kirkby. And then there were a few landowners who could afford to buy the best cattle in the county and proceed to take the credit.

The grain harvest was under way at

Badger's Gill; the oats had been stooked and were standing out in the fields, allowing the grain to ripen. 'They have to hear the church bells three times, that means they'll be in the stooks for three weeks to dry out,' Joe reminded Sally. There was time to get the oats in before the show, unless the weather changed. Oats were never sold, they were kept to feed all the farm stock through the winter. But the quality was important, especially for horses.

'The Kirkby Show's timed to follow the harvest and come before the cold weather, when the work is easing up a little before the winter,' Sally explained to Emma. And she suggested that the methodical Emma might like to try making a batch of butter for the show, to be judged against the High Side's best. 'There is a number on each brick, so the judges don't know whose they are. Why not have a go?' Sally was keen for Emma to be involved.

Robin added his encouragement to Sally, when he heard of the idea. 'Middle of September, we'll all have finished harvest by then. You'll enjoy the day out, Emma, and if your butter doesn't win a prize, you might learn something from the one that does!'

Robin and Emma, Sally noted, were gradually drawing together as allies. Sally admired the way in which Robin was quietly influencing the girl, without any dramatic declarations. It wouldn't be proper for him to spend much time alone with her, but he was often at Badger's Gill. Sally admired his mature attitude. It's a good job I got over him or I'd have been jealous, she told herself. Robin had always been her friend, but he'd never been so thoughtful and attentive to Sally as he was to Emma. The girl was growing up and perhaps Robin was too, Sally thought as she watched them together. And Robin's father was investigating the whereabouts of Emma's inheritance.

Without Simon, Sally felt the old loneliness returning, as it had after her father died. Especially since Marcus had now disappeared. But this time, Robin and Emma were a comfort to her. Their very youth made her feel lighter in spirit, less weighed down by responsibility.

While the corn was ripening, Sally and Emma turned to the guesthouse again. They turned out the main bedroom and changed the furniture round in the dining-room, where Simon's painting now hung above the mantelpiece. Sally felt an urgent need, as before, to change things, to look to the future rather than dwell on the past.

'We need another paying guest. Let's advertise!' Sally said, when all was ready, including a high polish on all furniture. She didn't want another critical woman finding fault with the housekeeping. In fact, when she thought about it, she didn't much like the idea of another stranger coming to live in her house. Emma and Simon had both become her friends and had changed her life. The next arrangement, she was sure would be merely a commercial one.

A week passed and then one morning the postman delivered a letter from Bradford. Sally pounced on it. 'A new paying guest, maybe!' She carried it into the kitchen where Emma was making toast. 'It's from a solicitor ... oh!' She looked up from the letter and the room seemed to be whirling round. From a long way off, she heard Emma's voice, full of concern.

'What's wrong, Sally?'

With great effort, Sally spread the letter on the table and read it again. 'This letter ... oh, Emma, he was so thoughtful!' And she felt the hot tears on her face. Simon, generous Simon, had remembered her in his will. On that rainy day when Mr Scott had come to help him draw up his will, Simon had arranged his affairs and Mr Scott had recorded his wishes. He had left some of his money to Sally, 'Because I know she wants to buy the farm'. Three thousand pounds! Quite enough money to buy back Badger's Gill and leave some over for future security. It was a huge shock, it changed everything.

It took time to sink in, but over the next few days, Sally realized that her money worries were over. 'But I'd rather have Simon back, alive! And anyway, I don't deserve all this!' So much money was almost a burden.

'How very good of him! And now, if you don't want to take another guest, you need not!' Emma, practical as ever, tried to comfort Sally. 'Simon was so happy here. He told me so. And so am I! You deserve the money, Sally!'

There was no message from Simon, although she looked for one. But then Sally realized that he'd already told her everything he wanted her to know. She remembered Simon's last day and the way he'd taken her hand and placed it on the picture frame, symbolically giving her the farm. She understood that, now.

'But what about his family? What will they think?' Sally was torn between joy and sadness. It would be quite natural for them to resent her.

Once the money was in the bank, Sally decided, she would write to Mr Radford again and make him an offer for the farm. The Scotts would know what it was worth. But she hardly dared to hope that Badger's Gill would ever be hers. Oliver Radford would not want to be cheated of his revenge. He might enjoy twisting the knife and refuse to sell the farm even when she could afford to buy it.

The next day, a letter arrived from Mrs

Drury and Sally opened it with trembling hands. But it was as kind and generous as Simon himself. 'We are pleased that you were included in Simon's will … he was able to leave the bulk of his fortune to his family, and no one was left out. Thank you for looking after him so well.'

Simon must have been a very wealthy young man, thought Sally. But he'd never talked about money.

It was time for one of those letters to Mr Radford. But this time she had power on her side, the power of money. Sally sat down after work that night, pen in hand.

Dear Sir,
I hesitate to contact you again, after your hostile letters. I know you have no wish to hear from me again, but I have inherited a sum of money, so I am now in a position to buy Badger's Gill. And I refuse to deal with your agent in Thorpe.

Since you have stated that you have no interest in the property and no wish to visit, I hope that you will agree to the sale.

Please name your price by return of post.

Yours faithfully,
S. Mason (Miss)

Sally couldn't rest until the letter was safely in the postbox outside the post office. This time, the reply came back swiftly. There was the familiar cream envelope, with the thick, spiky writing in black ink.

Dear Madam,
I believe it is unlikely that you can afford to buy Badger's Gill, as you suggest. A female is unlikely to have a grasp of values, particularly land and property values.

It is my duty to the family estate to sell the farm for its current value, which is two thousand pounds. I will not enter into any negotiations with regard to the price.

I expect this to be the end of the matter.

Yours faithfully,
Oliver Radford.

'Right! He can have his two thousand pounds. It's a high price I believe...' Sally showed it to Mr Scott.

'It is high, but I suppose that's inevitable, given the type of man you are dealing with.' The Scotts had always sided with the Masons. 'The annoying thing about this is that the farm is worth so much because your family has managed it so well!'

Sally wrote back to agree to Radford's price and soon received another letter, which made her dance with joy and rage, all at the same time. She felt the familiar fizzing inside and ran down the street to show the letter to the Scotts straight away.

Dear Madam,
I note that you agree to purchase Badger's Gill, Thorpe, for two thousand pounds, and will instruct my solicitors to proceed in the matter.

It is my wish that once the sale is complete, there will be no further communication between my family and yours. I look upon this as a condition of sale.

Any further correspondence should be addressed to my solicitors, Arnold and Sedgwick, of Ripon.

Yours faithfully,
Oliver Radford.

The main thing was that the man had agreed to sell the farm. But was he saying that Sally had to choose between Marcus and Badger's Gill? Did he know that she knew Marcus? Or was it just the old quarrel that made him so keen to sever any ties between them? This must be the last letter from the old rogue. And a good job, too.

That night, Sally took down the little china shepherdess from the mantelpiece in her bedroom. Carefully, she wrapped the figure in a soft cloth, and put it away, deep in a drawer. She would forget all about the Roman soldier. With a father like that he must be horrid, deep down, she told herself firmly. All her instincts, all her deep feelings, must have been wrong when it came to Marcus Radford.

Marcus, meanwhile had discovered that he could not forget about Sally, but he now had hopes of a solution. Saturday came and he rode over to see his father, to report on progress as requested.

Choosing his time carefully Marcus waited until after dinner to talk about what was really important to him, the discovery in Foxholes Wood. He waited until all the farm business had been discussed and the family news exchanged.

'I have something to tell you Father, that I found out the other day. About the affair of Grandfather's death.'

Oliver moved restlessly on his chair. 'I don't want to hear about it. All that is over now. And I hope you won't mention it to Mrs Russell. I dine there again next week. I am ... reaching an understanding with Mrs Russell.' The older man sat back to observe the effect of this statement.

'Do you mean to say you're going to get married?' Marcus tried to keep the surprise out of his voice.

Oliver smirked. 'Why not? If you would hurry up and get yourself a wife, you could look after the Grange here and I could go off with Mrs Russell – Dorothy – and enjoy myself a little! We thought of a European tour next spring.'

So the old boy had his future all worked out. Well, he was sprightly enough, why not? The trip abroad didn't sound like Oliver; it was probably the Mrs Russell's idea. Thank goodness he seemed to have forgotten about linking his son up with her daughter.

'You will understand that raking up the past at this juncture would be inappropriate, to say the least.' Oliver glared at Marcus.

'But please let me tell you this; that I have proof that Richard Mason did not kill Grandfather. He died by accident, from an overdose of an experimental drug.' Marcus tried to keep his voice level and unemotional.

Oliver closed his eyes. Marcus pressed on, determined to have his say. 'I met Professor Vernon, of whom you may have heard. He admitted that he killed Grandfather by accident and drugged Richard Mason enough to destroy his memory.' He described the death briefly and then there was silence for a while.

'Why did he not come forward at the time, and admit what had happened?' Oliver seemed interested, in spite of himself.

'He was at the start of his career and very ambitious. He said that a confession would not bring Grandfather back. But he seems not to have considered the effect on his family and on the Masons. The scandal would have ruined his life's work, he said.' Marcus thought back to that extraordinary day in the wood, and the deep impression that the professor had made on him. A complex character, but not evil, he thought, 'He's very old now, of course, but extremely alert. I believe he has the ruthlessness of an ambitious man. But he has done a great deal of good.'

'Tell me how you met him. Why would he let you into the secret, after all this time?'

So Marcus told his story simply, and Oliver said very little. 'It's a shock,' was all Marcus got out of him. 'I am going to bed, now.'

The sun was shining the next morning, as Marcus went down to breakfast. He'd hoped for a companionable walk with Oliver round the home farm before going home. But his father was there before him, dressed for church. His face was set in a stern, church-going mould.

Oliver got straight to the point. 'That tale you told me last night makes no difference to us, Marcus. I hope you realize that.'

Marcus felt his heart sink. 'What do you mean, Father?'

'Nothing can change the situation between us and the Masons, not now. The rift is too old and too deep, and you should under-stand that I have very strong feelings about it.' Oliver paused.

So Marcus was not going to influence Oliver's thinking by any logical argument, it seemed.

'I forgot to tell you that I have decided to sell the Badger's Gill farm at Thorpe. I'm selling it back to the Masons, the solicitors have it in hand. That will put an end to the whole affair, I hope. I should never have bought it in the first place and got involved with them.'

Good! So little Sally had got together enough money to buy back her farm. Marcus felt a rush of admiration for Sally and saw her in his mind's eye – her red curls bouncing with energy, clapping her hands because she was going to recover the Mason farm. Then it struck Marcus suddenly that Sally might be going to marry money. The fair-haired, idle rich lad he had seen with her that day in Kirkby, would be about to buy her the farm, as a wedding present. He felt sick at the thought. Marcus realized that Oliver had not finished.

'I am selling it for two thousand pounds, the current price for a farm that size, in good heart, with a large house.'

Marcus poured himself coffee and took a slice of toast, but he had no appetite. It was quite enough, he thought; in fact at about ten pounds an acre it was the same price as a farm lower down the valley. The old boy was after his pound of flesh. Two thousand! It was a lot of money for Sally to find. The theory of the rich boy was looking more likely.

Oliver smiled thinly as he delivered his final shot. 'And my condition of sale is that there should be no more communication between them and us.' His mouth closed with a snap.

Marcus was stunned for a moment. He ran his hand through his thick dark hair. 'But if you accept that Mason didn't murder Grandfather, why be so set against them?'

'I am not going through all that again, Marcus. But I must say that I will be most displeased should you communicate with any of that family again.'

Should he keep quiet, to please the old boy? Should he pretend to agree and then please himself? Marcus thought for a while and then made up his mind. 'I will explain my position, Father, since you have told me yours. I'm afraid you won't like it, but I must be honest and I have a right to a point of view.' He stopped and saw that Oliver was frowning at him. It was very unusual for Marcus to be so defiant.

'I do realize how you feel about Sally's mother. But it was long ago. You have lived a lot since then, and you're going to have a new lease of life with Mrs Russell. You might not want to meet the Masons and I can understand that. But I do.'

'You are against me, then.' Oliver's voice was bleak.

'Father, this is not personal at all. I happen to disagree with your opinion. I want to make peace with Samuel Mason, Sally's uncle, and talk to Sally herself.'

Oliver Radford poured himself more coffee with a hand that shook slightly. 'I am trying to advise you for your own good. I am much older than you, Marcus, and I don't want you to be hurt!'

Well, you are doing your best to hurt me, Marcus thought. 'I have met Sally Mason several times, and I am attracted to her and want to get to know her better. I am not sure whether she may be already engaged to someone else. I might have no chance.' As Marcus faced this possibility he felt depression settling again. He would have to see her immediately. 'But I am bound to tell her what I have learned about our families' history, for her sake. There is no need for a bitter feud between us any more.'

'Rubbish! Masons don't care about it,' Oliver snorted. 'It wasn't their father that died.'

'But Richard Mason's life was ruined. He was never the same again and I gather the family's fortunes started to decline from then on.' Why couldn't his father see anyone else's point of view? Marcus sighed. 'And so, whether you like it or not, I am going to see Sally Mason today to tell her the story. After that I am not sure what will happen. I will let you know.'

'Your grandmother will be bitterly disappointed.' Oliver turned on the family pressure, but Marcus did not respond. Breakfast proceeded in silence after that.

It's almost the twentieth century Marcus thought to himself. Surely a father can't expect to dictate to his children all their lives? Perhaps he should have stood up to Oliver years ago. But in general he got on well with his father and he'd often kept small differences of opinion to himself. Oliver was inclined to take any opposition personally, even if it were only opposition to one of his ideas.

As soon as the meal was over Oliver went off to church, as Marcus saddled his horse and rode out of Nidd Grange to visit Thorpe against his father's wishes. It was a strange feeling; he'd never really quarrelled with Oliver in his life. But he'd had to speak the truth. As he rode over the moor and past the Drovers' Inn Marcus recalled the day when he'd rescued Sally from the snow. That day, he'd wanted to stay with her for ever. How hard it had been that night for him to ride away! Now it could be too late; the fair-haired boy had probably taken over. Marcus realized that if Sally were now out of reach it was probably his own fault. He hadn't tried to see her for so long, he'd been kept busy by Oliver – probably on purpose, to keep him out of the way. But, Marcus thought as he trotted over the short moorland turf, if he'd lost Sally, there was no point in upsetting the old boy. It might have been all for nothing. There was an insistent drumming in his head as the horse's hoofs drummed on the turf. He had to know whether Sally was still free. He was afraid of what the answer would be.

As he neared Thorpe Marcus began to feel peculiarly hollow inside. He thought it might be love – could people actually become lovesick? But then he remembered the uncomfortable breakfast with Oliver, when he'd eaten very little. So the pangs might be hunger after all. He decided to call at the Crown for a bite to eat. The Crown would be closed as it was Sunday, but Mrs Bartram would find him something. He urged Odin on to a faster pace.

NINETEEN

'Now we've got the harvest in we can think about other things. Let's go on a trip to Fountains Abbey on Sunday! Will you come, both of you? Ma'll be coming too, when she hears about it.' Robin looked at Emma and Sally, eager to be off, to get out of Thorpe for an afternoon.

Sally was still quite tired after the effort of harvesting. All the stooks of oats were safely stacked in the barn, to be threshed out later. It was satisfying to look round the yard and see the corn and the hay, evidence of prosperity and hard work completed. But her arms still ached from throwing the sheaves up to the stacker and when she closed her eyes at night, she still saw the flying sheaves of golden grain.

'I'll stay at home just for once, but Emma should go. You'll enjoy the ride, Emma. And the beautiful old ruins by the river, they're full of history.' Sally was also thinking that Emma, although much braver than before, tended to shyness in company. It would be good for the girl to go out with the Scotts without Sally to hide behind. And it would be good to have a day to herself for a change.

As Marcus was riding down to Thorpe on that bright Sunday morning Sally was getting on with the farm work, still wondering about Oliver Radford's letter. What would Marcus think of the ban on further communication between them? Perhaps he would accept what Oliver told him. Thinking it over, it seemed to Sally that Marcus had a rather sad outlook on life at times. She'd seen it that day when they met in Kirkby. Perhaps he needed someone to remind him to look on the bright side? Even on that day, he'd seemed much more relaxed after he'd talked to her for a while.

Sunday was Joe's day off and so Sally had to milk the cows and do all the chores by herself. Emma had gone off to lunch at the Scotts before the trip to Fountains. It wasn't often that Sally was alone on the farm these days. With Joe and Emma as permanent helpers life was much easier. And she'd also been able to hire other workers when they needed them, such as a man and a wagon to help to lead in the sheaves of corn.

For most of the morning she was busy with the cows, feeding the hens and collecting the eggs and doing all the other small jobs round the yard. It was a reminder of just how hard her life had been when she had tried to farm all alone. Thank goodness that was over.

Once the work was done Sally sat down in

the kitchen for a cup of tea and a slice of teacake and cheese. It was very quiet, the village of Thorpe was enjoying its day of rest. The ticking of the old clock was loud in the silence and from the yard she could hear the loud call of a hen that had just laid an egg and wanted the world to know. What now? There was always a job to do on a farm, but most of them could wait another day or two. She had two or three hours before the evening chores would begin. Going out into the garden, Sally picked some of the last of the summer roses. She arranged a bowl of roses in the hall and then decided to take the rest of the flowers to her parents' grave. Sally often thought of her parents, but she'd had little time to visit their grave since her father died. Today was her first taste of leisure for weeks. But she couldn't walk up through Thorpe on a Sunday in her farm clothes.

Half an hour later, neat and wearing a pretty print dress, Sally put on her straw hat and walked sedately up the village street to the church. The morning service was over and people had dispersed to their homes. The Crown inn was next to the church and as she passed, Sally looked through the stone arch beside the inn. And there tied up to a rail she saw the horse that Marcus rode, Odin. It was the same chestnut, elegant head that had come between them while they were talking in Kirkby. Sally had a good eye for a horse and she certainly remembered this one. Sally's heart went down. Marcus was in Thorpe, and hadn't come near her. Marcus didn't care about her, or he was so afraid of his father that he dare not disobey him. Or – was she in danger of being as negative as he was? Sometimes, it was hard to work out the truth, especially of complex relationships. She wasn't sure what their relationship might have been, but no doubt it was over.

The churchyard was peaceful, with a pigeon cooing in the trees and Sally felt gradually calmer. She placed the flowers and then took off her bonnet and sat on a seat near the graves. What would Mother and Father have thought about Radford's condition of sale? Her father in particular would have been delighted that the farm was coming back to the Mason family. And a lack of communication with Radfords wouldn't have worried him. But what if I told him I wanted to see Marcus Radford? What would my father have said? Sally couldn't find the answer. Neither could she decide what she would have done if her father had forbidden her to see Marcus again. She had loved her father and wouldn't have wanted to cause him grief.

Sally sighed and went slowly to the churchyard gate. It was all too difficult and probably always would be. She looked across the wall to the inn; there was Marcus, leading his horse through the arch. Although she felt like hiding behind a gravestone Sally stood still, with her hand on the churchyard gate. Her heart was hammering and she felt herself turning bright red. I hope he doesn't see me...

'Sally!' Marcus called, and ran the short distance between them, with Odin trotting behind. 'I came to Thorpe to see you.'

His arms went round her out there in the sunshine, and Sally's heart experienced a surge of joy. This wasn't the gloomy man she'd seen in Kirkby! 'I-I didn't think you'd see me,' she stammered.

'Of course I saw you! You can't hide that hair!' Marcus was laughing with sheer lightness of heart himself. But suddenly a grave look came over his face as he looked down at her. 'Tell me quickly ... we have so much to talk about ... but – are you engaged, or promised to anyone else?' His voice was urgent.

Sally was puzzled for a moment and then she saw the problem. 'You mean my paying guest! Poor Simon. He was here for his health and he died not long ago. But I told you the last time we met, he was just a guest, Marcus.' She paused, considering what a real lady should say. And she could see that Marcus was still waiting. Sally was used to taking the lead and making up her mind; she knew she was sometimes seen as unfeminine, especially by Aunt Bertha. And she didn't want to appear forward and unfeminine with Marcus. She was not yet sure of him, however pleased he seemed to see her.

'I have no engagement, or involvement with anyone at all.' It came out primly, but it was probably the correct thing to say even though Sally felt like shouting, 'It's you I want, you idiot!' That would have been nearer the mark.

Marcus let out a long sigh. 'So that's it, that's the main thing. I was hoping, but I wasn't sure until I saw you!' He beamed at her. 'May I walk home with you?' He offered his free arm, the one that wasn't holding the horse.

'What if Sol sees us and tells your father? We're not supposed to communicate, ever again. It's a condition of sale for the farm.' Sally drew back.

Marcus looked grim. 'Come on, we'll walk down the street together.' So Marcus led the horse down the street, with Sally on his other side. There was still nobody about except a few ducks on the green, lazing in the afternoon sun and not in the least interested in whether Sally was walking close to Marcus or not.

'It doesn't matter, Sally. I can't be dictated to all my life. I have just been told of his "conditions" this morning. And I told my father that I was coming to see you today. I stopped at the Crown for a bite to eat, that was all.'

So Marcus had defied his revered father, to come to see her.

'I'll tell you more when we get to Badger's Gill.'

At the farm Marcus put his horse in the stable and they sat together in the garden, on an old stone bench. Bees were humming in the Michaelmas daisies and the scent of the fading roses rose up in the warm air. Sally brought out a jug of lemonade. 'When I got the letter with that condition, I thought it was the end–' Sally began.

The last words of this speech were smothered because Marcus leaned over and kissed her. 'All right, I should have come before, I know. But it seemed so hopeless and I thought you were set with that fair-haired boy, too. And then I had this idea of getting to the bottom of the murder. I thought that would end the quarrel for Father. But it didn't, of course.'

Sally took his hands in hers. 'Start at the beginning, Marcus. Did you get to the bottom of the mystery? What have you found?'

Sitting there in the sunshine, Marcus told Sally the story of Foxholes Wood and what had happened there fifty years ago.

'The poor things! Marcus, it sounds so likely. People often said that my grandfather couldn't remember anything. His memory was bad, we all knew it. I suppose that's why they didn't bring a case against him. Most people believed him when he said he couldn't remember what happened.' Sally sat quiet for a while, thinking about her grandfather. 'But it was worse for your family ... Mr Radford was left without a father, at a young age. It probably changed him, Marcus.' That strong, determined, ruthless face, Sally thought, had perhaps been formed as a result of the tragedy.

'You're right. But he's very – inflexible. I'd hoped that the truth would put an end to the hatred, Sally. But he said this morning that nothing had changed for him.'

Marcus stretched and looked across at Sally. 'Now that our grandfathers have been laid to rest, you and I at least have nothing to come between us. What do you say, little Bo-Peep?'

Sally looked down modestly. 'I don't want to come between you and your father. And I don't really know what will happen if I break the condition of sale, for Badger's Gill. But...'

Marcus smiled, and Sally thought his face was thinner than she remembered it. 'So there is a but, is there? I love you, Sally. And I am prepared to upset all the Radfords at once, if necessary, so long as you want me with you.' There was a long interval, with

Marcus and Sally very close together. 'My little Bo-Peep!' he murmured into her hair.

'Marcus, I have missed you more than I can tell. I want to be with you!' Sally felt her face flushing again, but she didn't care. This was happiness. 'I am so happy that you feel the same way! But I think we can be generous. Let's take things gently and hope that your father will change his mind about me. Give him time.'

In one way, Sally thought, Oliver's opposition was a good thing. Marcus had shown that he was prepared to stand on his own feet, make his mind up. She admired him for his independence, knowing how hard it was to achieve in a farming family. Marcus was his own man, thank goodness.

'I believe I know some of the problem: my grandmother. She's the one who is most implacable. The death soured her, poor thing. But there's something else.' Marcus was looking at her closely. 'It's only right that you should know the whole truth about my father. I know that judging by his letters he would seem to be an ogre to you. He's told me what went into them! I think he enjoys dreaming up scorchers, to tell you the truth. He likes words, he writes all his own business letters, doesn't trust it to Hill. I'm afraid he polishes up the insults as a hobby!'

Sally laughed. 'I rather wondered ... they

were so very rude!' But I was just as bad, she thought guiltily. That first letter ... I hope Marcus didn't see it.

'Well, one night I got it out of him. My father refuses to see you, won't visit Thorpe – because you're too much like your mother, Sally.'

Sally's eyes widened. 'But he didn't know my mother – did he? She never mentioned him!'

'He was in love with your mother, but she married your father instead. I don't know how well they knew each other, though. And there was no suggestion of betrayal, or of going back on a promise. She just chose Robert Mason. I don't even know whether she knew of Father's feelings. He told me he'd been very serious and devoted to business, as a youth.'

In the silence of the garden, the humming of bees was loud.

'And my father was – devastated.' Marcus took her hand. 'I can imagine how he felt.'

Sally sat quiet, digesting this thought. 'Poor Oliver! So it wasn't exactly hatred, after all.' She shook her head.

'Far from it. That's why he bought the farm, you see. Not out of revenge, but to help your parents without appearing to. Nobody else offered a bid and no doubt the auctioneer told him, knowing my father could afford to buy it.' Marcus took another sip of his drink. 'I learned quite a lot about Father that night. He's not as ruthless and hard as he pretends to be. But he cares what people think of him, more than I do. That's why he dresses so well. And he likes people, especially tenants, to see him as a tough businessman.'

'But later, he was happy with your mother? What was she like, Marcus?' There was a great deal that she didn't know about Marcus. And Oliver Radford was emerging as almost likeable! Sally couldn't quite believe it.

'Mother was calm, practical and warm-hearted. Just like me!' He laughed. 'Yes, they were happy. But I have a feeling that since she died, the past has come to mean more to him. He gets very agitated if I ask him to come to Thorpe.'

The shadows were lengthening across the green as they talked on, absorbed in learning about each other. At length Marcus looked at the sky and then across at the farmyard. Sally's cows were assembled round the gate, staring reproachfully over the wall into the garden. They knew it was milking time, even if those silly humans had forgotten.

'We may be trying to follow our destiny, but the cows still have to be milked! I'll give you a hand, lass – I suppose there's no one else to help on a Sunday?'

Sally and Marcus tied up the cows and

then under Sally's direction, Marcus helped with the evening chores. The sun was setting by the time they finished and turned the cows out again.

'That's a fine animal!' Marcus watched Primrose walking proudly out of the shed.

'She's to be shown at Kirkby, next week. We've decided to have a go at the championship.'

'Good, I'll hope to see you there. We're tied up with the show, of course.'

That might be interesting. If she talked to Marcus at the show, under Oliver's nose... Sally put the thought away. 'Colsterdale's a fair way to ride, tonight. Perhaps you should go now, before dark.' Sally felt she had to say it, although she wanted him to stay. But Marcus laughed.

'There's a moon tonight, Sally. I'll come round the sheep with you and perhaps have a cup of tea before I leave.'

Emma was not back, so probably she was having supper at the Scotts'. Down in the gill, the sunset was long gone but the moon was rising above the ridge. The Thorpe Beck gurgled its way down to the river with a peaceful, contented sound. Sally and Marcus were on a farm walk in the moonlight and for the first time, Marcus went with her into Badger's Gill.

'I can see why you love this farm. It's a beautiful spot. A bit lower down the hill than my place at Colsterdale. I like the big trees and the hedges. I suppose Kirkby is a bit warmer, but Thorpe's a civilized sort of place.'

'I've always loved it. See how the wood slopes down to the gill? That's where the badgers sometimes play. But of course I've never lived anywhere else. I've never been very far, Marcus, I'm afraid.'

'No need to go far, when you live in a place like this. And you've looked after it well, too.'

Sally glowed with pleasure; Marcus could not have said a better thing to her. Except for the next thing he said.

'Come and sit on this log, my lass. Little Bo-Peep, it's time we got serious. Now...' and his arms went round her. 'That's better. Will you marry me, little Sally? I want to live with you, happily ever after!'

Their moonlit shadows moved towards each other and merged. They could hear the quiet murmuring of pheasants settling down for the night, but neither of them paid any attention to the birds.

'Well!' Sally emerged rather breathless, from a long kiss. 'Er – live where, Marcus dear?' This was the crunch. She'd have to face it, now; the thought that if she married, it would mean leaving Thorpe. Miss Mason of Badger's Gill realized that she would lose her farm. And her name, too and the little business she was building up and that she was so proud of. It would be a big sacrifice.

'Colsterdale, I suppose, although Father was talking about going off and leaving me in charge of Nidd. But I expect you don't want to leave Thorpe?' Marcus looked guilty, as though he'd forgotten Sally's ambitions in the joy of the moment.

'I've had to fight for Badger's Gill. You don't suppose I'd want to sell it?' Sally drew away from him, just a little.

'What do you really want, my little Bo-Peep? Truly now! I can see that you've enjoyed the fight, you've kept the farm and beaten Sol Bartram. What next?' Marcus drew her to him.

Sally was quiet; she was saying goodbye to Badger's Gill. It would soon all be over.

'Yours is a hard life, my darling. I want you to enjoy a little more leisure ... but what do you want?'

'I want to be the best woman farmer in Yorkshire and for this to be the best farm! I want to win prizes at shows, and Badger's Gill to beat everybody!' Sally could feel the familiar fizz, but the words didn't quite ring true, even to her.

'Does this mean you're turning me down?' The dark face was worried.

'I'll be honest. I really want to have a loving husband and children. I don't want to live alone, to be successful Miss Mason, fading into a spinster ... oh, Marcus. It will be hard to leave! I never wanted to leave Thorpe!' Tears welled up as Sally looked around at the moonlit fields and woods.

'But you'll marry me?' Marcus persisted. 'We can keep Badger's Gill, my girl, for one of our children.'

Our children! Sally's deepest, most secret wishes were going to come true. 'I will marry you, Marcus, and leave Thorpe. There, my choice is made.' Marcus too may have to sacrifice, thought Sally. In his case, his relationship with Oliver. But he was evidently putting that aside. She sighed deeply. 'But you haven't said what you really want, my Roman soldier?'

'To develop our farms, with your help. I've always hoped for a wife who would take an interest in the farms – I want to try some of the new ideas, and improved breeds.' Marcus laughed. 'But only with you, Sally. That's what happiness means to me ... you, and eventually, our children.' He paused. 'I would like to continue to work with my father, but only if he accepts our marriage. If not ... I'll take my share of the estate, and leave him to the rest.'

They were speaking very quietly, but they'd been heard. There was a stealthy movement round them and a soft bleat or two. Sally looked round and realized that the Motley Flock had surrounded the log they were

sitting on. Mary and Lavinia jostled themselves between herself and Marcus, gently
but persistently. Marcus and Sally sat among
the sheep, laughing quietly, but almost
hysterically.

'These sheep are determined to come between us! I remember very well the day we
met on Camp Hill and you tried to disown
them!' Marcus could hardly speak for
laughing.

'But if they hadn't strayed, we would never
have met!' Embarrassing though they were,
Sally was grateful to the Flock.

Suddenly, Marcus grabbed Sally's arm.
'What's that noise?'

There was a strange shuffling, grunting
noise, a dragging noise at the end of the
gill... 'I think it's the badgers,' she whispered
back. 'But they sound different tonight.'

Marcus and Sally went forward in the
shadows, and there in a patch of moonlight,
they saw a strange sight. A human figure
was shuffling along, dragging a large sack
across the turf. It was heading for the gate
into the green lane, which now stood open.
A good job the sheep haven't seen it, Sally
thought with part of her mind. From the
heaving sack came a grunting and savage
snarling that sounded like badgers at their
rough games. It could only be– 'Somebody's
stealing the badgers!' Sally yelled and the
figure turned, then started to run.

Marcus sprinted ahead and grabbed the man round the knees, bringing him down. Getting one arm free, the man raised a cudgel. Sally caught up with them, twisted his arm and brought the weapon down hard on the man's own head. 'What have I done?' Sally was appalled, as the figure slumped forward. But then she saw who it was. Sol Bartram, her true enemy. The man who had set Oliver Radford against her. And now, in yet another act of treachery, he was trying to steal the badgers of Badger's Gill. She'd hit Sol! Sally almost felt like hitting him again.

Marcus wouldn't let Sally touch the sack. 'I'll cut a hole in it,' he said, drawing a knife from his pocket. 'Stand back, they're bound to be angry.' Two half grown badgers stumbled out of the sack and scuttled away into the darkness as fast as they could.

Sol Bartram began to groan, and Marcus looked down at him with contempt. 'Taking badgers for baiting! I didn't think anyone in Thorpe would stoop so low. But you've been trying to undermine Miss Mason for years! I know what you've been up to, Sol Bartram. I shall tell PC Brown all about you. And you're fired. You will never work for my family again!'

'Masons is rubbish! You should've let me have this farm. You Radfords don't know what's good for you! After all my years of slaving away for you lot and you treat me like this. I shan't forget, see if I do!' Rubbing his head, Sol slunk away.

'Well done, Sally, my love. That stick would have knocked me out, if he'd had his way.'

Sally stood still, with the stick in her hand. A worrying thought had come to her. 'Marcus, I – enjoyed hitting him. That's wicked! But he's been the chief cause of trouble, between Radfords and me... I suppose I'll feel sorry for him, now.'

They walked slowly up to the house, and as Marcus looked down at her, Sally wondered what he really thought about her wilder tendencies.

'You can be a bit fizzy, I've noticed. But you're not wicked, Bo-Peep. I think you are the most wonderful girl in the world!'

TWENTY

Sally watched, holding her breath as the judge walked round the line of cattle drawn up for inspection. Primrose, proudly led by Joe in his best suit, was somewhere in the middle. She's not the biggest cow there ... but I think she's the best! Sally just hoped that the judge agreed with her. In the end, wasn't it a matter of personal opinion?

The excitement of competition and the rivalry with the Scotts had kept Sally going all week. Badger's Gill had bustled with preparations; Jed and the trap had to be cleaned and polished and Emma needed to finish new dresses for herself and Sally. And most important of all, Primrose had to be in peak condition.

'I'll give her a drop of linseed oil,' Joe suggested in the middle of the week. 'Put a shine on her coat.' Primrose's tail and top line were trimmed, her hooves were polished and her coat was brushed every day. Sally rather wondered what she thought of it all, but the cow seemed to enjoy the attention. And now, on a fine and sunny Saturday in September, here they were!

The judge beckoned to Joe, and he walked slowly forward. Two other cows were also moved and there was a new line of three. Primrose was in the running for a place! This class was for the best milking cow and the winner would go forward to the championship. Best In Show.

'Well done Sally, you've been placed!' Uncle Samuel stood beside her, beaming. He sniffed the air. 'I love the smell of a show ... crushed grass, cows and horses ... oh, my goodness girl, your cow has won!'

The judge waved Joe and Primrose to stand in front of the rest and a red rosette was pinned to her halter. First prize! Sally could hardly contain her joy. Looking round the showground the girl drew a deep breath, trying to compose herself. The world was full of bright colours; flags fluttered in the sun, the women's dresses and hats were still in their summer brightness, although it was autumn now, a perfect autumn day.

A tall figure materialized at her other side. 'Congratulations, Miss Mason!' said Marcus formally and then he turned to Uncle Samuel. Sally hastily introduced them, hoping that Aunt Bertha wouldn't appear from the produce tent.

Sally had written to her uncle to tell him about the new evidence, soon after she heard the story from Marcus. As a Mason he had the right to know; and she wanted Uncle Samuel on her side. Aunt Bertha had gone into hysterics when she heard that Sally knew Marcus Radford and had firmly refused to believe any good of the family.

The two men shook hands and the Reverend Samuel Mason said graciously, 'I am very pleased to meet you, Mr Radford. Sally has told me that our families' quarrel was the result of a misunderstanding.'

Other people came to congratulate the winner then and Sally went forward to speak to Joe. 'It's all your doing, Joe! You take the credit!'

Joe smiled, the rare High Side smile of pure joy. 'Nay, miss, the breeding was there!

You can't make a silk purse out of a sow's lug!' He lowered his voice. 'We'll have a go at championship, but Best in Show is open to all comers. And Scotts have a good bull, won his class, we might have a job to beat him!' Sally hadn't really thought about beating her friends the Scotts, although Robin had teased her about the competition.

Joe and Primrose went off to the cattle lines to rest before their next appearance. Primrose walked proudly, as though she knew she had the red rosette. And because she was from Badger's Gill, Primrose was afraid of nothing and took the crowded showground in her stride.

Emma had been with the Scotts, but now she came back to Sally, her face shining with happiness. 'I've just been to the produce tent – your aunt is there, Sally, but she didn't remember me. My butter got second prize, I'm so pleased!' And she darted off again.

Soon after she saw Emma, Robin came over to Sally, laughing. 'We're in competition, Sal, by the look of it. I told you so! Our bull against your cow! Can you stand the excitement?'

'Oh Robin, I don't care who wins. This is just such a happy day!' Marcus was there, still talking earnestly to Uncle Samuel. All was right with the world. Sally couldn't remember a happier day since she was a little girl.

Robin moved closer. 'I can tell you something to make you even happier, Sal. I've come to an agreement with Mum and Dad ... a sort of trade-off.' He looked round at the crowd. 'Where's Emma? She should be here when I tell you this.'

'Gone back to gloat over her butter, I believe.'

'Well, I'll tell you quickly. I've agreed to give up the idea of Australia. Too far for Ma, you see. I'd never be home again, she says.'

'I am not surprised. But what's the bargain?'

'As soon as Emma turns eighteen we're going to get married and take over one of the farms. That will give her a year to get used to the idea. Sal, we'll be so happy!'

'I know you will. I am so pleased, Robin. Can't tell you my news just now, but soon, I will.' And Sally refused to say any more.

'It's that Radford chap, isn't it?' Robin's eyes were thoughtful as he looked at Marcus, who was just out of earshot.

Sally turned bright red.

'I just hope he looks after you. He'll have me to deal with, if he doesn't!'

He sounds just like a brother, Sally thought happily. She went towards the produce tent to see Emma's wonderful butter, but on the way, Marcus stopped her.

'Are you allowed to speak to me today?'

Sally regretted the grim High Side comment as soon as it was made. 'Sorry Marcus. It's not your fault!'

Marcus sighed, but Sally noticed that he looked full of suppressed excitement.

'I have just asked your uncle formally to approve of our marriage, Sally.' He spoke very quietly, with his back to the crowd. 'And he said that he will be very pleased to marry us, with the agreement of the vicar at Thorpe of course.'

So Uncle Samuel had agreed to put the past behind them. Dear Uncle Samuel, who had always been loyal to her. 'But – what about your family, Marcus?' Sally looked round the crowd. There were bound to be other Radfords about.

'Yes. My family is a problem, but we'll work on it. They will just have to get used to the idea.' Marcus looked very much like his father as he spoke. 'I'm not sure where to start, but with you on my side, I'll win in the end!'

In the produce tent many ladies were admiring the winning entries of classes for butter, cheese, jams and pickles and deep yellow sponge cakes. Badger's Gill had won second prize for both butter and cheese, Sally noticed with pleasure. She'd been too busy watching Primrose to see what happened when the cheese was judged. The fierce rivalry between Kirkby and Thorpe was nowhere fiercer than in the produce tent and Sally was pleased that she'd earned a few points for Thorpe, the smaller, poorer village higher up the hill.

Aunt Bertha was sitting on a chair at the side of the tent, fanning herself. 'There you are, my dear child! Why do you spend so much time out there with the men? A proper lady's place is here!'

'We've just won a prize with a cow, Aunt,' Sally said quietly.

Aunt Bertha would never understand what it meant to Badger's Gill that Primrose had won. That all the years of careful selection, all the preparation, had paid off.

'But you can leave that to the workers! It seems so vulgar to walk among cattle and have your dress smelling of the farmyard! So unladylike, my dear!' She lowered her voice and leaned towards Sally. 'Who made your dress? It is really rather too – modern, for my taste. Should you not be wearing black?'

Sally looked down at her pretty green dress, with the ruched bodice and fitted waist. Emma was a very good dressmaker and the dress made Sally look a little more rounded, without taking away from her slimness.

'You must give me the name of your dressmaker, Sally. I would like to guide her as to what would be suitable for you to wear. And with your unfortunate hair colour, black is really your only option, I feel.'

'Thank you, Aunt Bertha.' Sally escaped as soon as she could, leaving the stuffy tent with relief. Aunt Bertha had lost the battle for Sally's soul and was clutching at straws. Wait until she heard about the marriage! She hoped that Uncle Samuel would break it gently to his wife. But of course the Radford money and estates might eventually bring her round; Aunt Bertha had a healthy respect for money and possessions. Strange, thought Sally, I'd never thought of Marcus and money. Marcus himself, rich or poor, is my man. Goodness! I'll have to get used to that.

The band was playing and Sally wandered round the show-ground enjoying the festival atmosphere. It would soon be time for the final judging of the champion of the show. Sally went with Robin and Emma to the refreshment tent, where they drank home-made lemonade, ate scones and laid modest bets with each other on which animal would win. Marcus had disappeared, presumably on Radford business and Sally decided it was probably a good thing. In Ripon they had been hardly noticed. But at the Kirkby show, where everybody knew everybody else, a Radford could hardly be seen with a Mason without causing a stir. Eventually, as Marcus said, they'd all have to get used to it. But perhaps not yet.

'There's a big heifer from Dallagill, was in another class to ours,' Joe whispered to Sally, as he gave Primrose a last brush. 'That there might beat all us Thorpe folks.'

The championship took an agonizing length of time. Sally was at the ringside with Robin and Emma, as all the animals were slowly paraded round the ring. The crowd watched critically; most of them knew their cattle and they all loved competition. After what seemed to Sally like hours, the judge – a different one this time – drew out the Scott's bull. A pause. Then he beckoned forward the big heifer, which stumbled slightly, tripping over her feet as she went forward. There was another pause. And then, slowly, the judge walked around Primrose once again. The little animal seemed to pose for the judge, one forefoot in front of the other, head up, standing quite still. The way an animal stood could make quite a difference, Sally realized; the big heifer was graceless, compared to Primrose. The judge beckoned Joe forward. Primrose was in the final!

Afterwards, Sally couldn't quite remember the sequence of events. Primrose, after further agony of waiting, was the winner. The Supreme Champion of the Kirkby Agricultural Show. 'Hurrah!' The cheers went up from all the young lads of Thorpe, pleased to see their village on top. Emma, Robin and Sally hugged each other and Sally had tears in her eyes. 'If only Father were here!'

But soon, Robin reminded Sally that she would have to go up, be presented and make a speech. She would receive the cup, up on that platform, from the show president. In a few minutes' time! 'But I've never made a speech in my life!' Sally wailed, appalled. This was one contingency for which she was not prepared.

'Just look modest, if you can. I don't suppose you're feeling modest, Sal, but it's expected! You needn't say much, just thank you and all that. Blush prettily, you're good at that! The crowd will love it – much more interesting than a win by a noble lord, or a big estate.'

Robin was teasing her, but Sally was truly alarmed. She went behind a tent and tried to brush out her tangled curls and smooth her dress. Out of sight of the crowd, she was alone for a moment and took a deep breath. What Sally saw next took her mind off the ordeal to come. Looking over to where the horses were tethered under some trees, Sally automatically looked along the line for Jed, just to check that he was not too restless. It was a long time for a horse to wait. And she saw a figure creeping along, dodging from trap to trap, with something in its hand – a knife? Straining her eyes, Sally saw that it was Sol Bartram. When he reached Jed, Sol stopped and Sally saw the knife slash upwards as the man cut the tethering rope. Jed threw up his head and the knife flashed again. The horse had obviously been slashed; he reared and kicked and galloped off in the direction of the ring.

Seconds after the horse was released, another figure came out of the crowd with amazing speed, grabbed the halter rope and hung on grimly. It was Marcus, being dragged over the ground, but slowly winning. Before the horse reached the people, a farm boy had jumped to the rescue and between them, Marcus and the boy managed to halt the terrified animal. A few yards more, and Jed would have galloped into a group of children.

Sally ran down to the horse but PC Brown, puffing, was there before her. 'Saw the whole thing,' he said solemnly. 'Charges will be laid. And will you be a witness, sir? Are you all right, sir?'

Marcus was bleeding from grazes and holding his shoulder. But when he saw Sally's anxious face, he smiled. 'It's nothing, just a scratch or two. He was bent on real mischief, this time! That horse could have killed someone!'

Spitting and swearing, Sol was led away. Sally wondered why, if PC Brown had been watching, the crime couldn't have been prevented. And it now seemed that Marcus had been tailing Sol for some time. 'He came out of the beer tent half an hour ago, after an argument with someone and I thought he looked like trouble. It's my job in any case, to keep an eye on trouble makers... I'm on the show committee, we try to keep the peace.' Marcus wiped his face with a handkerchief. He looked rather the worse for wear, with green stains on his tweed jacket.

'Why pick on poor Jed?' Sally's eyes were blazing. She rummaged in the trap and found some salve, which she spread very carefully on the horse's wound. Then she looked round to see Marcus laughing.

'I could do with some of that salve, lass, when you've finished with the horse! You're a real farmer, that's quite clear!'

Sally was mortified. 'Oh, Marcus, I'm so sorry! I should have attended to you first!' She put the herbal ointment on his bleeding hands, which had rope burns. 'Comfrey, it heals very quickly,' she assured him.

Marcus pulled his jacket on and looked over to the show ring. 'It's time for the presentation, Sally. You'd better hurry!'

There was no time now for composing dignified speeches. This was it. Stepping up to the platform, Sally saw the sea of faces and her heart nearly stood still.

'They've called your name! Go up there!' A steward called her urgently and Sally went up the steps and advanced timidly to meet the show president. She looked up and found herself staring into the implacable face of Oliver Radford. The enemy! She'd had no idea that *he* was the president of this show. Why hadn't someone told her?

Between them on a table stood the enormous silver cup, the championship cup, which was hers for a whole year. But Sally hardly noticed it. She was trying to arrange her features, to move towards the man she hated ... but she had to watch the platform, which was uneven. It would never do to fall over. Head back, grim, Oliver Radford held out his hand. Whatever he thought about her he was going to go through the ritual; the president must congratulate the winner. No doubt he was gritting his teeth, doing his duty.

A few steps nearer and to her surprise, Sally found her hand taken in a warm clasp. He took her hand in both of his. Looking up from the floor, Sally saw a gradual transformation of the president's face. Oliver Radford was smiling at her, his eyes were twinkling, his face was radiant, as though the sun had come out. What a good actor! Sally thought. Or – could it be genuine?

The president spoke quietly, privately. 'Dear madam!' He said it almost lovingly.

Sally's sense of humour took over, and she felt a laugh bubbling up. 'Dear sir! You write terrible letters, you know!'

'So do you!' Oliver responded. 'Perhaps

we should have met before!' He turned to the attentive crowd and cleared his throat. It was time for the president's speech.

'This presentation gives me more pleasure than any such before at Kirkby Show, and I am sure you will all agree with me. Miss Sally Mason is this year's winner of the Championship Cup. She has succeeded where many would have failed. My estimation of the young woman's capabilities has had to be revised.' He looked at her briefly. Echoes of that rude letter, last winter! But only she would know what he meant.

Sally hung her head modestly. She could hardly believe her ears.

'Miss Mason was left to carry on her family's business and traditions alone, which she has done extremely well. Not only is the farm a credit to her,' and he winked at Sally, 'but she has won this cup today by sheer hard work and good judgement.'

Oliver paused and someone clapped.

'I must admit that I did not believe a young woman to be capable of success in farming. I was wrong.' He turned to look at Sally with that warm smile again. 'Of course, I had not then met Miss Mason. Those of you who know her will not be surprised.'

There were cheers. Sally felt like crying.

'I would like to say in conclusion that I have formed the highest regard for this young lady. And in presenting her with the cup, I congratulate her on the high standard of her cattle and wish her well for the future.'

The clapping and cheers were deafening, and Sally had no trouble in blushing. Taking the cup, Sally found her voice. 'Thank you so much, Mr President, for those kind words. Nobody knows how much they mean to me!' They signified the end of the quarrel. Sally dared to look round at the audience; there was more she had to say. 'This achievement was only possible with the help of my friends. I was alone, but not for long! My friends and neighbours have all helped me to keep the farm going and I am so grateful. And my loyal staff at Badger's Gill ... thank you all.' Sally stepped down very carefully, carrying the cup and at the bottom of the steps it was taken from her gently by Marcus Radford. His face wore a look of great relief.

'We're going to be approved, very soon,' he whispered. 'Come into the president's tent.'

There were several people sitting on canvas chairs in the tent. Oliver Radford was leaning on a table, quite at ease. Sally didn't know what to say. Mrs Russell was there, beaming at Sally. 'I told him you were a fine young woman! You're just like your mother, Sally!'

'I do so like a winner,' said Oliver warmly. 'You've shown a lot of spirit, young lady.

And I was impressed when you bought the farm, just like that. But your winning the championship really convinced me!'

'Convinced you of what, Mr Radford?' Sally stole a look at him, but he was still smiling at her.

'That Marcus was right and Sol was a villain, and I was a silly old ... but we won't worry about all that. I don't intend to apologize, it's not my style. But we'll look to the future. Nothing should spoil the day for you!'

A little while later, Oliver drew Sally outside the tent for a private word. 'I meant what I said, up there on the platform.' He smiled again. 'You're a grand lass!' He added, in broad Yorkshire. 'Dorothy Russell has been telling me so for some time. With her and Marcus on your side, I just had to give in.'

'And you forgive me the letters?'

Oliver laughed. 'I deserved them. The letters showed your spirit. I was fighting you off, you see, and it was a good fight, but I lost, in the end.' He paused. 'And another thing. When I tried to end your tenancy, I was doing it for your own good. I knew how hard your life would be... I imagined you just like your mother, Sally. And it seemed to me that any future was better than trying to run a farm with no money and no help. There. You needn't tell anybody else, they all think I'm tough and cynical ... here comes the lad himself.'

Marcus came out to join them. 'May I present my fiancée, Father?' He took Sally's hand and looked his father firmly in the eye.

The three of them were away from the crowd, in a little world of their own.

'You don't waste any time, do you, lad?' Oliver smiled grimly. Then he relaxed and laughed. 'Bless you both. The first grandson had better be called after me! Oliver Mason Radford. How does that sound?'

The publishers hope that this book has given you enjoyable reading. Large Print Books are especially designed to be as easy to see and hold as possible. If you wish a complete list of our books please ask at your local library or write directly to:

Magna Large Print Books
Magna House, Long Preston,
Skipton, North Yorkshire.
BD23 4ND

This Large Print Book, for people
who cannot read normal print,
is published under the auspices of

THE ULVERSCROFT FOUNDATION